Behind Enemy Lines

Hellhounds Series: Book 2

Theo Mann

The Invisible Publishing Company

Hellhounds Series

Contents

Chapter 1

Gunfire slammed Captain Owen LeMaine hard against his safety harness and he ducked his head aside to avoid getting hit in the face. Blasts ripped into the Elian Military bomber *Lucidity*. More shots shrieked into the open flight deck where LeMaine waited.

The *Lucidity* jolted back to starboard and enemy fire skated past the hatch to pound the hull. Attack cruisers whizzed back and forth beyond the opening and four of them exploded under continuous enemy assault.

A thin EM field kept the deck pressurized from open space. Stars pricked the black sky beyond, but LeMaine couldn't see the enemy from here. They were too far away.

Attack cruisers screeched through the gap and skidded across the deck. Some crashed in flames against the wall only a few yards from LeMaine's position. More attack cruisers launched from their anchor points, rocketed into space, and joined the firefight raging outside.

"How much longer?" Lieutenant Elliot Polasek yelled from LeMaine's right.

"How the hell should I know?" LeMaine hollered back. "The order should have come down by now."

Polasek looked past LeMaine's shoulder to the other Hellhounds jerking and tossing against the wall. Their safety harnesses kept them from cartwheeling head over heel through the protective field.

This position left them exposed to enemy fire coming from the outside and flying debris from exploding cruisers that managed to land before they burst.

LeMaine glanced down at the remote panel on his sleeve. It was already 1827, nearly half an hour after the time when he and his squad should have deployed.

He raised his right hand to tap the remote when a siren went off near the end of the line. A signal came through LeMaine's remote. *Lieutenant Stuart Peterman, Attack Cruiser* Icarus, *Deploy.*

"That's my cue!" Peterman called from LeMaine's other side. "Watch and learn, children."

He ripped the release cord on his harness, landed on his feet on the deck, and took off running as another attack cruiser hurtled through the EM field. She twirled once, slid a dozen yards to face backward, and screeched to a halt right in front of Peterman.

The cruiser's rear hatch slammed open and Peterman raced inside before the cruiser launched and disappeared.

"Children!" Corporal Glenn Heckler snarled through gritted teeth. "He's the only chump on this squad small enough to be a child."

LeMaine's heart sank as he watched Peterman go. LeMaine always prided himself on deploying first. How many more of the Hellhounds would he have to watch go out into open battle while he stayed behind?

"This is not good," Polasek yelled in his ear. "It shouldn't be taking this long."

LeMaine almost answered when his remote vibrated again. He dreaded finding out which of the Hellhounds would deploy next, but he perked up when he read the order. *Captain Owen LeMaine, Attack Cruiser* Valhalla, *Deploy.*

Polasek clapped him on the shoulder. "Lucky bastard! See you down there."

"Make sure you come. Don't stay home filing your nails."

Polasek laughed and LeMaine ripped his cord. His harness released and he slammed down into a crouch.

A punished barrage of gunshots hit the *Lucidity* at that moment and the bomber staggered. LeMaine checked his balance, but when he looked around for his cruiser, none came through the field.

More plasma erupted outside, and this time, a single cruiser wheeled beyond the gap to face outward. She shuddered there taking a brutal assault on her forward shields. She protected the flight deck alone until the bombardment pivoted somewhere else.

The cruiser hesitated and LeMaine held his breath to see what would happen. A bunch of mechanics and armory crewmen hunkered against the walls waiting for the cruiser to reenter the flight deck, but she still held off.

A second later, more cruisers whizzed across the opening and the *Valhallah* retreated inside. She floated into position, extended her landing gear, and pointed her nose back into space.

The hatch popped and LeMaine sprinted forward to charge inside. He pulled up short when a tall, blonde woman stormed down the ramp toward him. She wore a Military-issue pilot's jumpsuit with lieutenant's bars on the collar.

She pointed at the armory crew rushing in to work on her ship. "The starboard cannon is twenty degrees out again. I told you to fix it last time. How the hell am I supposed to shoot anything with it like this?"

Someone called back, "Yes, Ma'am."

The woman glanced another way and spotted three mechanics surrounding the port engine housing. She walked straight past LeMaine, thrust her arm up to the elbow in the engine fins, and fiddled with something. "I took a hit on it earlier. I think it's fried. You'll have to install a new one before I go back out."

"Yes, Ma'am. We'll replace it right away." One of the mechanics raced off to the parts store.

The woman came back to the ramp as though she'd just noticed LeMaine for the first time. She saluted him. "Captain Owen LeMaine? Lieutenant Riley DeYoung."

LeMaine saluted her back and then held out his hand. "It's a pleasure to meet you, Lieutenant. Your record speaks for itself."

"As does yours. Are those the infamous Hellhounds? It's going to be an honor to serve with such a decorated squad."

"You say that now. You might not find it such an honor once you get to know them. They can be a little rough around the edges."

"Sounds perfect." A shout distracted DeYoung and she looked behind her. The mechanics were pulling back from the engine housing and the armory crew was retreating to their own positions. "That's us. You better show me how you earned that commendation on Sapis."

She led the way back inside the cruiser. LeMaine shot one last look at Polasek and followed her.

She made it halfway across the rear compartment on her way to the cockpit when more gunfire exploded outside. It struck the cruiser's nose and knocked the whole craft sideways.

The *Valhalla* tilted onto one landing skid and screeched across the deck to slam into the wall. The mechanics had to leap out of the way and both LeMaine and DeYoung pitched against the hull.

"The bastards are laying into the *Lucidity*!" DeYoung yelled over the noise. "They see the cruisers launching from here and...." Another smash cut her off.

"No more talk!" LeMaine ordered. "Get us out there pronto."

"Yes, Sir!" She sprang across the compartment and vanished inside the cockpit. LeMaine scrambled into the cannon placement above the rear compartment.

This cruiser only had one placement unlike the Hellhounds' most recent transport. The ship was so small that the cockpit, the compartment, and the gun placement comprised the entire craft.

LeMaine didn't have time to strap himself in before DeYoung blasted the engines to full throttle and rocketed off the deck. The *Valhalla* skimmed sideways and erupted into a headlong sprint straight for the thickest firefight.

More cruisers raced past LeMaine's placement. He wedged himself into his harness while he swept his cannon back and forth across the battle. He took in the scene in a blink and didn't like what he saw at all.

Dozens of Elian cruisers swarmed around a formation of bombers standing guard over the Elian system's outer rim. Four planets occupied orbits on this side of the system where Elia butted against the Axichis system.

No Elian Military craft or personnel had ever patrolled this part of the system before. Now dozens of formations dotted the boundary zone to defend against the Axichis invasion. The Axichis had been Elia's closest allies and trading partners until just a few days ago. Not anymore.

The Axichis had tried to establish a base on Iumia first when the planet migrated closest to their system. The Hellhounds had helped the Iumians repel that attack. Now Iumia was moving farther away from Axichis space.

That left Toreon in the firing line, but no Axichis warships patrolled around the planet. In fact, LeMaine didn't see any Axichis spacecraft around Toreon at all.

Thousands of lasers erupted from the planet's jungle surface. The shots came from hundreds of placements surrounding an Axichis base buried in the jungle. Those guns targeted Elian vessels with pinpoint accuracy.

"Here we go!" DeYoung called through the communications system. "I hope you emptied your bladder before you came on board."

"If I didn't, it will all be dripping down into your cockpit if you screw up."

Gleeful laughter answered him. DeYoung gunned the engines and drove the *Valhalla* into a steep dive toward Toreon.

LeMaine trained his cannon at the surface and opened fire. He targeted as many Axichis gun placements as he could, but the *Valhalla's* systems had trouble locating them in the mayhem.

More fighters plunged alongside the *Valhalla* and the *Icarus* pulled abreast. "Did you miss us, Sir?" Peterman asked.

"Captain LeMaine is always trying to get himself killed without us," Sergeant Mason Kellogg added from a different cruiser.

"Fan out, Hellhounds," LeMaine ordered. "Don't give them such a concentrated target."

"Attack pattern Reliri!" DeYoung barked. "Bring it around to the Belina Continent."

"Yes, Ma'am," another pilot replied and four cruisers peeled off to port.

"What are you up to, De Young?" LeMaine asked.

"Just a little trick we picked up during the Chiuliv campaign. Are you in position, Carver?"

"Locked and loaded, Ma'am," another male voice replied.

"Stand by to give 'em a big fat knuckle sandwich, Hellhounds!" DeYoung added.

"Who the hell is this lady?" Heckler snarled.

"I'm still not sure," LeMaine replied, "but we're about to find out. Execute, DeYoung."

"You heard the man! Open fire, Carver!"

DeYoung and ten more cruisers whirled south, cut a wide path away from the heaviest Axichis fire, and came pelting in with guns blazing. Two more formations did the same thing and circled Toreon from the north and the west.

All three groups converged and carpeted the planet's surface with heavy fire. They blasted several enemy placements that erupted in flames.

"Lemon: one!" Sergeant Krista Lemon called from Carver's group. "You Hellhounds are letting the whole squad down."

"Peterman: two," came Peterman's calm voice. "You kids need to take some lessons."

"I am going to slap that bitch if he....." Heckler began.

"Break it up!" DeYoung cut in. "The gunners are correcting. Reverse attack pattern!"

"Come and get it, assholes!" Heckler snarled and he swung his cannon downward as his pilot rocketed over another placement.

Heckler opened fire and Kellogg joined him. The rest of the Axichis placements turned their guns on the Elians as they joined up into one horde.

The pilots tried to split apart into three separate groups, but they only made it a few miles before the Axichis bombardment cut them apart. Shots zinged past the *Valhalla* and smashed into another cruiser.

"We're hit!" Carver bellowed. "We're losing altitude!"

"Keep moving, people!" DeYoung ordered. "Get back to the *Lucidity* on the...."

Another smash cut her off. It punched through the *Valhalla's* hull and kept on going to hit Sergeant Brien O'Hara's cruiser. The shot ripped the cockpit to shreds and the communications system cut out.

"DeYoung!" LeMaine yelled. "Are you okay?"

"Hanging by a thread, Sir! We have critical hull breaches in the belly and in the roof. We're depressurizing."

"Abandon ship!" LeMaine scrambled to unlock his safety harness. He climbed down into the rear compartment just as DeYoung came to meet him from the cockpit.

Both of them got busy unzipping their jumpsuits in a hurry. Another blast rocked the *Valhalla*. "There goes the port engine!" DeYoung hollered.

"No more talking! Let's go! Follow me."

He kicked off his jumpsuit to reveal a skin-tight black drop suit covering his whole body. He charged the rear hatch and punched the release to open it just as the cockpit exploded.

He and DeYoung barely had time to pull their masks over their faces before LeMaine grabbed DeYoung's arm and they both launched themselves into the atmosphere.

Chapter 2

LeMaine tucked his chin and curled into a ball as searing heat bit into his suit. He buried his face under his arms for protection and hurtled at terminal velocity toward the green jungle far below.

Axichis laser fire sizzled past him and a deafening boom told him it had hit the *Valhalla*. That was the end of that ship. Now he and DeYoung were stranded on a planet crawling with enemy aliens.

One explosion after another resounded through the atmosphere behind him, but he couldn't uncoil to see which cruisers got taken out.

He only unrolled when the familiar buzz of his remote told him he was safe. He flung out his arms and legs. Webbing between his limbs and body caught the atmosphere and he soared over the treetops.

DeYoung steered over next to him. She kept checking her remote and adjusting her trajectory. LeMaine spotted more people falling toward the ground from destroyed cruisers, but they were too far away to see who they were.

LeMaine skimmed the canopy until he found an open place. He made sure it was deserted and dropped between the branches.

He still didn't see anyone while he yanked off his suit and got his carbines in position. He checked and double-checked the surroundings before he made his way over to DeYoung.

"Where are we?" she asked.

LeMaine took advantage of DeYoung's weapons to make a closer study of his remote. "We're seven miles from the Axichis base. Peterman and Kellogg are nearest. Let's meet up with them. Then we can decide what to do."

She followed him between the trees while LeMaine used his remote to track down Peterman. "Is it true you picked up a Maczhi on your squad when you were deployed on Ziea?" DeYoung asked.

"It's true. He's the first non-human we've ever had."

"What is he like?" she asked. "Word on the streets is the Maczhi are weak and submissive."

"Most of them are, but Buca isn't like that. He's one of the best Hellhounds we've ever had."

DeYoung cracked another grin. "I can't wait to meet him."

"Why did you become a pilot if you wanted to join the Special Forces instead?"

"I'm an adrenaline junkie. I just can't get enough of breaking my neck and blowing things up."

"Blowing things up I can understand. Our sapper Nunn can't get enough of blowing things up, either, but breaking your neck is NOT allowed on my squad, Lieutenant. You break your neck on someone else's watch."

She only smirked at him. "Yes, Sir. You can count on me."

He snorted and didn't answer. He could tell he was going to have his hands full with this woman. He could just imagine what would happen when she met up with the Hellhounds.

He and DeYoung kept scanning the area for any threat, but the whole jungle lay still and quiet except for birds and insects chirping in the canopy. That sound should have put LeMaine's mind at ease, but it only made him edgy.

They found Peterman and Kellogg bending over Kellogg's pilot. The guy jabbered and babbled while Kellogg and Peterman worked full tilt to seal the blood vessels of the pilot's severed arm.

"I didn't do anything!" the young man stammered. "I'm telling you I was flying the cruiser and it hit me out of nowhere."

"No one blames you, Lexington," Peterman murmured. "You did a great job of...."

"Hand me that scalpel," Kellogg snapped.

Peterman turned to Kellogg's backpack that lay open the ground, but Peterman couldn't reach it with his hands full of Lexington's bloody limbs.

Peterman's pilot stood off to one side gaping at the scene in stark horror.

"Cameron!" Peterman yelled. "Help us!"

LeMaine hustled to Kellogg's side. "I'll get it. What happened?"

"We go hit, of course. God damn it!" Kellogg hissed. "Give me that staple gun, Sir."

LeMaine got busy handing Kellogg things as fast as possible. DeYoung wandered over to watch. "Can I do anything?"

"Talk some sense into Cameron," Peterman replied. "We can't take him with us if he doesn't snap out of it pretty quick."

"Lie him down," Kellogg ordered.

Peterman and LeMaine helped Kellogg lie Lexington on his back. The young pilot kept running on at the mouth about how the Axichis hit that destroyed his cruiser wasn't his fault.

Peterman held Lexington's arm in place while Kellogg reattached the joint. Blood soaked LeMaine's fatigues, but that was nothing compared with how Kellogg and Lexington looked.

Finally, Kellogg fixed the bone electrolyzer to Lexington's shoulder and fired it. The young pilot collapsed, unconscious, and silence fell over the scene.

Kellogg sank back on his heels. "Jesus H. Christ, he was driving me crazy!"

"Are you two all right?" LeMaine asked.

"We're fine." Peterman glanced at DeYoung over LeMaine's shoulder. She had taken Cameron far enough away that none of the Hellhounds could hear what she was saying to him. "How's the big war hero?"

"She's great. Nunn and O'Hara are going to love her."

Peterman snorted. "Just what we need—another wise ass."

"How long before Lexington will be ready to move?" LeMaine asked Kellogg.

"He should be fine as soon as I administer the antidote and wake him up. Just give me a minute to enjoy the peace and quiet."

LeMaine checked his remote. "Do it now. We need to assemble the rest of the squad and we'll need you if anyone else is injured."

Kellogg got his syringe out of his pack and loaded it with antidote while LeMaine went over to DeYoung and Cameron.

DeYoung gave LeMaine a knowing look while Cameron stared at the ground. "Is this your first deployment, son?" LeMaine asked him.

Cameron nodded without looking up. "Yes, Sir."

"Which flight academy did you graduate from?"

"I....I didn't, Sir," he croaked. "I was in my third year when the war broke out. We all got conscripted on the spot. I.....I only got assigned to the *Lucidity* last week....Sir."

LeMaine glanced over at DeYoung's understanding smile and LeMaine cringed. This put a whole different spin on the mission.

LeMaine checked his remote again. Polasek, O'Hara, Monk, and Heckler were all within walking distance with three more pilots. How many of them would be totally green, too?

LeMaine unbuckled one of Cameron's carbines from his backpack and handed it to him. "Have you been trained in how to use one of these, son?"

"Yes, Sir."

"Take it, then, and be ready to use it." LeMaine turned to DeYoung. "What do you know about the other pilots?"

"Lexington has been in our squadron for over two years and he was at Soclitese, so he's solid. I guess he was just in shock when he lost his arm, but he should be fine now. Same with Carver. He's seen ground action and he knows the drill."

"What about the other two...?" LeMaine read their names off his remote. "Orr and Stivers?"

"They've both been out of the academy for about a year. They're good pilots, but I don't think they have any ground experience." She shot her eyes to Cameron, who still didn't look up.

LeMaine heard what DeYoung wasn't saying. That made Cameron the least experienced of the whole group.

"We're ready to go, Sir," Kellogg called. "Lexington is clear for active duty."

"All right. Let's move it. It looks like Polasek and O'Hara have met up. We'll rendezvous with them first."

He made sure everyone was armed. Lexington conducted himself smoothly and easily, now that he had full use of both his arms. DeYoung was right about him.

The rest of the group arranged themselves in a single file line with LeMaine at the front. Kellogg and Peterman took the rear.

LeMaine became aware of Cameron hovering close on his heels, but LeMaine pretended not to notice. New people always acted that way—except Buca. That man came prepared and ready to roll.

LeMaine checked his remote again and again, but he still didn't see any sign of Buca, Nunn, or Lemon. Where were they?

Polasek, Carver, and O'Hara came through the jungle to meet the rest of the squad. LeMaine was pleased to see Carver scanning the surroundings. He jumped to alert every time a noise disturbed the stillness.

Polasek slotted in next to LeMaine. "What's the plan, Sir? Do you want to keep searching for the rest of the squad or head for the base?"

Just then, Monk and Heckler caught up to the group along with Orr and Stivers. LeMaine frowned at his remote. "Let's pull it up here and talk shop. If the others don't turn up soon, we'll head for the base, which means we'll have to reconfigure our assault."

"That shouldn't be a problem," DeYoung suggested. "We just send in fewer people on each front."

"That's easy to say from out here," Peterman argued. "We don't know how many the Axichis will have posted around the base."

"If we use stealth the way we planned, how many they have posted around the base shouldn't matter."

"Our whole strategy depends on O'Hara taking out any sentries and Nunn distracting the rest with explosions. We don't have Nunn or Nunn's explosives. We don't even have the explosives to blow up the transmission array the way we planned."

"What about.....?" Kellogg began.

"Quiet!" LeMaine interrupted. "We got a serious problem."

Everyone looked at him and saw him scowling at his remote. Then they all looked at their remotes, too.

"Son of a bitch!" DeYoung whispered. "The Axichis are coming out after us!"

"They aren't coming after us." LeMaine jerked his carbine to his shoulder. "They're going after the other three. Move it out, Hellhounds."

He took off at a fast clip toward where Nunn, Lemon, and Buca appeared on his remote. LeMaine picked up speed, but he couldn't reach them fast enough before the Axichis got there first.

The Axichis party crawled across the landscape. The enemy spread out to encircle the three Hellhounds and, out of nowhere, gunfire erupted in the jungle ahead.

LeMaine broke into a run with his carbine still jammed to his shoulder. Heckler caught up with him, but they still didn't make it.

The Hellhounds burst through a patch of trees and almost ran headfirst into a firefight. Nunn, Lemon, and Buca had backed against a rock outcropping to the left. Lemon and Buca stood over Nunn while she worked hard and fast arranging Plaostine blocks on top of her backpack.

Fifteen Axichis ringed the three Hellhounds and unloaded lasers at the trio. LeMaine had a split second to pull his carbine up before half the Axichis turned on him and opened fire.

Lasers ripped the trees next to his head and spat in the dirt at his feet. He dove aside and shoved Cameron behind a thick tree trunk. His party distracted the Axichis away from the three friends pinned under the cliff face.

The rest of LeMaine's party scattered. DeYoung, Carver, and Monk ended up taking refuge twenty feet to the right. They attacked the Axichis from the rear so now the Hellhounds surrounded the attackers who had been surrounding Lemon and Buca.

LeMaine's party traded shots with the Axichis. The next time he stuck his head out, he saw Nunn standing up with her prepared Plaostine blocks ready.

LeMaine unloaded another barrage of carbine fire, but he didn't try as hard to hit the Axichis. He only cared about keeping their backs turned away from Nunn.

She lobbed four blocks one after the other. They sailed past Buca's shoulder and landed amongst the Axichis attackers. LeMaine pulled Cameron behind the tree and covered the young pilot's head.

Four rapid booms rocked the forest. Dirt and bark peppered the trunk behind LeMaine's head, and when he dared to look out one more time, only four Axichis remained.

Buca stormed forward shooting fast and straight. Monk, Heckler, Polasek, and Peterman converged from the other side, and by the time LeMaine got there, all the Axichis were dead.

"You okay, Corporal?" LeMaine asked Buca.

Buca nodded. "We're all right. They got the jump on us."

"How could they?" DeYoung asked. "Your remotes should have picked them up."

"Were they using masking technology like we saw on Ziea?" Peterman asked.

"I don't know," Buca replied. "One minute we were all clear, and the next minute, they came out of nowhere. They were already too close for us to get away. We were lucky we found this cliff or we would have been dead."

"I didn't see them, either," LeMaine replied. "By the time I realized you were in danger, they were already within range."

"That makes no sense," DeYoung countered. "The Axichis don't have any masking technology."

"It looks an awful lot to me like the Axichis have been doing things behind our backs that they didn't tell us about," Heckler growled. "They pretended to be our friends while they were secretly arming this invasion. They could have all kinds of technology waiting in the wings to spring on us."

"Exactly," LeMaine replied, "which is why we need to get to their base and carry out our mission. O'Hara, we'll need you in position on the high point beyond their south perimeter. Nunn and Heckler, you two will pull the old tiptoe-and-decimate routine."

Heckler laughed his big, rumbling, rolling laugh. "I think I'll get that one tattooed across my chest. Tiptoe and Decimate. I like it."

"You can use that as a pickup line for girls you meet in bars," Kellogg told him.

"Lemon, you know what you have to do," LeMaine went on.

"Tiptoe and decimate," Peterman explained.

"The rest of us will just decimate," Monk added and the Hellhounds laughed.

"What about us?" DeYoung asked. "Will there be any decimating to do when you finish with the enemy or do you just want us to stand around and watch?"

"You wish," Nunn added.

"I want you five to do nothing BUT decimate," LeMaine replied. "Nunn, Heckler, and Lemon will do the tiptoeing. As soon as Nunn and O'Hara trigger the attack, the rest of us will be on clean-up duty. Polasek, you'll go straight to the transmission dish and broadcast the frequencies to the whole Axichis fleet."

"You got it, Sir."

"Uh...Sir?" It was Cameron. "Uh....I don't understand. What am I supposed to do?"

"Shoot," Polasek told him. "You can tell the difference between an Axichis and an Elian, can't you? You stick with Captain LeMaine here. As soon as the shooting starts, blow away any Axichis you lay your eyes on. That's all you have to do."

Cameron looked back and forth between LeMaine and Polasek. "That's it?"

"Yeah." Polasek clapped him on the back and laughed. "You do that and you'll be an official Hellhound."

The rest of the Hellhounds burst out laughing at the awed look on Cameron's face and LeMaine turned away. "Let's get to it, Hellhounds."

"Sir!" Lemon interrupted.

"What is it, Sergeant?"

"I can do my tiptoeing now, Sir. It will be easier to get inside the base if I go now."

"Do what you have to do, Sergeant. We'll see you inside."

"Yes, Sir."

She pulled off her backpack, threw it on the ground, and started unbuttoning her fatigues.

The pilots stared at her when she started peeling off her shirt and pants until she stripped down to her underwear. Cameron had his mouth open and Stivers blushed furiously, but he didn't look away.

"You got yourself an audience of admirers, Lemon," O'Hara teased.

"That's more than you'll ever have, shithead," Lemon hissed.

She pulled her camouflage suit out of her pack, stuffed all her clothes into her backpack, and shimmied into the suit until it covered her whole body, including her head.

"What are you going to disguise yourself as?" DeYoung asked.

"You'd love to know, wouldn't you?" Lemon took a step backward and vanished into the moss-covered rock face behind her. Her disembodied voice came from nowhere and everywhere at once. "Don't trip over yourselves, Hellhounds. I'll see you in there."

Her voice evaporated and there was nothing left to see. LeMaine bumped Heckler's shoulder. "Let's go. You and Nunn get around to the north side. O'Hara......"

A buzz on LeMaine's wrist cut him off. Everyone present looked down at their remotes. "Shit!" Peterman whispered.

"How do they keep getting the jump on us?" DeYoung asked, but no one answered her.

The Hellhounds moved into a circle facing outward. Carver, Lexington, and Stivers stepped into place with Hellhounds, but Orr and Cameron took longer.

LeMaine aimed his weapon in the direction his remote told him the Axichis were coming from, but no matter how hard he looked, he didn't see anything. The whole jungle was empty except for him and his squad.

LeMaine backed into Heckler, pushed the group deeper into the jungle, and inched parallel to the cliff. "Let's get out of here."

The Hellhounds started to move off. LeMaine hated to tear his eyes away from the jungle to look down at his remote. The trees and undergrowth breathed with hidden menace. The jungle would disgorge some terrible threat if he took his gaze off it for a split second.

He glanced down. A much larger cluster of dots flowed closer and closer. It should be right in front of him. His eyes darted from one tree to the next, but he still didn't see anybody there. This was much worse than the situation on Ziea.

Carver sidestepped and stumbled on LeMaine's foot. None of the Hellhounds could see where they were going with their eyes locked on the surroundings.

LeMaine rotated to his left and took five steps to pass the cliff face. He couldn't wait anymore.

He waved to Polasek and the Hellhounds fell in behind LeMaine. They set off toward the Axichis base, but the instant they passed the cliff, an Axichis platoon materialized out of thin air right on the spot where LeMaine had just been looking.

The Axichis became visible within a dozen yards of the Hellhounds. All the Hellhounds spun around and opened fire, but it was already too late.

The Hellhounds smashed together in a tight knot just as more Axichis appeared on top of the cliff. They fired down into the squad from above and Cameron screamed.

LeMaine whipped up his carbine to return fire on the Axichis above him, but at the same moment, the Axichis on the jungle floor charged in with guns blazing.

LeMaine had half a second to see Polasek, Nunn, Monk, and O'Hara take off running into the jungle. LeMaine adjusted his position to plant himself behind them. He faced both Axichis groups together to guard the Hellhounds' retreat.

He brought up both his carbines, aimed one up at the cliff, and the other to his left. He roared his challenge and sprayed Crossfire bursts everywhere.

He rotated farther left and found Heckler at his side along with Buca and Lexington.

LeMaine lost sight of the others, but he didn't care anymore. He could buy them enough time to get clear and make it to the base. One or two people lost on this rotten planet didn't matter as much as saving the whole Elian system from the invasion.

The Axichis on the cliff jumped down and the Axichis in the jungle inched closer. LeMaine and his men closed tighter together, but their shots didn't seem to touch the Axichis.

LeMaine couldn't understand it in the fog of rage and confusion. He kept firing everything he had and the thunder of gunfire blocked out all else....until his ammunition ran out.

Heckler's carbines belched a few more times and then a deadly silence fell over the jungle. LeMaine's head cleared and he found himself face to face with the enemy.

The Axichis glared at him with small, beady eyes. Dozens of finger-like cilia wriggled all over their faces.

The Axichis surrounded the four men. Buca stepped forward to confront them, but LeMaine held him back.

Four people. LeMaine. Heckler. Buca. Lexington. They were the only ones left. Everyone else was gone. The Hellhounds and the other three pilots had vanished into the jungle. Were they safe?

Whatever the Axichis did to LeMaine and his men wasn't nearly as important as carrying out the Hellhounds' mission to the base. LeMaine didn't care about anything as long as Polasek and a few other sturdy characters survived to transmit those frequencies.

Chapter 3

LeMaine raised his arm only a few inches to give himself a glimpse of his remote. He didn't dare lift it any higher in case the Axichis saw.

His remote would trace his route through the jungle—not that it mattered. The Axichis led him and his men into the Toreon jungle. They were taking LeMaine to their base.

He didn't see any other Hellhounds around, which meant they were either dead or hiding.

About an hour into their hike, Lexington muttered to Buca, "How long have you been a Hellhound?"

"Keep quiet," Heckler snarled under his breath. "The Axichis can speak English."

Lexington didn't say anything after that. He kept Cameron's old place behind LeMaine with Buca behind him and Heckler in the rear.

Seven Axichis went in front with another seven behind the prisoners. More flanked the party on either side. The Axichis had to hack their way through the jungle to hold their formation. It slowed the whole journey down, but they didn't slacken their vigilance at all.

LeMaine caught Heckler and Buca glancing at him on the way, but they didn't talk. The Axichis were taking them to the base which was where the Hellhounds wanted to go in the first place.

Even so, they couldn't carry out their mission without Polasek. He had the frequencies in his backpack communications array.

LeMaine had one contingency plan in case anything happened to Polasek's array. Once LeMaine hacked the transmission dish—assuming he *could* hack the transmission dish—he could contact the Elian Military Command.

He could get the frequencies from them and then broadcast the frequencies to the Axichis invasion force. Then the Axichis would become vulnerable to Elian weaponry. The war would be over.

That was the plan, anyway. First, LeMaine had to get inside the base, find the dish, and eliminate the Axichis who would sure as hell be guarding it from an attack just like this one.

He scanned the jungle one more time. Where were his Hellhounds now? Where was Lemon?

She was too smart to show herself during that skirmish in the woods. If LeMaine knew anything about her, she could have been all the way to the base by the time LeMaine finished talking.

Was O'Hara out there setting up his sniper rifle? Was Nunn preparing to lay her Plaostine blocks around the base to surprise the Axichis?

Heckler was with LeMaine, so that was one less infiltrator than LeMaine planned. LeMaine would give anything to question Lexington right now. LeMaine needed to know what resources Lexington could bring to this mission, but LeMaine couldn't do that with the Axichis listening to their every word.

LeMaine kept a close watch on the countryside, the Axichis, and his people. Pretty soon, he had plenty more to keep a close watch on as the base came in sight.

Armed Axichis patrolled the outer perimeter wall on top and on the ground. Fighter craft buzzed back and forth in the air overhead.

They kept up a constant flight pattern, especially around the giant transmission dish that poked its nose high above the wall. That must have been the whole reason the Axichis established such a powerful base on this planet—to control communications inside the Elian system.

The patrol fighters' guns swiveling around to aim at the ground. Then they pivoted upward to target the party as it got nearer. The fighters zoomed over the approaching platoon and its prisoners.

The Axichis guards advanced to the entrance gate. It rumbled out of the way and the platoon escorted LeMaine and his men inside. Now the shit would really go down.

The instant they got inside, the Axichis grabbed LeMaine and yanked him away from the others. He fought their hold trying to get back to his people. "No! We're staying together."

Heckler and Buca both tried to pull him back into their group, but one of the Axichis that LeMaine mistook for a common soldier shoved him away.

He slammed LeMaine against the wall and pinned him there. "You are the captain. You will come to the commandant and explain yourself."

"There's nothing to explain. We crashed on this planet."

"You are Elian Special Forces. The Elian Special Forces do not crash on planets."

"I'm telling the truth!" LeMaine gave one last almighty effort to break free, but the Axichis proved way too strong. "Let me go!"

The creature didn't answer. He ripped LeMaine off the wall and knocked him sideways. LeMaine staggered to keep his balance, and by the time he turned around, the rest of the platoon was already leading Buca, Heckler, and Lexington away.

Four more Axichis caught LeMaine and hustled him in the opposite direction. They pushed him and jostled him every time he turned around to see where the other three were going.

In the end, the biggest one snatched him by the fatigues and sent him stumbling into one of the base's many buildings. The soldiers marched him to a standing workstation where a different Axichis worked over his controls.

The workstation and all the electronics were Elian and this Axichis certainly acted like he knew what he was doing. Why shouldn't he? The Elians had been sharing technology with their Axichis allies for generations. The Axichis knew everything about Elian society. Too bad the Elians couldn't say the same thing about the Axichis.

The creature stopped what he was doing and fixed LeMaine with hard, small eyes. "State your name and rank."

LeMaine hesitated only an instant. He didn't see any reason to lie. The Elian Military had been sharing all kinds of secrets with the Axichis, including access to all the Military's personnel databases, duty rosters, and ship movements.

This Axichis probably already knew everything about LeMaine and his squad. Hell, LeMaine's name was printed on his fatigues for all the world to see.

"Captain Owen LeMaine, Elian Special Forces."

"Ah, yes...." The Axichis punched the instruments in front of him. "You are the commanding officer of the infamous Hellhounds Special Operations Squad. We have heard enough about you and your exploits. I am Commander Naelxad. Now we have been properly introduced, Captain. Now you can tell me what you are doing on this planet."

"I already told your man here. We crashed."

"That is your cover story," Naelxad countered. "What is the real reason you're here?"

"I just told you. We were helping the bombers and your forces shot us down. That's pretty straightforward."

"You assembled your squad on the ground. You would not have done that if you weren't planning some operation on Toreon."

"I wanted to make sure my people were all right. Do you honestly think we would bring five untrained pilots with us if we were planning some operation here? My squad always works alone."

Naelxad looked down at his instruments. "You brought Lieutenant Riley DeYoung with you. She is also highly decorated."

"We also have a conscript from the flight academy who doesn't even have a commission yet. The Elian Military wouldn't send someone like that to work with the Hellhounds. I wouldn't allow it. I'm telling you the truth. This was totally unplanned."

Naelxad snorted and his cilia wavered. "I don't believe you, Captain. Your men will be interrogated until they tell us what you are doing here. In the meantime....."

He trailed off and the Axichis solders attacked LeMaine even more roughly. They yanked at his backpack and ripped it off. "Hey!" he yelled. "What are you doing?"

Naelxad pulled the backpack toward him, unzipped it, and started going through it item by item.

LeMaine watched him and thought fast. Neither Heckler, Buca, nor Lexington had anything on them that could give away the mission. Heckler had his swimming goggles. This Axichis knew all about the Hellhounds, so Naelxad must already know that Heckler was a swimmer.

Polasek. Polasek's communications array had all the frequencies pre-programmed into it. LeMaine had to stop the Axichis from getting their hands on it.

If the Axichis found out what the Hellhounds were doing—or worse, if the Axichis got hold of the frequencies themselves—Elia would have no way to defeat the Axichis. The Axichis would be able to counter the frequencies. No Elian weapon would be able to stop the Axichis then.

LeMaine had to get word to Polasek somehow. How could LeMaine warn Polasek not to come to the base? LeMaine didn't even know if Polasek was still free or if he was already dead.

Either that or LeMaine had to get word to Polasek to destroy his own array. Using the transmission dish to get the frequencies from Command would make the Hellhounds' mission exponentially harder, but it was better than giving away their plans to the enemy.

Naelxad didn't stop until all LeMaine's gear lay scattered across the workstation. Naelxad waved LeMaine away. "Never mind. We will discover your real mission, and when we do, we will thwart it. You can go, Captain, but when you see the fate in store for your subordinates, you may consider being more cooperative."

The guards yanked LeMaine out of the building. They shoved and prodded him across the base to a large, barred cage constructed against the wall.

LeMaine's heart sank all over again when he saw Buca, Heckler, and Lexington already inside. If Nunn laid charges against this wall to blow her way in, she could end up killing the prisoners into the bargain.

He had to get word to her, too.....somehow, but right now, he had bigger problems. The guards pushed LeMaine over to the cage and shoved him in with the others.

Heckler and Buca caught him and set LeMaine on his feet. The guards shot the four prisoners dirty looks and then left.

"What do you think, Sir?" Heckler growled. "How do we get out of here?"

LeMaine assessed their situation. "They aren't guarding the cage."

"They don't have to," Buca pointed out. "There are already too many soldiers patrolling the grounds, too many sentries on the walls, and too many patrol ships in the air."

"There has to be a way out of here," Lexington insisted. "It can't be totally hopeless."

"Hold your horses, son. Our objective was to get inside the base and we've accomplished that."

"But we can't hack the dish from in here. We can't accomplish our mission when we're locked in a cage."

LeMaine grinned at Lexington calling the Hellhounds, 'we'. Now Lexington was thinking the right way.

"We can't hack the dish without Polasek anyway," Heckler pointed out. "We might as well sit tight in here where we're safe until we find a way to *actually* hack the dish."

"How do we hack the dish, then?" Lexington asked.

"We don't. Only Polasek can do that."

LeMaine turned his back on the outside world. "Listen. The Axichis are going to interrogate you to try to find out our mission. Lexington....."

LeMaine broke off observing the young man. LeMaine didn't worry about Heckler and Buca keeping their mouths shut. Lexington was a total unknown.

Lexington read his mind. "You don't have to worry about me, Sir. I'm tougher than I look."

LeMaine laughed. "I can believe it if you were at Soclitese. I'm just wondering....."

A high-pitched yowl startled LeMaine into spinning around. He scanned the base, but he didn't see where the sound could be coming from.

"What was that?" Buca whispered.

"It wasn't any animal native to this planet," Lexington murmured back. "I don't recognize it."

"How would you know what animals are native to this planet?" Heckler countered.

"My dad is a cosmozoologist. He studies the habits, ranges, and vocalizations of every animal in the system. I'm telling you whatever made that sound didn't come from any Elian planet. I'm certain of it."

LeMaine didn't answer. He already knew Lexington was right. That sound didn't match any animal in the whole Elian system, which meant it came from something else.

The Axichis guards, patrols, and sentries all jumped at the sound, too. They turned their weapons in every direction and scanned the skies and the trees, but nothing showed itself.

The Axichis broke out in tense whispering. Someone must have ordered the patrols to search for the source. Squadrons of fighter craft soared over the jungle swiveling their weapons everywhere.

The Axichis barely snapped alert before the sound came again. It sounded like it came from all directions. It drove the Axichis into a heightened state of anxiety and some of the guards and sentries left their posts.

A third screech set LeMaine's hair on end and Buca moved closer to Heckler. "What is it? It sounds like a ghost."

"It isn't a ghost, fool!" Heckler hissed back.

Buca trembled. LeMaine had never seen him so rattled—ever. Buca could handle the hottest battle and any kind of hardship, but this really got to him.

He laced his fingers together again and again and kept shooting terrified glances outside. He looked more agitated than the Axichis.

"It's Lemon," LeMaine whispered. "She's here. She's doing this to unnerve the Axichis."

"Are you sure?" Buca choked. "How can you be sure?"

"You heard what Lexington said. No animal in the whole system makes that sound. It has to be her."

"How do we contact her?" Heckler asked.

"We don't. We wait for her to come to us."

"That could take hours." Lexington squinted up at the sentries on the wall. "What if something happens before then?"

Almost in answer to his words, the same troop of Axichis guards stalked over to the cage, unlocked the door and one of them pointed at Lexington. "You—come with us."

Lexington cast a desperate glance at his companions before the guards yanked him out the door. Lexington shot out a grasping hand to LeMaine. "Captain—don't let them.....!"

The guards didn't give him a chance to finish. They started dragging Lexington away and Lexington panicked. He tore out of their grasp, charged the bars, and thrust his arm through to grab LeMaine's hand.

LeMaine gripped it once and brought his own face close to the bars. "It will be all right, Ensign. This is your chance to show me how tough you are. This is your chance to show us all you're a true Hellhound."

Lexington's face spasmed with emotion. He tried to smile, but it didn't work. He crushed LeMaine's fingers one last time before the guards hauled him away.

LeMaine's heart twisted watching them kick and punch Lexington out of sight. LeMaine never should have agreed to let these pilots come on this mission. He knew it was a bad idea when Colonel Nicholson and Commander Lodge told him about it. LeMaine should have stood his ground.

No Hellhound mission was any place for civilians or even lesser trained military personnel. LeMaine kicked himself now for violating that one most fundamental rule of his command.

If Cameron had been here in Lexington's place, it would have been a thousand times worse. Cameron would never have been able to stand up to Naelxad's interrogation. He would have been crying and spilling the squad's secrets the first time Naelxad made a nasty face at him.

LeMaine didn't like to think ill of anyone, but he couldn't help but cringe at the thought of Lexington facing the Axichis commander. How long would Lexington be able to hold out?

"Figures they'd take the weakest first," Heckler muttered.

"What do we do if he talks?" Buca asked.

"If he talks," Heckler growled, "we're sunk."

LeMaine didn't answer. He needed Lemon now, but he couldn't do anything to help Lexington or anyone else. LeMaine just had to wait.

Chapter 4

Deep darkness hung over the Axichis base. Flood lights illuminated the grounds inside and search lights swept the jungle beyond the walls, but nothing could dispel the pall hanging over the base.

That spine-chilling shriek kept resounding over the landscape at random times throughout the day. It left everyone on edge, especially the Axichis.

LeMaine squatted against the wall straining his ears to pick up any other sound in between the unearthly yowls piercing the night.

The base's lights didn't extend inside the cage, so LeMaine and his men sat in total darkness as shadows enveloped Toreon.

LeMaine struggled to hear if Lexington was screaming, but LeMaine didn't hear anything. He almost wished he *could* hear Lexington screaming. Then he would know just how bad things were getting in Naelxad's office. Lexington had been in there for hours.

Buca and Heckler had stretched out on the floor side by side, but LeMaine already knew they weren't asleep. No one could sleep with that ghastly sound stretching everyone's nerves to the breaking point.

Arguments kept breaking out among the Axichis. If Lemon was the one doing this—and LeMaine became more convinced by the hour that she was—she was doing one hell of a job of unnerving the enemy. That woman could get under a person's skin like no one LeMaine had ever met in his life.

She was sure doing a bang-up job of getting under LeMaine's skin, too, and Buca had been going half out of his mind.

He kept whispering about ghosts and then falling into even more petrified silences. For a man so self-possessed in combat and at every other time, this situation got to Buca in ways no mortal danger ever could.

Buca's panic had started to leak over into Heckler's iron reserve. LeMaine almost collapsed in relief when the two Hellhounds finally laid down, closed their eyes, and pretended not to hear the sound anymore.

LeMaine stayed upright. He couldn't stop watching the situation outside. Naelxad didn't show himself, but someone at the top was sure getting antsy about that sound.

The patrol craft kept whizzing back and forth, changing their flight patterns, and searching different parts of the jungle trying to find whatever was causing that noise.

Different officers appeared, ordered their men out into the jungle, and then changed the watch in different parts of the base. No one knew whether they were coming or going and no one knew what to do.

Out of nowhere, a long, low hiss breathed in LeMaine's right ear. He jumped out of his skin and then the hiss turned to a whisper. "Ssssssss....... captain........ sssssssss"

"Lemon!" he whispered back. "What the hell!"

"sssssssss.......... we're......... waiting........"

LeMaine gasped to catch his breath. He had to keep quiet. Neither Buca nor Heckler heard Lemon whispering in his ear and LeMaine didn't want them to find out. "Where?" he whispered back.

"sssssssss......... south......... side............ O'Hara.......... ready........"

LeMaine gulped. "Are they all there?"

"sssssssssss......... DeYoung.......... and Nunn............ north.......... with........ Carver......... sssssssss"

"Listen to me!" LeMaine whispered. "I need you to get a message to Polasek. I need you to tell him to stash his array somewhere in the jungle.....somewhere the Axichis will never find it. It's important. We can't let the frequencies fall into Axichis hands. It wouldn't be so bad if any of you get caught and spill the beans about the frequencies as long as the Axichis don't get their hands on the frequencies themselves."

"sssssssssss........the transmission........sssssss"

"Forget that!" LeMaine breathed. "This is more important!"

"sssssssssss.......assault.........at..........dawn.........captain.........sssssssss"

That hiss evaporated in a breath that became one with the night. LeMaine slumped and buried his face in his hands. His one contact with the outside world was gone, but at least he wasn't alone.

The Hellhounds were alive and they planned to mount an assault. Lemon would tell Nunn where LeMaine and the others were. Nunn wouldn't blow up the cage with her Plaostine-happy explosions.

He considered waking up Buca and Heckler and telling them, but he decided against it. The Axichis would be watching the prisoners.

Better to let the enemy think the captives were cowed and beaten. Seeing LeMaine and his men on their feet preparing for something would tip off the Axichis that something was up.

Sitting still drove LeMaine bananas. He would give anything to prepare, but he didn't have anything to prepare with. The Axichis had taken all his gear.

LeMaine didn't dare to check his remote to see if the Hellhounds really were there—not that he doubted Lemon.

Then again, their remotes had been going haywire since the squad landed on this planet.

He made a mental note to have Command check the technology when he got back. He couldn't let his squad get ambushed like this again. This was the second planet where remote malfunction had left the Hellhounds in danger. He couldn't let it happen again.

Now he just had to wait for dawn and he hated waiting. He considered again if he should wake up Heckler. Then at least LeMaine would have someone to talk to. Heckler would be annoyed when he found out that LeMaine kept him in the dark until the last minute.

Buca and Heckler would be going out of their minds from impatience, too, if LeMaine knew anything about his people. They would want to talk about all the possibilities and scheme how best to help the assault.

LeMaine forced himself to sit still, but his eye kept ranging around the base. The patrol craft returned, descended to a spot behind the buildings, and then took off again. That must be the Axichis flight range. How many more ships did they have over there?

Colonel Nicholson and Commander Lodge had told LeMaine on board the *Lucidity* that the Axichis were keeping a sizable force here. LeMaine had seen huge Axichis warships and freight vessels coming and going on his way through the atmosphere.

As long as the Axichis had to hold this planet to control the transmission dish, they might as well use it as a full military installation. Large ships rose from and sank onto the flight range even now. Not all of them were fighters and warships. Some were freighters and personnel transports.

Doors slammed in the darkness and a scuffle broke out somewhere on the base. The noise attracted the guards' attention and woke up Buca and Heckler. Both men got to their feet as the hubbub got closer.

"What's going on?" Heckler growled.

"Not sure," LeMaine replied, "but it can't be anything good."

The noise came from the direction of Commander Naelxad's office. Sure enough, a bunch of guards burst into view dragging Lexington with them.

The young pilot put up one hell of a fight. So many guards had to come over to help subdue him that LeMaine lost sight of Lexington for a minute.

The guards surrounded him, and a moment later, the cluster broke apart to reveal Lexington on the ground with at least ten Axichis standing over him.

They pummeled him and smashed their weapons into him, but he still fought back. He kicked, punched, and grappled their weapons nearly out of their hands.

Three times he succeeded in grabbing a guard's weapon and slamming it back at its owner. Two of Lexington's victims staggered away bleeding from their noses.

More guards gathered from all over. They finally buried Lexington under so many bodies that he couldn't do anything. They restrained his arms and legs, dragged him over to the cage, and pinned him down in front of LeMaine.

Five Axichis aimed their weapons through the bars. "Back away and stand against the wall!" More Axichis held Lexington at gunpoint. "Stand back or we'll shoot."

LeMaine pushed Buca and Heckler back. The Axichis unlocked the cage and pitched Lexington inside before they locked the prisoners up again.

Buca dropped on his knees next to Lexington. "What did they do to you?"

Lexington gave a hollow laugh and ran his wrist across his bloody nose. "You should see the other guy, Captain."

"I don't think I want to, son." LeMaine squatted down next to Lexington and examined the young man's face. "Is anything broken?"

Lexington forced another laugh. "Yeah. Commander Naelxad's temper is broken. I didn't tell him anything, Sir."

"Good for you, son. I need to check you for injuries. It will only take a minute."

LeMaine patted down Lexington's head, neck, and shoulders. When LeMaine got to Lexington's torso, the young pilot winced and pushed LeMaine's hands away. "Don't, Captain. It's nothing."

"I'm sure you're the toughest nut on the block, Ensign, but it's my job to know the fighting condition of all my people. Are your ribs broken?"

"One of them, at least." Lexington winced again and his cheery exterior cracked. He hugged his arm tight to his ribs and slouched over to the bench against the wall. He sank onto it and sat there doubled over under LeMaine's critical eye. "I'll be all right, Captain. I promise. Just....." He glanced at the other two. "Don't tell anyone about this."

"Why not?" Heckler rumbled. "Getting injured in the line of duty is the greatest honor a Hellhound can hope for. You took these injuries defending Elia and protecting your squad mates. No one can ask better than that, man."

Lexington tried to smile, but he was looking greyer by the second. "Thanks, Corporal."

"How many are broken, son?" LeMaine asked. "I won't touch you again. Just tell me how bad it is."

"I....I don't know, Sir. It hurts to breathe."

"All right, son. I won't make you, but if we tie something around your ribs, it will stabilize them until we can get Kellogg to electrolyze them. We're gonna need you on your feet pretty soon, so anything we can do to help ease the pain will benefit all of us."

Lexington winced again. "Do what you have to do, Sir. You're the boss."

"He sounds like a Hellhound already," Heckler growled.

LeMaine stripped off his jacket, peeled off his t-shirt, and put his jacket back on without the shirt. He tore the shirt with his teeth and ripped it into strips. "Take your fatigues off, Ensign.

"I......." Lexington gasped. "I don't know if I can, Sir. It hurts too much."

"All right, Ensign. No big deal."

LeMaine cast a backward glance at the base while he got to work tying the strips tightly around Lexington's chest. How much longer did he have before the Hellhounds launched their assault?

Having to worry about an injured man didn't help matters, but LeMaine agreed with Heckler on this one. Lexington deserved a medal for standing up to Naelxad. LeMaine would make damn sure the young pilot made it off this wretched planet to receive the decoration he so bravely earned.

Heckler sat down next to Lexington. "The other Hellhounds are gonna want to know about this. Hell, you might even get posted to our squad permanently like Buca here."

Lexington tried again to smile, but it came out more as a grimace. "I don't think I'm ready for that, Sir."

Heckler squeezed his shoulder. "You're a credit to the Military. You stick with piloting. You've got a great career in front of you."

"Heads up!" LeMaine whispered. "They're coming back—probably for one of you two."

Chapter 5

Heckler got to his feet. He and Buca moved forward to flank LeMaine. The three men instinctively shifted closer together to block Lexington from the approaching guards.

The guards glared at the cage. They were definitely coming for Commander Naelxad's next victim. LeMaine braced himself for a fight when a catastrophic boom shook the ground beneath his feet.

The guards spun away aiming their weapons toward the noise, and at that moment, the whole base erupted in pandemonium. Continuous explosions shattered the night and columns of fire roared skyward.

"So much for waiting until dawn!" LeMaine grabbed Buca and Heckler. He towed Lexington and the others into the middle of the cell. "Get away from the walls! That crazy bitch is going Plaostine-crazy again!"

"What are you talking about?!" Heckler bellowed. "What happens at dawn?"

LeMaine didn't get a chance to answer before an answering explosion echoed across the base. This one came from directly over Commander Naelxad's office. One of the patrol vessels detonated in a fireball of destruction.

Naelxad burst out of the building just in time to avoid the wreckage smashing through the roof. Guards raced everywhere trying to find some enemy to fight, but there was no one in sight.

Naelxad caught a troop of guards who were running around like headless chickens. He pointed toward the cage and the whole platoon charged the bars. LeMaine braced himself. This couldn't be good.

The guards raised their weapons to shoot, but the shots that followed didn't come from the guards. Carbine fire blasted from somewhere and half the guards bit the dust.

Naelxad checked himself, wheeled, and still didn't see anyone. He hardened his resolve and rushed the last few feet to the cage.

He pulled a key from his pocket and started fumbling with the lock. "Oh, hell no!" Heckler snarled. "Don't even think about it!"

At that instant, a small, compact body materialized right behind Naelxad. It began as a blur against the backdrop of the base and reformed into a short, dark-haired woman.

Lemon grabbed Naelxad from behind and snapped his neck in a split second. She dropped his body on the ground and grabbed the key.

"Man, you're a sight for sore eyes, Sergeant!" LeMaine breathed.

Lemon pulled the bars aside and hauled LeMaine out of the cage. "Go, Sir! I'll deal with Lexington."

"Heckler, you and Buca come with me." LeMaine spotted Peterman, Polasek, Kellogg, and Monk all gunning their way onto the base. "Let's go!"

The three men charged between the panicked guards. Patrol craft whizzed overhead unloading on the squad, but the enemy kept their fire to the base's perimeter. They must be going after Nunn and O'Hara.

LeMaine grabbed Peterman. "You and Monk come with me. Polasek, get to that dish and transmit the frequencies now!"

"Yes, Sir! I'm all over it!"

"Kellogg, go find Lemon. Lexington is injured. Go!"

Kellogg and Polasek bolted in opposite directions. LeMaine took off at a run with Buca, Heckler, Peterman, and Monk.

"Where are we going, Sir?" Peterman asked. "Shouldn't we be defending Polasek?"

"That's what we're doing, Lieutenant. Look."

LeMaine ducked behind a building and ran onto the flight range. He was right. Most of the warships and freighters had launched when the Hellhounds started their assault, but quite a few unmanned patrol craft sat there abandoned.

"Each of you get one of those craft in the air," LeMaine ordered. "Give Polasek as much cover as you can. Understood?"

"Understood, Sir," Monk replied and locked another Crossfire gel cartridge into his carbine.

LeMaine did a quick check on the other three. He almost gave the order to go when DeYoung came around the building with Carver and Cameron.

She cracked a grin. "You did NOT think you were gonna steal those ships without taking us with you, did you?"

"Actually, that's exactly what we were going to do," Heckler snarled. "Please tell me you know how to fly one of those things."

"Do *you*?" DeYoung bumped Carver. "You hear this, boys? We get to crash a few more fighters today. Yippee."

"I don't want to hear the words 'crash' and 'fighters' in the same sentence, Lieutenant," LeMaine cut in. "You pilots get in the air and do your thing. Give the Axichis hell and draw them away from the dish so Polasek can work."

"We can do that." DeYoung smirked at Carver again. "No one gives the enemy hell like we do, Sir."

"Unless it's the Hellhounds," Peterman corrected.

"Of course." DeYoung crept another few inches to the edge of the building. "Are we deploying or not?"

LeMaine hesitated. He wasn't sure what he was waiting for—a sign from On High, maybe. His gut told him not to give the order yet. Something on the flight range didn't look quite right.

The instant he thought that, another even bigger Plaostine concussion blasted through the wall to his right.

Mortar and rubble erupted across the range and hit four of the parked patrol vessels. Two exploded and the noise coming from the base behind LeMaine spiked to an ear-splitting din.

"Go!" he roared. "Go now!"

He pushed Buca forward, but none of the waiting Hellhounds needed any encouragement. Everyone charged onto the range and fanned out to the remaining patrol craft.

LeMaine had no idea what to expect once he got inside the cockpit. He raced through an open hatch and got a pleasant surprise when he sat down at the controls.

The craft had been configured in an almost perfect replica of an Elian attack cruiser. The Axichis had incorporated Elian technology even here. Even the readouts were in English.

More patrol craft rocketed into the air beyond LeMaine's cockpit window and he scrambled to fire up his engines. The Axichis patrols either got tired of trying to target Nunn or they realized what was going on at the base. The patrols came racing back in a big hurry.

"Come on out and play, suckers!" DeYoung sang through the communications system.

"How about we give 'em the old pinch-squeeze, Lieutenant?" Carver asked.

"What the hell are you two talking about?" Heckler growled. "Speak English, why can't you?"

DeYoung laughed. "Watch and learn, sonny. Let's go, Carver."

"Yes, Ma'am."

DeYoung peeled one way and Carver banked the other. They split off and the Axichis pursuit parted to follow them.

LeMaine rocketed up into the mix and got caught in a firefight with Peterman, Cameron, and Monk all gunning for the enemy.

Peterman wheeled his cannons outward and sprayed shots at three Axichis attackers coming in hot. They outraced him and flew straight into Cameron's guns.

The young recruit pilot hadn't even flown anywhere. He stayed in one spot and waited for Peterman to chase the enemy right into the line of his fire.

"Holy f-ing shit, Batman! Did you see that?" Peterman crowed. "Cameron: three. Hellhounds: zip. You boys are falling down on the job."

"Bring 'em in, Sir!" Cameron called. "Set 'em up and knock 'em down just like a spider catching flies in a web."

"Are you people listening to this?" Heckler rumbled from the other side. "He's talking like a Hellhound now."

"Coming straight at you, son." LeMaine pulled his ship into a steep curve to surround the attacking patrols. "Stand by to eat 'em up."

The enemy fell for the bait and ten of them enveloped LeMaine in cannon fire. He maneuvered his ship in wild somersaults to avoid as many shots as he could. He unloaded his guns in all directions to keep them close and he plunged nose first into Cameron's trap.

Cameron rotated his vessel at blinding speed and erupted cannon fire in a whirl. LeMaine didn't see how the young pilot was keeping up with so many attackers.

LeMaine didn't have time to wonder. He had all he could do to stop the enemy from destroying his ship and blowing him to kingdom come.

He pushed the throttle to the wall racing for Cameron's covering fire, but Cameron had his guns aimed in the opposite direction. He didn't even see LeMaine.

LeMaine hunkered low in his seat waiting for the attack that blasted him to smithereens. Without warning, without the slightest hint what he was about to do, Cameron jerked his cannons backward.

He didn't move his ship at all. Anyone looking at him would think he didn't know what was going on.

The next second, all his cannons unloaded on LeMaine's pursuers. Blasts enveloped LeMaine and blocked out the cockpit.

Fire and noise pounded the cockpit window. When it cleared, LeMaine saw himself diving full tilt into Cameron's ship.

LeMaine peeled sideways and barely scraped past, but Cameron never budged. He trained every shot on the patrols hounding LeMaine and left none intact.

"You better wake up and smell the coffee, Buca!" Monk called. "This boy is giving you a run for your money."

"How many is that so far?" Buca asked.

"I make it twenty," Peterman replied.

"I make it twenty-eight," Cameron corrected.

Heckler cackled with glee. "Spoken like a true Hellhound, boy. Keep your kill count. Hellhounds hang their hats on kill count."

"Just don't tell Nunn and O'Hara," Monk warned. "They're gonna be in a foul mood when they find out."

"Considering how many explosions Nunn set off and how many Axichis guards O'Hara shot, I don't think they'll be too concerned." LeMaine broke off. "Looks like someone wants to join our little tea party."

LeMaine's scanners detected another contingent of Axichis patrols returning from the forest. They hurtled for the flight range on an intercept course with the Hellhounds' position.

"Got any more bright ideas?" Heckler asked.

"It doesn't look like our spider will be able to stand up to all these," LeMaine replied. "Monk, Heckler, and Peterman, get down into Cameron's web and defend the range."

"What are *you* going to do?"

"I'll draw them in. Just don't let them kill me, all right?"

Peterman laughed. "Don't worry, Sir. No one in the whole Elian Military would be stupid enough to try to replace you."

LeMaine had to join in the joke, but the Axichis patrols were coming in way too fast. LeMaine raced out to engage them.

The patrols spotted him and pounced. They surrounded him in such a thick knot that he couldn't break free to fall back.

His ship staggered. The Axichis revolved around him in tight orbits of punishing cannon fire.

Out of nowhere, another barrage struck the craft right behind him and he broke through into open space. He got a clear view of his own people fifty yards ahead.

He gunned his engines and darted into their midst, but the Axichis spotted the trap, held off, and unloaded on the defenders from out of range. The Hellhounds could only retaliate by breaking out of their cluster.

LeMaine throttled forward to make another feint when two more patrol craft rocketed out of nowhere. LeMaine had half a second to recognize DeYoung and Carver blasting in from opposite sides.

They both opened fire at the same instant and pounded the Axichis with dozens of shots. Axichis vessels exploded as the two pilots streaked past each other and whizzed skyward again.

The instant the devastation cleared, an emergency alarm went off on LeMaine's controls. He adjusted the helm for a second before the whole cockpit started going haywire. None of the instruments or the helm would respond.

He tried to correct, but nothing worked. The controls flashed on and off and half his console shut down.

"Mayday, mayday!" Cameron yelled. "My ship is malfunctioning! I'm losing stability and cannons are nonoperational."

"The frequencies are transmitting!" LeMaine replied. "Polasek is shutting down the Axichis. Everyone get down on the ground—now! Land your ships and get out!"

LeMaine fumbled to descend, but the engines didn't respond. The alarms squealed louder and the fuel system started to overload.

The ship lurched and shuddered. He got the fighter thirty feet above the tarmac before one engine cut out and the other exploded.

The craft slammed down hard with one wing in flames. LeMaine sprang out of his seat, but with the systems shutting off one after the other, he couldn't get the hatch open.

He searched the ship for some weapon he could use, but he didn't find any. He kicked at the controls a few times, but they didn't respond until the hatch released from the outside.

The hatch banged down on the tarmac. DeYoung and Peterman ran over to him. "Captain....."

"Fall back!" he yelled to the Hellhounds who were gathering from all over the range. Patrol craft were going up in flames all over the place. "Get off the base! Get back to the jungle on the double."

He pushed Peterman ahead of him. LeMaine made sure the rest of the group made it off the range and into the trees.

LeMaine snatched up fallen Axichis weapons on his way back to the base. He had to find the rest of his squad. The frequencies had just gone out to the whole Elian fleet which meant Polasek was still working on the transmission dish.

LeMaine swept every nook and cranny for enemies, but all the Axichis seemed to have fled. LeMaine didn't want to trust that, though. The Axichis went to a lot of trouble to establish this base and to hold it throughout the war. They were too slippery and too cunning to just abandon it.

LeMaine headed for the dish keeping out a sharp eye for the rest of the Hellhounds. Nunn, O'Hara, Lemon, Kellogg, and the other pilots were around here somewhere, but LeMaine didn't see any sign of them. Did they already escape to the jungle....or did something happen to them?

LeMaine ducked through a door in the dish's large pedestal. A structure as big as a small house supported the dish off the ground.

The wall with the door in it was the only part of the structure not covered in electronic equipment. Polasek whizzed from one component to another like a kid in a candy store. He fiddled with this, tinkered with that, adjusted something else, and peered into various screens and diodes LeMaine couldn't hope to understand in a million lifetimes.

"Bail out, Lieutenant," LeMaine panted as soon as he burst inside. "The frequencies are away. We have to fall back to safety."

"No problem, Sir. I wasn't sure how to tell if the frequencies had worked or not."

"They worked. Now come on." Polasek started to unhook his portable communications array from the vast web of equipment in front of him, but LeMaine stopped him. "Leave it. We don't need it anymore."

"Are you sure, Sir? Lemon said you wanted to stop the Axichis from getting their hands on the frequencies. If I leave my array behind, they might be able to hack it and get the frequencies."

"Oh. You're right. Go ahead, then, Lieutenant."

Polasek went to work, but LeMaine couldn't calm down. He stood guard at the door to make sure no one interrupted Polasek.

LeMaine kept scanning the base for any sign of the remaining Hellhounds. He even checked his remote, but he no longer trusted it to tell him what was really going on. He was flying blind.

He tensed when more Axichis warships thundered overhead, but they didn't come from or stop at the base. They raced across the sky toward the distant horizon.

Polasek came up behind LeMaine. "I'm ready, Sir."

"Good man. You did real good, Lieutenant."

Polasek beamed at him. "Thanks to you and your covering fire. You drew the whole Axichis force away. No one even saw me come in here."

"Then we did our job. Let's rock and roll."

LeMaine and Polasek inched out of the building. LeMaine made one last sweep of the surroundings and tugged Polasek's sleeve. "Let's go."

They took off running for the jungle. LeMaine veered around the wreckage of Naelx-ad's office when a resounding boom rocked the whole planet. Thunderous crashes and deafening explosions shook the air.

LeMaine and Polasek darted behind one of the few buildings still standing. LeMaine tried to hide and check the situation at the same time.

He stuck his head out only to yank it back when a giant Axichis warship plummeted out of the sky. It exploded in a shower of burning fuel and smashed into the ground right on top of the cage where the Axichis had imprisoned LeMaine and his men.

A shockwave flattened LeMaine and Polasek against the wall. Blistering heat scorched LeMaine's cheeks. The minute he dared to open his eyes, he saw two more warships blazing a fiery path through the planet's atmosphere.

"Let's get out of here!" Polasek yelled and both he and LeMaine burst into the open.

From here, LeMaine could see Elian bombers pounding through the Axichis invaders. Warships exploded in all directions and they all plunged to crash on top of the base.

LeMaine seized Polasek's shirt and tried to dodge one crashing enemy after another. The pair worked their way across the base, but the battle built to an ever more devastating pitch as dozens of Elian bombers descended on the scene.

Each Axichis warship and fighter detonated in a ball of destruction. Torn fuselages, burning engine housing, and torched Axichis bodies rained around LeMaine's head.

Polasek shrieked something as a metal fragment pelted on top of him and he stumbled. LeMaine caught him, held Polasek up, and practically dragged him into the trees.

Polasek collapsed and LeMaine lowered him against a tree. Blood poured from Polasek's scalp. Where the hell were Kellogg and the rest?

LeMaine inched to the edge of the jungle and peered through the leaves. He had to get Polasek to some medical help. More Axichis warships crashed all over the base, but the Elian bombers didn't disperse as the Axichis force dwindled.

LeMaine held his breath as three bombers eased down to land on the base. They extended their landing gear and set down on the flight range. Their giant struts crushed the patrol craft LeMaine and the others had been flying.

No Axichis came out to shoot at them and no Axichis craft launched to attack them. LeMaine breathed a heavy sigh of relief. The battle was over. The Elian Military was back in control of Toreon.

Chapter 6

LeMaine stood back and watched the *Lucidity* medical staff buzzing around Polasek's bed. They had fixed a cranial scanner to his forehead that fed continuous readings to the nearby scanner station.

Nurses reported the data to doctors who were examining Polasek all over. Several more nurses work to clean up his hair and face to find the source of the bleeding.

LeMaine could already see there was nothing wrong with Polasek except a really bad gash on his scalp, but LeMaine didn't want to leave. Polasek saved the whole Elian system. Now the Military had the Axichis on the run.

One of the nurses bumped into LeMaine. "I'm sorry, Sir, but you'll have to leave. We'll notify you if there's any change in his condition."

LeMaine took a step backward, but he still didn't leave. The nurses went into an even more confused flurry around Polasek's bed. They started to lower his head to make him lie down flat

Some of the medical staff unlocked the rolling casters on the table and they started to wheel Polasek away. "Where are you taking him?" LeMaine demanded. "There's nothing wrong with him."

"We have to take him down to the deep tissue scanner," a different nurse told him. "We need to assess whether there was any blunt force trauma to the cranial bones."

LeMaine took a step forward to follow them, but the nurse stopped him. "Please, Captain. There's nothing you can do here except get in the way. Go out to the waiting area and we'll notify you if there's any change."

They swiveled the bed around and Polasek's head passed LeMaine. Polasek looked up between several arms and bodies. "I'll be all right, Sir. I have to make it out of this so the Hellhounds can chap my hide about getting hurt. I couldn't miss that."

LeMaine shot out a hand and grabbed Polasek's arm. "You did real good, son. I couldn't be prouder to have you on my squad."

Polasek beamed at him. "Tell Kellogg I'm glad I have some real medical professionals working on me for once in my life."

LeMaine had to laugh. "I think you better tell him that yourself, Lieutenant."

Polasek burst into a huge grin and pressed LeMaine's hand deeper into his own arm before the medical people tore him away. A second later, Polasek's bed slammed through the swinging doors toward the elevator and the whole party disappeared.

LeMaine turned away with a heavy heart. He could handle one of his squad getting injured in the field. Then maybe he and Kellogg would be able to do something about it.

Having one of his injured people taken away where he couldn't see and help them, even for a minor injury, was more than he could bear.

He dragged himself out to the waiting room. That was the last place in the universe he wanted to be. He despised medical waiting rooms more than anything.

He only stopped there because he found the rest of the Toreon ground team in there waiting, too. Heckler, Peterman, Buca, Monk, DeYoung, Carver, and Cameron all turned around when LeMaine came in.

"How's Polasek, Sir?" Monk asked.

"He's fine. He's got a cut to his head, but there's no brain damage. He was making jokes when they wheeled him away to the deep tissue scanner. I'm sure he'll be just fine."

The others exchanged glances and Peterman asked the question they were all thinking. "What about the others?"

LeMaine sighed again and passed his hand across his eyes. "I don't know. I guess I better go debrief with Command and find out why the rest of the squad didn't make it back. I hate to hear what they have to say."

"It can't be anything good," Heckler growled. "The Elian Military is all over Toreon. If the rest of the squad was there to be found, we would know about it."

"Not necessarily," DeYoung countered. "One of the other bombers could have picked them up and word just hasn't gotten back to us yet."

LeMaine turned to her. "You and yours should go report to your superiors. You aren't part of this anymore."

"To hell with that," Cameron cut in. "The Hellhounds are our people, too."

"Lexington, Orr, and Stivers are missing, too," Carver pointed out. "We're just as concerned about what happened to the squad as you are."

"You don't worry about Lexington," Monk told him. "He'll be just fine as long as he's with Kellogg."

"Cool your jets, all of you," LeMaine cut in. "Wild speculation about where they are and what they're doing won't do us any good. DeYoung, you take your people down to the flight deck and report to your superiors."

"Yes, Sir."

LeMaine turned to Carver and especially Cameron. "I'm telling you now that it's near impossible any of you will be assigned to the Hellhounds again. If you want to put in for a post on my squad, you'll have to go through the proper channels. I'll give all of you my personal recommendation, but that's the best I can do. Understand, Cameron?"

Cameron nodded and he didn't lower his eyes the way he did before. "Yes, Sir. I'm staying on the flight crew."

"Me, too," Carver replied.

"All right, boys. You did great down there. You did your ship and your crew proud. I couldn't ask for better."

Cameron blushed. "Thank you, Sir. It was an honor to serve with you."

LeMaine held out his hand, and when Cameron shook it, they both pulled each other in for a hug.

LeMaine clapped the young pilot on the back, held him at arm's length, and beamed at him. "What do you say, Ensign? You earned your first decoration before you even graduated from the Academy. Not many pilots can say that."

"Hell, not even I can't say that," Monk grumbled.

Cameron blushed furiously. "Thank you, Sir. I guess I surprised even myself."

LeMaine shook hands and hugged Carver and then turned to DeYoung. "What about it, Lieutenant? Do you fancy yourself a Hellhound?"

She wouldn't stop grinning. "Naw. You slouches spend way too much time on the ground."

"Oh, here we go with the wisecracks," Heckler growled. "Where's O'Hara when we really need him?"

"All the more reason to get rid of her while we have the chance," Peterman added. "Another wise ass is the very last thing we need on this squad."

DeYoung beamed at them all. "If you Hellhounds ever want to take some lessons on how to get it done, you're welcome to come on back to the *Lucidity* anytime. We'll be happy to school you, won't we, Cameron?"

Everyone laughed and LeMaine pretended to push DeYoung away. "Get out of here, all of you. I don't need another mouth war breaking out in the damn medical ward."

The three pilots laughed and shared hugs and handshakes with the rest of the squad before they left to go back to the flight deck. LeMaine was sorry to see them go. He was always happy to meet good people who threw down and did the job for his squad. He really couldn't have asked for a better result from the *Lucidity* pilots.

"You better get upstairs, Sir," Peterman told him. "The sooner we find out the position, the sooner we can all stop worrying and get back to work."

"You're right. You Hellhounds can stand down until further notice. Go get yourselves a shower and something to eat. Grab a few winks and I'll let you know as soon as I find out where our people are."

"Yes, Sir." Peterman waved to the others. "Let's beat it."

He, Heckler, and Buca headed for the door, but Monk stayed behind. "Do you want me to go with you, Sir?"

"Thanks, Monk, but I better go alone. You go on and try to relax some. If the position isn't looking good, we'll be bound to deploy again soon so enjoy yourself while it lasts."

Monk sighed and looked away. "I don't think I can, Sir."

LeMaine squeezed his shoulder. "I know how you feel. Maybe don't enjoy yourself, but at least go downstairs and clean yourself up. Get some food and some sleep with the others. Think of it as preparing yourself for our next deployment....." LeMaine glanced behind Monk. The others had already disappeared. "If it looks bad and our people are captured or pinned down somewhere, getting some food and some rest will be the best way you can help them."

"Yes, Sir. Thank you, Sir."

Monk left the medical ward. LeMaine waited until he was alone before he let himself feel the full weight of worry and dread. What would he find out when he debriefed with Colonel Nicholson?

LeMaine didn't want to relax, either, not until he knew where his people were and that they were out of danger. He wanted to deploy again right away so he could find them and bring them back, but he couldn't do any of that.

He still hadn't been called up to debrief, so he had no choice but to go to the *Lucidity's* officers' quarters, take a shower, change his fatigues, and get something to eat, too, but everything he put in his mouth made him feel sick.

Did the total lack of communication with Command mean something? Did it mean the missing Hellhounds were already dead? They could be on a different ship like DeYoung said. Colonel Nicholson might be in a high-level brass meeting and hadn't had time to notify LeMaine that his Hellhounds had been found.

LeMaine exchanged a few snatches of casual conversation with other officers in the mess, but his heart wasn't in it. He didn't want to talk to anyone except Lemon, Nunn, O'Hara, and Kellogg. LeMaine didn't want to be anywhere other than looking for them.

He finally gave it up and decided to go downstairs to the enlisted mess to find the rest of the squad. At least they would understand how he felt. They could all wait together, but when he went out into the corridor, his remote buzzed. *Captain Owen LeMaine: Report immediately to Captain's Ready Room.*

His heart skipped a beat and he veered off to the elevator.

Chapter 7

LeMaine steadied himself before he walked into the ready room to find Colonel Nicholson and Commander Lodge waiting for him.

"I won't beat around the bush, Owen," Colonel Nicholson told him. "Your people are captives of the Axichis. They're being held on Nainia. The Axichis are holding them hostage in exchange for concessions from Command."

LeMaine buckled, propped his arms on the table, and let out a shaky breath. "Shit!"

"As far as we know, your people are all alive and well," Commander Lodge added. "We've scanned the planet and located their life signs on board the Axichis warship in question. All their vitals are reading as normal....although Ensign Lexington is showing extreme stress responses. We can only assume he's injured, but the Hellhounds are all fine."

"Thank God for that!" LeMaine breathed.

"Which means you're going in after them, Owen," Colonel Nicholson finished. "You and your Hellhounds will deploy on Nainia within twelve hours."

"We can't spare anyone to assign you additional personnel," Commander Lodge added. "I know it's asking a lot, but you'll just have to go in with the five men you already have."

"Don't worry about it," LeMaine replied. "We'll handle it, and once we get inside, we'll have the other seven to help us out."

"We just received a medical report on Lieutenant Polasek," Colonel Nicholson went on. "He's clear for active duty. He's on his way down to the enlisted barracks right now."

"What can you tell me about the position on Nainia?" LeMaine asked.

Colonel Nicholson waved at a chart already displayed on the screen behind him. "The Axichis have retreated there. They've set up a temporary command center here, near Thailiv."

"That's a major Elian population center!" LeMaine exclaimed.

"Which is exactly why they're using it as cover," Commander Lodge replied. "We can't bombard their cluster without risking the city, which is where you come in."

"The Hellhounds are being held on the *Scagrak*, an Axichis warship," Colonel Nicholson added. "We haven't seen the Axichis take your people off the ship even once."

"Any ideas on how we can get inside?" LeMaine asked.

"We're leaving that up to you, Owen," Colonel Nicholson replied. "We're rallying the whole fleet for a major offensive to drive the Axichis out of our system. It's going to take the combined efforts of every ship we've got so we can't dedicate any resources to this. We need you to work the old Hellhounds magic and just handle it."

"Oh, I'll handle it. If it means getting our people out, we'll go to town."

"Good man." Colonel Nicholson clapped him on the shoulder. "We'll be launching our offensive in twelve hours. Plan to execute and complete your maneuver before then. Once we launch it, the *Scagrak* will leave Nainia with the Axichis fleet. You'll need to drop on Nainia, locate your people, and get them off the *Scagrak* before the ship launches. We won't be able to help you if you're on board once it engages the rest of the Elian Military. Understood?"

"Yes, Sir. I understand completely."

"You're dismissed, then. Good luck, Owen."

LeMaine saluted them and got back into the elevator with his head spinning. Twelve hours. That left him virtually no time at all.

He had to work fast. He hustled down to the enlisted barracks and found Polasek with his face buried in the biggest sandwich known to mankind. "On your feet, Lieutenant. We're going on a rescue mission to get our squad back."

Polasek choked on his sandwich, but he didn't stop eating. "What—now?"

"Yes, now. I need you to find the rest of our squad and get down to the flight deck on the double. Get your hands on every weapon available and get suited up to drop. Go, Polasek. It's urgent."

Polasek didn't argue and LeMaine got back into the elevator. He had to think and he had to think fast. He stepped onto the flight deck and looked around. He was hoping for DeYoung, but he set off when he spotted Cameron instead.

The young pilot had his hands deep inside an attack cruiser's guts and grease smudged Cameron's face. He smiled when LeMaine showed up. "Did you bring my Medal of Valor, Sir?"

"Put your tools away, Ensign. I'm commandeering you for the duration."

Cameron blanched. "Sir?"

"I need you to drop me and the Hellhounds on Nainia. It's an emergency and we're leaving right away. Is this your ship?"

"No, Sir, but I can get one if you need one."

"Get it. Oh, good. Here comes DeYoung."

DeYoung strolled over. "That was quick. You couldn't live without us, could you, Sir?"

"I'm taking Cameron, Lieutenant, and a ship. It's critical and I'm under direct orders from Colonel Nicholson."

"Okay. I'll take your word for it." She turned to Cameron. "Go suit up, Ensign."

"Yes, Ma'am." Cameron dropped his tools and skedaddled. A second later, he returned somewhat cleaned up and wearing his usual uniform instead of his jumpsuit.

He started working on a personnel transport vessel across the deck. "What's going on?" DeYoung asked.

"The Hellhounds are being held hostage by the Axichis and we're going to get them," LeMaine replied.

She grinned again. "Goody! Can I come?"

"You had your chance, Lieutenant. Besides, we're going down on the ground and you wouldn't want that."

She laughed and LeMaine crossed the deck to where Polasek, Peterman, Monk, Buca, and Heckler were just coming out of the elevator. LeMaine was delighted to see them all suited up and armed to drop.

"Cameron is taking us out. Go strap in on that ship over there. I'll be with you in a second."

LeMaine crossed to the nearest weapons locker and started loading himself with everything he could find. He took carbines, gear, and finally pulled a drop suit over his fatigues. So much for getting some rest.

He found his five remaining Hellhounds strapped into the back of Cameron's transport. The young pilot went up to the cockpit and started powering up. "Strap in to launch, Sir!" he yelled to LeMaine. "We just got clearance from the bridge."

"Take us out, Ensign!" LeMaine called back and took the seat next to Monk.

LeMaine wriggled into his safety harness as the ship launched into the stars. Cameron punched the engines and the ship rocketed away.

It had only been traveling for ten minutes when Cameron called again. "Coming up on Nainia, Sir! Any particular place you want me to drop you?"

"Drop us over Thailiv!" LeMaine bent close to the other Hellhounds. "Get down into Thailiv and converge on the Axichis cluster. We'll rendezvous once we get on the ground, but we need to get as close to the enemy as possible. Don't wait around to meet up with the rest of us. Just get there as quick as you can."

"Entering orbit now!" Cameron called. "Stand by to drop!"

LeMaine and the others unbuckled, lashed their safety leashes to the ship's interior anchor points, and pulled on their pressure masks.

LeMaine went down the line checking each Hellhound in turn, but he already knew they were ready. The Hellhounds didn't make mistakes with their gear and time was of the essence.

"In position!" Cameron yelled. "You're all clear to deploy!"

LeMaine couldn't answer with his mask on. He would have liked to go up to the cockpit and thank Cameron, but that would have to wait for another day.

The hatch cracked open and pelting wind snatched at LeMaine's body. It tried to rip him out into the sky.

LeMaine gave the thumbs up to his squad and then hurtled himself out of the compartment. He plunged through the atmosphere dropping fast.

Chapter 8

L eMaine curled into a ball as heat seared his drop suit. He stayed in that position until his remote buzzed.

He flung out his arms and legs and soared over Thailiv. The city sprawled far and wide covering hundreds of miles. Farmland surrounded the city with dense, boreal forests beyond that. Nainia would have been a beautiful planet if the Axichis hadn't been here.

LeMaine flew over the city and steered toward the Axichis warships parked at the edge of town. He had no idea where to land or what to expect once he got on the ground, so he chose a random street.

He veered downward, hit the pavement, and ran to slow his momentum. He darted into an alley and started stripping off his drop suit. He checked and rechecked his remote. It seemed to be working just fine now, thank Christ.

It showed him the *Scagrak* with its seven human life signs. The remote also showed him four more human life signs and one Maczhi landing in the city. The Hellhounds were the only humans on the planet. Everyone else belonged to one of the native alien groups.

Dozens of natives meandered through the streets minding their own business. They cast sidelong glances at LeMaine when he landed. Some even raised their eyebrows when he stepped out into the street fully armed and wearing Special Forces fatigues. They couldn't be seeing this every day, but he didn't have time to be discreet.

He checked his remote again. Monk and Buca had landed only a few streets away and they were already on their way toward the Axichis cluster.

LeMaine headed for them and then discovered Polasek, Peterman, and Heckler coming toward him. This was lucky. He wasn't hoping to meet up with his men so soon.

"What's the plan, Sir?" Heckler growled when the squad reformed.

"We're going to get ourselves caught," LeMaine informed them. "That will be the quickest way to get the Axichis to take us to our people."

Peterman's eyes widened. "You....*want*....to get caught by the Axichis?"

"That's right, Lieutenant, so you keep your negotiating skills to yourself. Don't tell the Axichis who you are or that you speak for Command. You're nothing but a grunt on this mission."

Heckler laughed and punched Peterman's shoulder. "Just a lowly grunt like the rest of us, Lieutenant. Try not to cry into your corn flakes."

Peterman only grinned at him. "Maybe if I can be a grunt like you, Corporal, I'll make a bigger target for the enemy to shoot at."

"Ouch!" Polasek exclaimed.

"Peterman might be small," Buca added, "but he can shoot better than anyone....exc ept for me, of course."

The others howled with laughter. "This boy has been taking lessons from O'Hara on how to mouth off," Heckler announced. "You better watch out, Sir. Buca will be busting your ass with the best of them before long."

"I couldn't be happier if he did." LeMaine cocked his head and frowned. "I hear gunfire."

The whole squad looked down at their remotes and LeMaine jumped. "Shit! Get back here—into that alley."

He herded his people off the street. They crowded into an alley just as a mixed mob of Nainians swarmed around the nearest corner. The group consisted of at least four different local alien species all jumbled together. They were all armed, but they didn't see the Hellhounds.

LeMaine shouldered his carbine and prepared himself to go down shooting, but the Nainians didn't pose any threat to the Hellhounds. The locals dashed around the corner, spun backward, and fired up the street at something LeMaine couldn't see.

The Nainians made their stand, but only for a few seconds before lasers skittered from behind the nearest building. LeMaine tensed and then his worst nightmare came true when an Axichis platoon stormed around the corner.

They laid down punishing fire on the Nainians, but it still took a long time for the Axichis to drive off these sturdy locals. The Nainians cut down plenty of Axichis in the process.

The Nainians retreated one painstaking step at a time and the Axichis sent in more ground troops to hunt the locals down. The Nainians drew level with LeMaine's hiding place and he sprang out to join them. He stormed into the battle firing at as many Axichis as he could hit.

The Hellhounds angled in to join the Nainians, and for a second, it looked like they might actually win. The Nainians advanced a few more paces and pushed the Axichis toward the corner where they came from.

LeMaine almost called to his Hellhounds. His plan to get captured wasn't working out the way he hoped. He would have to adjust, but at that moment, a howl echoed out of the distance.

He automatically swiveled his carbine upward and the Hellhounds did the same. In fact, all the Nainians rotated their guns upward, too. They all knew that sound as well as LeMaine did.

A squad of Axichis fighter craft lifted from the outskirts of town. They came from the area the Axichis were using as a base and the fighter craft shot straight into the battle.

The ground troops took advantage of the distraction and unloaded on the defenders with all their firepower. They hit four Nainians and Peterman went down.

Heckler and Buca charged over to defend him, but he was already sitting up, twisting onto his seat, and shooting right back at the enemy. His face twisted in a furious mask of hate. He bared his teeth and roared at them. LeMaine had only seen Peterman like this a handful of times since he joined the squad.

More fighter craft screamed down from above. Their lasers ripped the whole street to smithereens.

The Nainians whirled away and bolted into the city. Lasers struck them from behind and bodies pitched all over the street. The fighter craft streaked past LeMaine's head to gun the Nainians down. Then the enemy wheeled a block away and came racing back to target the Hellhounds.

"Get him up!" LeMaine bellowed to Heckler. "Pick him up and make tracks!"

Heckler fired a few more times, but the oncoming fighter craft cut such a deadly swatch of lasers across the street that he had to give it up.

Buca, Monk, and Heckler ran one way and got cut off by fighter craft swiveling to intercept them. Buca stood his ground to return fire until a vicious barrage smashed the pavement right next to his foot.

Monk grabbed him and yanked Buca out of the way just in time. They tried to stagger back to the LeMaine, only to run into another assault from more fighter craft veering into their path.

The three friends backed together for protection. Heckler grabbed Peterman's free arm and swung Peterman across his back. Peterman held on with one hand and kept firing while Monk defended their retreat.

LeMaine headed for the alley where the squad had been hiding before. He didn't see any other way out. The streets left the squad too exposed. The fighter craft would still be able to target the Hellhounds here, even between these narrow walls.

Seconds kept ticking by. Every minute LeMaine spent out here was another minute lost before he could free the captured Hellhounds. He had to do something.

He spun around to make sure the rest of the squad was coming with him, but Buca, Monk, and Heckler couldn't break through. Too many enemy fighters blocked them from rejoining their comrades.

LeMaine started forward. He didn't see anything he could do against so many fighters. He had nothing but two carbines to fight them with.

He took four steps before another band of Nainians charged out of some hidden corner. They overran the Hellhounds in a split second. LeMaine took a fraction of an instant to realize they were the same people he'd seen fighting the Axichis to begin with.

They flooded the area, but they didn't come for the Hellhounds. They descended on the Nainian casualties sprawled around LeMaine's feet.

Seven Nainians bent down trying to pick up their fallen comrades and the fighter craft pivoted to target them instead. Buca, Monk, and Heckler broke away and sprinted to join LeMaine and Polasek.

LeMaine turned his carbine back upward at the enemy. None of them was targeting him. They were all gunning for the defenseless Nainians.

LeMaine barged out into the street, planted himself between the enemy and the retreating Nainians, and defended them while they helped their wounded get away.

The fighter craft pivoted back toward him and he looked right up into their laser ports. He braced himself for the end when a missile screamed out of nowhere and smashed the nearest fighter to pieces right in front of him. The craft exploded with a bone-shattering boom and all the other fighters whirled backward to confront their new attacker.

LeMaine straight-armed his people toward the alley. He glanced up and down the street and spotted a whole crew of Nainians manning artillery pieces farther up the street.

They fired three more rockets and took out three more fighters with expert precision. The other fighters gunned their engines and blasted up the street training their lasers on the ground guns.

LeMaine traced his carbine across the skies to follow them, but they rocketed away so fast he didn't get off another shot. They shrieked toward the artillery and the Nainians opened up.

Rockets corkscrewed down the street and devastated the fighter craft in punishing explosions. Another five detonated and the last three raced away into the sky.

Chapter 9

L eMaine herded his squad closer to the alley when one of the Nainians called to him. "This way!" a big Buzath yelled. The guy was one of those helping pick up the Nainian wounded. "Follow us! You can't go in there! It isn't safe! Come with us!"

LeMaine already knew it wasn't safe, but he didn't see any alternative. He shouldn't even be out here shooting at fighter craft. He should be getting captured and taken to the Axichis ships.

The Buzath and his friends hoisted ten wounded off the pavement and headed up the street. The artillery gunners defended the locals all the way. How soon would the Axichis ground troops come back? They might show up at any time....but wasn't that what LeMaine wanted?

The Nainian wounded staggered behind the artillery pieces. The gunners hopped down and started dismantling the guns to join their comrades.

LeMaine threw caution to the wind and signaled the Hellhounds to follow. These Nainians might know a way to help the squad fulfill their mission, but LeMaine became painfully aware that he was moving away from the Axichis airfield instead of toward it.

The Nainians left at least half their casualties where they lay. The locals retreated up the street with the Hellhounds pivoting and guarding every corner.

The Nainians finally turned into a different alley a hundred yards from the battle site. A stone arch covered this one to protect it from the skies.

The locals laid aside their wounded and Heckler put Peterman down. LeMaine ripped open his pack, gave Peterman an injection of painkillers, and got to work sealing the gash on his thigh.

Peterman shut his eyes, gritted his teeth, and rested his skull against the wall. He kept his lips pinched shut and didn't make a sound until LeMaine finished.

LeMaine checked the rest of Peterman. "You're clear for duty, Lieutenant."

"Thank you, Sir," Peterman croaked.

LeMaine got to his feet and sliced his finger at the rest of the Hellhounds. "On your feet, people. We gotta make tracks."

The big Buzath from earlier called to LeMaine from across the alley. "Where are you going, Captain?"

"We're here on a rescue mission to free Elian prisoners from the Axichis." LeMaine stuck out his hand to the man. "I'm Captain Owen LeMaine of the Elian Special Forces."

"What prisoners are the Axichis holding?" a woman asked. "We haven't heard anything about any prisoners."

"They're members of our squad. They were captured on another planet and they're being held here. We're under a very tight time window. I'm sorry we can't help you defend your city and give your people medical treatment, but it's a matter of life and death."

"We'll come with you." The big Buzath stood up. "My name is Xars and this is....."

"I can't ask you to do that," LeMaine interrupted. "You stay here and protect your people. We have a mission to fulfill."

"Our mission is to defeat the enemy. If we can help you, we will."

LeMaine cast a critical glance over the group. More Nainians started getting to their feet, collecting their weapons, and advancing to join Xars and LeMaine.

Many of these Nainians were even injured. LeMaine assessed each one and recognized the unmistakable stamp of hardened warriors. These people were nothing to trifle with. "How much training do you people have?"

"We're all ex-Military and we've kept up our training in the Nainian militia. Just tell us what you want us to do."

"Just keep doing what you've been doing. I can't take you with me into the....." LeMaine's remote interrupted him and the other Hellhounds all looked down at their sleeves. "Shit!"

"What?" Xars asked.

"An Axichis patrol is coming straight for us." LeMaine snatched up his carbine. "Take your people and retreat deeper into the city—now! Don't ask any questions. Go! Get as far away as possible."

The Nainians started to follow him to the mouth of the alley, but LeMaine pushed them away. He pointed back into the alley, put his finger to his lips, and they finally retreated.

The Hellhounds came forward to join him and Heckler helped Peterman to his feet. Peterman stamped on his injured leg a few times, grimaced, and hefted his carbine. He was ready to go.

LeMaine paused at the head of the alley and checked his remote again. He grabbed Heckler and prodded him toward the street. "Take Monk and Buca. Get as close to the Axichis as possible, and once they come in sight, engage them. Understood?"

The others nodded and snapped their carbines ready. The squad set off at a fast clip on an intercept course for the patrol. LeMaine only hoped he could carry out his plan without taking too much damage.

He checked behind him to make sure the Nainians were out of sight. The alley appeared deserted from here. The Axichis wouldn't find the locals hiding there.

He dodged behind a pile of broken vehicle parts and peered out at the street from that vantage point. His remote showed him the Axichis patrol coming straight for this intersection. The enemy would pass right in front of him.

Peterman and Polasek flattened themselves behind LeMaine. Heckler, Monk, and Buca took a position across the street between two more buildings.

LeMaine held his breath as the Axichis got nearer. They advanced into the intersection sweeping their laser rifles over the whole area. They left no corner uncovered and inched nearer to LeMaine's trap.

They reached the corner and Monk lunged into the open. He roared at them and unloaded his carbine to mow them down. Heckler and Buca advanced right behind him.

Monk's shots dropped three Axichis first and the rest of the patrol rotated into line to defend themselves. At that signal, Peterman, Polasek, and LeMaine sprang out and attacked from behind.

The Hellhounds closed the enemy in their dragnet, and in a moment, the whole patrol lay bleeding on the ground.

"Well, Sir," Monk panted. "That didn't go as planned. We still aren't captured."

"Not so fast, Corporal." LeMaine looked down as another alert came over his remote. "There's a backup patrol coming in."

"How do you want to play this one?" Peterman asked. "Do you want to do the same thing?"

"No. Stay put. We'll pretend to be rifling the bodies. When the reinforcements show up, let them open fire and we'll all fall down like we've been hit. We need them to take us into custody."

"You mean just give up?" Heckler snorted. "That ain't the Hellhound way, Sir."

"It's the Hellhound way if we want to get our people out of here in time. If it makes you feel better, you can shoot back. Just don't kill too many of them. Leave enough of them alive so they can convince themselves that they captured us." LeMaine squatted down near one of the dead Axichis. "Oh, look. They have remotes, too. They're using a lot of Elian technology. That should make them easier to defeat."

He went over the dead alien and searched the man's pockets. Then LeMaine checked the Axichis's weapon while he watched the reinforcements inch nearer on his remote.

"Go on," he murmured to the others. "Don't let them see you standing up or they'll shoot you first."

"I *want* them to shoot me first," Heckler growled.

"Is that the Hellhound way?" Buca asked. "I may have signed up for the wrong squad."

Heckler laughed and the squad spread out to carry out LeMaine's orders. The men started searching the bodies in between keeping an eye on their remotes.

LeMaine kept his carbine in hand, but this position didn't give him much chance to defend himself. He resisted the urge to stand up. That would only make him a bigger target.

He shuffled over to the next body and did the same thing. The patrol was only one block away when it split in two. LeMaine tensed for the coming fight, but the patrol was moving too fast.

As soon as it divided, the Axichis started moving incredibly fast. The first group rushed into the street with guns blazing. LeMaine brought up his carbine and realized his mistake a second too late. The second group rushed around a different building and jumped out behind him. They pulled the same trick LeMaine just pulled on these dead Axichis.

Monk and Polasek leapt to their feet. They moved together to lay into the first Axichis attackers. A laser shot hit Polasek in the shoulder and he went down at Monk's feet.

LeMaine rotated backward to cover the flanking group, but he was the only one who did. Heckler, Buca, and Peterman all headed for Monk and left LeMaine alone to defend their backs.

He ripped his carbine up, scattered shots among his advancing enemies, and they spread out to surround him. He pulled his second gun forward and wheeled both ways at once. This definitely wasn't the way he planned to get caught.

Someone screamed behind him and the Axichis moved in for the kill. All thought of falling down and pretending to get hit evaporated out of LeMaine's mind. He had to protect his squad at all costs.

He swung left to gun down the Axichis creeping in on him, and in that moment, a searing jet of pain hit him in the chest. He dropped like a ton of bricks, and the last thing he saw was Monk standing over him unloading his carbine in all directions.

Chapter 10

LeMaine blinked to unstick his eyelids. He tried to clear his vision to look around, but his neck didn't seem to be working.

"Lie still, Sir," someone said. "Don't move or you might tear the seals loose."

LeMaine groaned. "Kellogg!"

"You're all right, Sir," Kellogg told him. "Just let me finish working on you before I clear you for active duty."

"Don't worry, Sergeant," LeMaine grumbled. "I don't think I want to hear the words 'active duty' ever again."

O'Hara snorted nearby. "I think the captain is going to live."

"I told you he would," Kellogg replied. "Don't move, Sir. I need to electrolyze you."

"I can't wait." ," LeMaine muttered.

He barely got the words out when a crushing blow struck him across the chest. It detonated his mind and he blacked out again.

A second later, he snapped wide awake with a roar of pain. Kellogg pushed him down on the floor. "Stay where you are, Sir. Just a little longer."

"He's been saying the same thing for the last three days," Lemon growled from somewhere out of sight.

"Lexington...Polasek...." LeMaine began.

"They're all here," Kellogg told him. "They're all fine. You're the last one."

LeMaine groaned again when Kellogg bent over and started working on his ribs. LeMaine clamped his eyes shut against the pain. "What happened?"

"You tell us," Nunn added from LeMaine's right. "We've been stuck in this damn hold ever since we left Toreon and then they brought you in."

"Buca says you got captured on purpose," O'Hara chimed in. "Is that true, Sir? Did you really do all this just because you love us so much?"

"I'm starting to seriously regret that, Sergeant. Aaarrrgh!"

"Sorry, Sir," Kellogg told him. "I've already given you the legal limit on painkillers and I can't give you any more. Please just lie still until I finish and then you can forget all about this."

"I won't forget all about this, Sergeant," LeMaine spat. "And you don't sound sorry at all."

"There's no one in the whole galaxy more sadistic than Kellogg," Heckler growled from above LeMaine's head. "He feeds off this shit."

"Tell them, Captain," Buca interjected. "They don't believe me when I tell them you planned this mission to get us captured by the Axichis."

"It's true," LeMaine replied. "For some reason, I thought rescuing you people might be a good idea."

"You see?" O'Hara chirped. "He really does love us."

"All except you, jackass," Lemon snarled. "No one loves your mouth."

"Aw, come on, Lemon. You know you really want to cuddle up to me and give me a nice, big, wet....."

"Knuckle sandwich," someone else cut in from LeMaine's other side. It was Lexington.

LeMaine looked instinctively toward the voice, and this time, Kellogg didn't try to stop him. "How are you, Ensign? How are the ribs?"

"They're fine now that he's had a nice healthy dose of Kellogg," Nunn replied. "We really need to find a way to make some money off this boy. He's a gold mine."

Kellogg laughed. "One more seal, Sir, and then you can sit up."

"Famous last words," Lemon muttered. "It's always one more seal."

"Until you get hurt again, right?" Peterman added. "It's never one more seal."

Nunn started to say something else, but at that moment, Kellogg sealed something else on LeMaine's stomach and his own piercing scream cut off the conversation.

Blistering pain destroyed his mind and he collapsed whimpering on the floor. No one said anything for a minute until one of Kellogg's tools clinked onto the floor near LeMaine's head. "You're finished, Sir. You can relax now."

LeMaine threw his arm over his face and rolled onto his side. He huddled in a ball doing his best not to fall apart from the pain. He had his fatigues off. The chilly floor burned his shoulder and side. That cold hurt almost as much as the wound being sealed.

Someone laid a comforting hand on his shoulder and no one said anything for a minute. He sniffed into his elbow willing himself to pull it together. How much time did he have left before the Elian fleet launched their strike? Was the *Scagrak* already airborne? Was he already too late to save the squad?

He fought himself under control and opened his eyes. All the Hellhounds and the three captured pilots crouched on the floor around him. They watched him out of the corners of their eyes and then looked away.

He pushed himself up and wiped his hand down his face. Now was not the time to fall apart.

Kellogg handed him a clean shirt. "So what's the plan, Sir? How do we get out of here?"

"What time is it?" LeMaine asked.

Heckler checked his remote. "Fourteen hundred by the Command clock."

"We have four hours to get off this tub." LeMaine looked around him more closely. The Hellhounds sat on a vast floor packed with prisoners. All of them belonged to Elian races and many bore the unmistakable signs that they'd been in battle. He even saw a few Military uniforms in the crowd.

He started to put the shirt on and then noticed the mat of sealed wounds on his chest and stomach. He must have been in terrible shape when the Axichis brought him in.

He winced when he pulled the shirt over his head. It was tighter than one of his own and the name, *Kellogg*, had been embroidered across the shoulder where LeMaine's own name should have been.

O'Hara clapped him on the back. "You're Kellogg now, Sir. You can spend your days electrolyzing your friends and making them writhe in agony."

"That's my ambition in life," Kellogg replied. "Lie down here and let me electrolyze you just for fun. Go on, Sergeant. You know you love it."

O'Hara laughed and Peterman interjected. "So how do we get out of here, now that we're caught?"

"What do you kids know about the lay of the land?" LeMaine asked.

Nunn nodded behind LeMaine's back. "They change the guard every five hours. They bring in food and water every twelve hours."

"They have the perimeter walls electrified with a high voltage current to drop any prisoner stupid enough to try anything," Lemon added. "See the space everyone leaves between themselves and the walls? A section of the floor is electrified, too. If anyone touches that wall or goes near it, they get fried."

"Any clue where they keep the controls?" LeMaine asked.

Nunn didn't turn around. "You can see the panel behind me. They activate and deactivate it every time they have to enter the prison floor to bring in food."

"How do they activate and deactivate it if the wall is electrified?" Peterman asked. "They would electrocute themselves just touching it."

"That's where you come in, Lieutenant," O'Hara told him. "We're going to send you over there to throw yourself against it. When the wall shorts out, we'll all escape taking your unconscious body with us."

"But don't worry," Kellogg added. "I'll revive you as soon as we're free."

The others laughed. "Seriously," LeMaine interrupted. "How do they work the panel without getting shocked?"

"We haven't been able to figure that out," Nunn replied. "So far, we've only ever seen Axichis work the panel, so maybe they've programmed the panel not to electrocute anyone with Axichis DNA."

"That's just a guess, though," O'Hara added.

Kellogg passed his scanner up and down in front of LeMaine. "You're clear for active duty, Sir."

"Just don't get shot in the chest again, will you?" Peterman added. "None of us wants that."

"Because none of us wants to take your place in command of this lunatic squad," Polasek chimed in. "You have to stay alive, Sir. You're the only thing keeping me sane."

LeMaine had to laugh with the others. He was starting to feel better now. His body didn't hurt as much, but that might just be the painkillers kicking in.

"You might not have such a bad idea about throwing someone at the panel to take the hit for us," he told Peterman.

"Hey!" Peterman countered. "I wasn't volunteering!"

"You can tell us the truth, Lieutenant," Nunn chided. "You just don't want to be next in line when the captain dies and Polasek gets shot."

"We aren't joking about that," LeMaine replied. "We're coming up with a strategy to short that panel so we can get out of here. We have four hours to get off this ship."

"I have an idea."

All eyes turned to Orr. He sat off to one side with Stivers. Neither of the two pilots had said anything since LeMaine woke up.

"Well, don't keep us in suspense," Lemon shot back. "Lay it on us."

"The mess workers who bring in the food aren't Axichis. They're Ongu from Imeon. If you're wrong about the panel being safe for Axichis to touch, we could use one of the Ongu to turn it off."

"How do we do that?" Nunn asked.

"Didn't you see the shackles on the Ongus' wrists and ankles when they brought the food in?" Stivers interjected. "They're prisoners just like we are."

Nunn turned all the way around and scowled at him. "I didn't see any shackles."

"You weren't paying attention, then. The Ongu keep looking at the Axichis like they were afraid of them."

"How does that help us use the Ongu?" LeMaine asked. "We're down to three hours and fifty minutes. We don't have time to contact the Ongu and explain our plan—whatever that is."

"The Axichis are scheduled to feed us again in twenty minutes," Kellogg pointed out. "The Ongu will be here. The only problem is how to communicate with them without the Axichis finding out what we're up to."

"That's easy," Stivers replied. "One of us has to go over there and cause a disturbance when the Ongu bring in the food. The Axichis will come out on the floor to break up the fight."

"Fight?" Lemon asked. "Who do you say is going to start this fight?"

"I am." Stivers looked straight back into her eyes and then faced LeMaine. "I'll do it, Captain."

"I see where you're going with this, Ensign, and I can't go along with it," LeMaine replied. "The Ongu are prisoners and living in fear of the Axichis. I can't condone throwing one of them against a highly electrified wall to help us escape. Whoever it is could be killed doing that."

"I'm not volunteering to throw the Ongu against the panel."

"What are you suggesting, then?" Peterman asked. "What are you going to do when the Axichis come over to break up the fight?"

"And don't tell me you're going to electrocute yourself, either," LeMaine added. "That's out of the question, too."

"I wasn't going to suggest that," Stivers replied. "I won't have to because the wall will already be deactivated. The Axichis will deactivate it so the Ongu will be able to bring the food onto the prison floor."

LeMaine shut his eyes. "Let me get this straight. You plan to go to the panel when it's already turned off....and then...."

"Turn it back on once the Axichis are on the floor," Orr finished. "The Axichis will deactivate the wall and the Ongu will come out on the floor to distribute the food. Stivers will start the fight. The Axichis will come out onto the floor to break it up. The rest of us will escape and then I'll reactivate the wall so the Axichis are trapped in here."

"That won't work," Polasek replied. "You and Stivers would be trapped in here along with the Axichis. You would still be on the ship while the rest of us got away."

Stivers shrugged. "It's a small price to pay so the rest of you can get away."

"No can do, Ensign," LeMaine replied. "Nice try, but no. We aren't leaving you and Orr behind."

"You won't have to," Orr countered. "Once you get out of this hold, you'll be able to figure out how to free us."

"I can't take that chance," LeMaine returned. "You would be trapped in here along with the Axichis. They would destroy you and we'd never see you or Stivers again. Come up with another option."

"There is no other option," Buca interjected for the first time. "We have four hours to escape and only twenty minutes until the Ongu come in. If we're going to do something, we need to do it now."

"Fifteen minutes, actually," Nunn corrected.

LeMaine winced. "This is a very bad idea."

"Says the man who deliberately got himself imprisoned on an Axichis warship to save a bunch of grunts no one cares about," Heckler growled.

LeMaine squinted between the prisoners toward the panel Nunn mentioned. "Too bad we don't know enough about the layout of this ship outside the hold."

Orr's eyes shot open. "I have it! I have the solution."

"What are you waiting for?" Nunn demanded. "We only have ten minutes left."

"As soon as you get outside and we're trapped in here with the Axichis, they'll chase us and try to catch us."

"And tear you apart," Lemon pointed out.

"We lead them back to the wall and get them to charge into it. Bzzzt! Problem solved."

The whole squad erupted in laughter and many other prisoners turned around to stare. Even the guards glared at the Hellhounds.

"You're betting your lives that this will work," LeMaine pointed out. "You realize that, don't you?"

Stivers cracked a wicked grin. "Isn't that what the Hellhounds do?"

LeMaine didn't answer. He didn't like that the Hellhounds bet their lives on flimsy plans like this. He especially didn't like that the Hellhounds were notorious throughout the whole Elian Military for doing just that.

LeMaine surveyed the Axichis guarding the hold. "Those stairs lead up to the catwalk where the guards stand. The guards must have an entry and exit point up there. We should get up there after Stivers reactivates the electric flow to the walls."

"The guards will try to stop us," Monk pointed out.

"I hope they do," Heckler growled. "I've been waiting too long to bust some Axichis heads."

"Things are going to get messy in the meantime." LeMaine nudged Stivers. "Are you and Orr sure you want to do this?"

"Don't ask them that!" Kellogg interjected. "They were the ones who suggested it. Don't give them a chance to back out. Just order them to do it."

"I wouldn't order them to do something I wouldn't do myself. Make sure you boys really want to do this because, once we start, there's no going back."

"We understand, Sir," Orr replied. "We're doing it."

LeMaine concentrated on Stivers. "The current to the wall could be strong enough to kill you. Do you realize that?"

"Yes, Sir. I understand. I also understand that these people are at war with Elia. If you and the Hellhounds get out of this hold, you'll be on board an Axichis warship in battle against the Elian fleet. You might be able to commandeer this ship and do some damage with it. That plan makes it worth it for me."

"Yeah, well, I'm not sure it makes it worth it to me."

"Do you really want to take that chance?" Stivers asked. "Time is running out, and if we don't carry out this plan now, we'll have to wait another twelve hours before the Ongu come back for another food run."

LeMaine sighed and looked away. "You missed your calling, son. You really are a Hellhound."

Stivers blushed and Orr elbowed him and grinned. Heckler gripped the young pilot's neck and gave him an affectionate shake.

LeMaine went back to studying the situation from a tactical point of view. About twenty-five guards patrolled the catwalk overhead. A high-security gate blocked the stairs leading down to the floor. Were the stairs electrified, too?

Chapter 11

L eMaine tensed when a door slammed on the catwalk overhead. The Axichis guards
patrolled the prison hold with their laser rifles aimed at the floor.

"It's time," Nunn murmured. "The Ongu will come in with the food now."

Sure enough, the guards on the catwalk unlocked their security gate and filed down
to the floor. "That answers my question about the stairs," LeMaine murmured. "They
aren't electrified."

"Does that help us?" Peterman asked.

"It might buy us a few extra seconds."

"No one will be able to reach the stairs once the wall is reactivated," Kellogg pointed
out. "Look."

Half the guards descended the stairs. They waited on the lowest steps while a different
door opened somewhere beyond the sea of prisoners.

LeMaine held his breath watching a section of the wall slid out of the way. Another
group of guards appeared escorting a crew of stooped, grey aliens. They Ongu pushed
wheeled trolleys into the hold. Shackles and chains bound each Ongu to its trolley.

The Ongu shuffled to the threshold and the guards stood watch on either side, but
none of them entered the prison hold. They hung back and none of the prisoners approached them, either.

LeMaine studied the whole process in detail. The forwardmost Axichis stepped onto
the floor and crossed to the control panel. He stayed close to the wall without venturing
out onto the hold floor. That section of floor must not have any current....or maybe he
turned it off from a different location.

He pressed his hand to the panel on the wall by the entrance. It buzzed and beeped
until green light flashed on it. Then the guard waved to the Ongu and the Ongu pushed
their trolleys onto the floor.

All the prisoners started getting to their feet. They jostled for the spots nearest to the Ongu, but no one crossed the section of floor between themselves and the wall, not even now that the electric current had been deactivated.

The guards flanked the Ongu until the mess workers took positions at the edge of the mob. Orr and Stivers elbowed their way into the throng. They kept whispering to each other, nodding, and pointing.

LeMaine suffered grave misgivings about this plan. He hated sacrificing any-one—ever—especially not good people who proved themselves brave, resourceful, and committed in combat.

Orr and Stivers turned out to be as tough and brave as any Hellhound. LeMaine hated putting them in danger like this, but he didn't see any choice.

He wouldn't go along with this at all if they hadn't volunteered to do it themselves. He considered calling them back, but in a second, the crowd swallowed them and he gave it up. It was too late now. The plan was already underway.

The Ongu started unpacking their trolleys and the prison crowd got more agitated. They shoved and scrambled to get closer. A few scuffles broke out and the guards had to step in to enforce order.

The Ongu pretended not to notice. They worked over their carts and unpacked stacks of bowls and serving utensils. The Ongu cast furtive glances at the prisoners and up at the guards. The Ongu gave all the signs of being as afraid of the Axichis as the prisoners were—maybe even more so.

Orr and Stivers worked themselves right up to the front. Only a few rows of prisoners separated them from the Ongu. The two pilots positioned themselves as close as possible to the control panel.

Another pang of doubt seized LeMaine, but before he could do anything to call them back, the two pilots rounded on each other. At some unspoken signal, they both started punching, kicking, and clawing at each other.

They went down among the prisoners and the whole prison hold exploded in pande-monium. LeMaine barely got a glimpse of the two friends locked in combat before they both struck out at people on either side of them.

The Axichis tried to wade into the throng to break it up, but it was too late. Unsus-pecting prisoners got caught in the mayhem. They either tried to hit back or they mistook the blows as coming from other prisoners.

Different aliens and a few Military personnel got dragged into the fight. In a matter of seconds, the whole thing devolved into a massive hand-to-hand battle with everyone fighting everyone else.

LeMaine shoved Buca and Monk forward. "Go! Get near the stairs!"

"When will he......" Polasek began, but he didn't finish before Stivers erupted out of the chaos and charged the control panel.

Five Ongu saw him coming the instant he broke cover. They lifted the tops off their trolleys and pulled out Axichis laser rifles hidden there. The Ongu turned them on the prisoners and especially on Stivers.

LeMaine started to turn back. Stivers came up with this plan to spare the Ongu. The Hellhounds assumed the Ongue were downtrodden prisoners like themselves.

That plan went right out the window when the Ongu turned their guns on the whole prison population. LeMaine froze in place watching the catastrophe unfold. The other Hellhounds paused at the base of the stairs to see what would happen.

The Ongu rotated their rifles downward and three of them opened fire. Their lasers skittered through the crowd and prisoners fell away screaming. The Axichis who had waded into the crowd to subdue the fight started to gain the upper hand, but only for a second.

Stivers checked himself for an instant. He reacted so fast that not even LeMaine realized what Stivers was going to do before he did it.

Stivers veered, seized the nearest Ongu by his ragged clothes, and flung the creature full force into the control panel. The Ongu struggled. Its leg caught on the chain binding it to the trolley, but Stivers attacked the poor alien without mercy.

Stivers hauled the Ongu to the wall against the little alien's best efforts to break free. Stivers's features twisted in fury and he crammed the Ongu's face right into the panel.

A sickening crack echoed through the prison, but no one heard it except LeMaine. The prisoners were too busy fighting each other.

Stivers flung the senseless Ongu down on the floor and the pilot went to work on the panel. LeMaine had no idea what the hell Stivers was trying to do. What happened to reactivating the wall to trap the Axichis inside?

All trace of a plan evaporated when Stivers yelled something to the prisoners nearest him. They took a minute to disentangle themselves from the mix, but when they realized what he was saying, they responded instantly.

The full horde of prisoners charged Stivers's position, overran the Ongu in seconds, and stripped away their rifles. LeMaine and the other Hellhounds got caught in the stampede as the whole population charged the opening where the Ongu had first entered the hold.

Lasers blasted out of the crowd as the prisoners gunned down the Ongu and the remaining Axichis. As soon as the Axichis went down, the prisoners took their weapons, too.

The guards on the catwalk fired down onto the hold floor, but the prisoners pivoted their stolen guns upward to return fire. No one seemed to care when prisoners fell. The rest of the mob was too excited to get out of here.

Hundreds of prisoners swarmed the Ongu's passage leading out of the hold. Orr reached Stivers first, and in a second, the rest of the Hellhounds joined them.

"Consider your decoration cancelled, Ensign," LeMaine shouted to Stivers over the noise.

Stivers laughed. "I have a better idea. Let's steal us a ship instead."

"That's what I'm talking about," Monk chimed in.

LeMaine pulled Polasek's arm toward himself and checked Polasek's remote since Kellogg's t-shirt didn't have one. The device showed LeMaine a layout of the ship outside the hold. "We're gonna need weapons to take the bridge."

"We're gonna need people for that, too," Kellogg pointed out.

LeMaine noticed a bunch of Elian Military personnel rushing past him. He grabbed a lieutenant by the sleeve. "Hold up, son."

The guy spun around. He wore dirty, torn fatigues stained with blood. His name patch read, *Porter.*

Porter scowled at first and then noticed the Hellhounds. Porter's eyes dipped to LeMaine's shirt. "Um....."

"I'm Captain LeMaine of the Elian Special Forces. Who do you have here with you, Lieutenant?"

Porter straightened up instantly. "I beg your pardon, Captain. There's me, Altman, Gwinn, McFarlane and all our men. We were just...."

"Go get them," LeMaine interrupted. "We're making a run on the bridge."

Porter's eyes popped and then he spluttered, "Um....yes, Sir."

"Nice to know someone around here still respects the chain of command," Heckler growled.

"'Cuz you sure won't, right?" O'Hara teased.

"Say that again to my face, asshole," Heckler spat through gritted teeth.

"Stow the attitude, Sergeant," LeMaine told O'Hara. "Keep your heads screwed on straight. The Axichis won't just let us waltz onto the bridge without a fight."

"They better not or I'm putting in for a transfer," Lemon grumbled.

Just then, Porter came back with three more lieutenants and a bunch of enlisted people. Several of them had Axichis weapons. "Some of the Xuvax got a weapons locker open down the corridor, Sir. Your people can arm up there."

"Holy shit!" one of the other lieutenants murmured. His nametag read, *Altman*. "You're the goddamn Hellhounds!"

"That's right, Lieutenant, so if you people are ready to throw down, let's go do some damage. Show me where these weapons are."

A ripple of excitement went through the group. LeMaine pretended not to see them grinning and elbowing each other as the news spread that they were all going to fight alongside the elite Hellhounds.

Porter led the way to the weapons locker. Not all the enlisted people were armed, but they stood back and waited for the Hellhounds to go first. They even let Lexington, Orr, and Stivers arm up first.

LeMaine checked Polasek's remote again. "Let's go. The bridge is this way."

He started off with the group behind him. They swept every corridor on their way to an internal stairway leading to the upper decks.

Laser fire and screams echoed through the ship. Running footsteps vibrated the floor and distant explosions punctuated the air. "Sounds like the prisoners are getting some payback," Nunn remarked.

More Elian Military personnel came out of the woodwork to join the group and gangs of aliens merged with the squad, too. By the time LeMaine reached the stairs, nearly forty people straggled out behind him. They blocked the corridor until no one could get through at all.

LeMaine made one more check of Polasek's remote. "All right, folks. That corridor up there leads to the bridge. As soon as we get upstairs, you all fan out and take up positions along the corridor. Don't let anyone else get up there unless you can personally vouch for them. Understand?"

Everyone nodded.

"Stand guard while the Hellhounds take the bridge. Lexington, Orr, and Stivers—you're with us."

Lexington pumped his fist. "Yes!"

"Porter, you, Altman, Gwinn, and McFarlane will be in charge out here. Open fire on any Axichis that try to flank us."

"Yes, Sir."

"You Hellhounds stand guard at the bottom of these stairs while our boys take the corridor."

"You bet, Sir," Monk replied.

"Deploy."

The group dispersed in waves. The Hellhounds spread out at the base of the stairs. LeMaine took his place with his squad and turned his guns outward to make sure no Axichis approached.

The four lieutenants went upstairs with their people, but LeMaine spun around fast when gunshots broke out up there.

He inched toward the stairs to back up the lieutenants when another burst of lasers erupted from nowhere. He whipped the other way as lasers pelted the stairs and along the upstairs corridor.

Shouts and yells echoed back and forth, but LeMaine didn't have time to see what was going on upstairs. A whole mob of Axichis stormed out of passages and hallways behind the Hellhounds' position.

The Axichis tried to overrun the squad. The Hellhounds returned fire, but the Axichis took cover in rooms and corners farther up the passage. They entrenched themselves where they could harass the Hellhounds and the Hellhounds couldn't hit them back.

LeMaine tried to glance up to see if his people were making any progress toward the bridge. Another curtain of lasers pinged off the stairs right near his head and made him duck.

"You cocksuckers!" Heckler roared and lunged out of his hiding place.

He plastered the Axichis and tried to make it to the stairs, but the Axichis were too well protected. LeMaine spotted an Axichis head sticking out with its eye pressed to a rifle sight.

"No!" LeMaine yelled and grabbed Heckler's fatigues. He yanked Heckler down just in time, but at that second, a deafening alarm blared overhead. It sounded like an air raid siren and it didn't let up.

All the Axichis looked up at the ceiling and then backed away. They retreated into the corridors. "What the hell is the matter with them?" Lemon yelled. "They didn't just give up and hand us the ship."

"It's the assault! The Elian Military is attacking!" LeMaine sprang to his feet. "Get to the bridge! Hurry!"

He swept his rifle back and forth, but none of the Axichis returned. That only increased LeMaine's anxiety. The Elian fleet was assaulting this planet to finish off the Axichis warships. LeMaine didn't have a second to lose.

Chapter 12

The Hellhounds pounded up the stairs and into the corridor on their way to the *Scagrak's* bridge. Porter and his crew guarded the place with dead Axichis lying around on the floor.

Polasek ran to the bridge door. "It's barricaded from the inside."

"Nunn....." LeMaine began and then broke off.

"I don't have any Plaostine, Sir, but I have something just as good."

She took off her laser rifle and wrapped the strap around the latch mechanism on the bridge entrance. She cinched it tight so the gun hugged right against the wall. "Everyone back away."

"You want to do more than back away when Nunn starts blowing things up," Kellogg told Gwinn. "You want to pack up and move to the next planet."

Gwinn stared at him in blank incomprehension. "Why?"

"Definitely not Hellhound material," Heckler growled and the other Hellhounds laughed.

They retreated down the corridor and LeMaine made sure all the soldiers guarding the area got a safe distance away. Then LeMaine handed Nunn his rifle. "Go to town, Corporal."

"Shouldn't I be the one to shoot it out?" O'Hara asked.

"Not on your life." Nunn put the rifle to her eye. "You aren't the only one who knows how to shoot."

"Even though you like to tell yourself you are," Lemon added.

Silence fell over the corridor as Nunn sighted down the rifle. Only the blaring siren disturbed the moment.

She fired and the rifle tied to the door exploded. A cloud of smoke and debris filled the corridor. "Go, Hellhounds!" LeMaine ordered. "Go, go, go!"

The crew charged the bridge. The four lieutenants and their people resumed their posts to guard the area, but no more Axichis showed their faces.

LeMaine rushed the threshold and slammed his shoulder against the wall where no one on the bridge would be able to hit him. He ducked out, swept his rifle across the bridge, and pulled back.

Lasers burst through the door right behind him, but that split second was enough for him to see the situation inside. The bridge staff, the captain, and all the technicians worked at their stations while the captain gave orders in his own language.

Four Axichis guarded them and trained their weapons at the door. They bombarded the exit with laser shots every time the prisoners showed their faces.

The smoke started to clear and LeMaine blinked at Polasek, Monk, Buca, Stivers, and Lemon across the gap from him. That left Nunn, O'Hara, Kellogg, Lexington, Orr, and Peterman on LeMaine's side.

Polasek cracked a grin. "You ready, Sir?"

LeMaine dipped his chin once and he and Polasek both leapt out at the same time. LeMaine and Polasek dropped to their knees with Monk and Buca standing behind Polasek. Nunn and Kellogg stood behind LeMaine and all six of them opened fire as the same time.

LeMaine aimed for the captain and dropped the guy with one shot. The four guards got into a firefight against the Hellhounds, but the Hellhounds overpowered them in no time.

Three more officers wheeled around to join in, but LeMaine finished them off, too. He vaulted to his feet and stormed the rest of the way onto the bridge. "All of you, get down on the floor! Get your hands above your heads and don't move!"

The bridge staff hustled to comply and the Hellhounds stood guard over them. Stivers raced to the pilot's station. "The fleet is moving in on Nainia, Sir! The Axichis warships are arming to defend themselves, but the order to launch hasn't gone out yet."

"Can you get this ship off the ground?" LeMaine asked.

Lexington sat down in the captain's chair and checked some readings on the consoles. "The alert is going out to all decks. The Axichis are scrambling fighters and arming laser cannons. They're preparing an all-out assault on the Elian fleet."

"Let 'em keep arming," LeMaine replied. "We can use this to our advantage."

"Sir," Stivers cut in. "If I may suggest....."

"Suggest away, Ensign. We're all at your command."

Some of the Hellhounds laughed and Stivers flushed. "I was going to suggest, Sir, that we do some shooting while we're still on the ground."

"I had the same idea, Ensign," LeMaine replied. "Can you target them?"

"The targeting station is....." O'Hara sat down in a different station across the bridge. The young sniper grinned like a fool adjusting the targeting system to his liking.

"This doesn't look good," Polasek remarked.

"What's wrong, Lieutenant?" O'Hara chirped. "Are you worried about what will happen when I start blowing things up instead of Nunn doing it? Some of us have to have a little fun sometimes."

"You Hellhounds get outside and make sure the place is secure," LeMaine ordered.

"It is," Lexington replied from the captain's chair. "The whole crew locked down when the alert went out. The cannon crew and the fighter teams are all active. Everyone else is under lockdown."

"Good," Heckler growled. "Dealing with them is the last thing we need right now."

"Sir!" Lexington called. "The order is coming down for the warships to launch."

"Fire at will, Sergeant!"

O'Hara responded in a heartbeat. The bridge's front screen gave a full view of the battle raging outside.

The warships also used plenty of Elian technology and the screen fed information in familiar patterns. Stivers, Lexington, and O'Hara had no trouble using the warship's controls and weapons.

O'Hara wheeled hard to starboard and unleashed a hellish barrage on the warships parked next to the *Scagrak*. Four of them detonated while they still trained their weapons toward the skies.

The Elian fleet descended on Nainia in droves. Bombers loomed high in the atmosphere pelting the Axichis cluster with concussions. Attack cruisers whizzed through the sky making run after run over Thailiv.

The warships to port swung their cannon around to counter the *Scagrak's* attack, but that only left the Axichis vulnerable to the Elian assault. O'Hara hammered another three warships before all hell broke loose.

The bombers thundered down on Thailiv and explosions smashed the city. The Elian fleet showered the Axichis with indiscriminate shots.

"I guess they didn't get the memo that we're down here!" O'Hara yelled.

The Axichis took their eyes off the enemy to destroy the traitorous ship. Warships on either side of the *Scagrak* opened fire and the hull boomed with explosions. LeMaine staggered against the wall. "We have to contact Command!"

"You'll have to do it!" Lexington hollered back. "The communications system is over there."

LeMaine stumbled under heavy bombardment and toppled over to a different station. He fumbled with the controls trying to find an open channel. "Mayday, mayday! This is Captain Owen LeMaine of the....."

A crushing boom shook the *Scagrak*. "The cannon crew is rebelling!" O'Hara called. "They're blowing up their own cannons! We're defenseless!"

"Get us off the ground, Ensign!" LeMaine yelled to Stivers. "Get us out of the line of fire and get us closer to the fleet."

Stivers shook his head. "I'm not sure that will work, Sir."

"Do you have a better idea?"

Stivers didn't answer. He bent over the controls working fast. More concussions rocked the ship while the engines cycled up to full power. Lexington didn't say what the problem was and LeMaine didn't ask.

The *Scagrak* no longer had any cannons left so O'Hara couldn't fire. LeMaine cast one glance toward the front screen and instantly turned away when he saw the Elian fleet preparing to strike.

Devastating smashes pounded the tarmac and more warships exploded under the assault. The Elian cannons crawled closer to the *Scagrak*, but just at the moment when they would have hammered the ship into the ground, Stivers punched the throttle and took wing.

The *Scagrak* zoomed off into the clear blue sky, but that hardly made LeMaine feel better. The ship hurtled straight into the line of Elian fire and the whole fleet turned on the ship.

"Get that communications system working, Sir!" Lexington called. "We have to let them know we're friendly."

LeMaine attacked the communications equipment again, but he saw at first glance that it was useless. "The Axichis crew has sabotaged the system. We're sunk."

No one answered him, and the instant the *Scagrak* got near the fleet, a gut-wrenching boom resounded through the ship.

"All systems shutting down!" Orr reported. "The frequencies are short-circuiting everything! We're going down hard!"

The frequencies shutting down the *Scagrak's* systems wasn't enough. Continuous crashes and pounding gunshots ripped into the hull. LeMaine held onto his workstation against G force that threatened to haul him off his feet.

O'Hara and the four pilots huddled low in their seats as the Elian fleet moved in for the kill. They attacked the stricken *Scagrak* without mercy and smashed it down toward the tarmac. Every cannon shot lurched the ship lower out of the atmosphere.

"Brace for impact!" Lexington roared and the very next blast slammed the *Scagrak* down with bone-crushing force.

The blow knocked LeMaine to his knees and the entire fuselage groaned under punishing strikes. The ceiling caved in and the next shot ripped half the bridge apart.

Daylight streamed through the breach. Smoke and venting gas diffused the light and more strikes echoed from outside. "Abandon ship!" LeMaine ordered. "Get out now!"

He vaulted down the stairs and had to land in a crouch as more blasts made the *Scagrak* tremble. How much longer before the fleet completely flattened the ship?

He charged O'Hara and hauled the young sniper out of his seat. "Get Lexington, Orr, and Stivers outside now, Sergeant! I'm going back for the Hellhounds."

"Yes, Sir!"

O'Hara pushed Stivers toward the gap. LeMaine sprang back up the stairs to the bridge entrance. His last view of O'Hara was of the young man guiding Orr and Lexington outside, but they could hardly be getting to safety. The situation outside would be as deadly as the one on board.

LeMaine couldn't wait a second longer. He rushed into the corridor to find the whole ship in chaos. The Hellhounds and the remaining Elian personnel knelt behind the railing trading gunfire with Axichis on the floor below. The Elian assault kept smashing the ship again and again. The deafening noise drowned out the zing of lasers from both sides.

LeMaine grabbed the first Hellhound he came to. It was Monk. "Get out through the bridge! Take everyone with you."

Monk leapt to his feet and started towing Buca and Porter after him. LeMaine ran down the line calling everyone to retreat through the bridge. He reached Heckler and Kellogg, the last two on the far end of the corridor, but they were too pinned down for LeMaine to say anything.

He leaned close to Heckler to order the Marine to retreat when a laser struck the wall right next to LeMaine's head. He swiveled his weapon over the side and spat several shots down at the floor.

Twelve Axichis returned fire from the lower level. Another group tried to sneak up the stairs under their comrades' covering fire. They were trying to flank the bridge.

More lasers punched into the railing and erupted in LeMaine's face. He ducked with Heckler and Kellogg right next to him. "Get out!" LeMaine bellowed over the noise. "Get out through the bridge. The Axichis are storming the corridor. We have to get out now."

Kellogg stole a peek in that direction. "They're coming! We have to go now!"

LeMaine nodded and all three men jumped to their feet. Lasers showered the corridor from below, but LeMaine didn't try to fight them. He turned his weapon forward and fired into the Axichis rushing up the corridor.

He made it ten feet before Heckler stumbled over a body on the ground. He tripped and went down next to McFarlane and Gwinn, both lying face down on the floor.

Kellogg crouched at Heckler's side and checked McFarlane's pulse. "He's alive. We should take him with us."

At the same moment, Gwinn pushed himself up on his elbows and extended a hand to Heckler, but Gwinn's eyes didn't register. "Please....." he croaked.

"Hang tight, boy," Heckler growled. "We're getting you out of here."

"You take Gwinn, Heckler," Kellogg ordered. "You cover us, Sir. I'll take McFarlane."

"Yes, Sir," LeMaine replied and he stepped over the two injured men.

LeMaine traded shots with the Axichis while Heckler and Kellogg picked up Gwinn and McFarlane. The Axichis took up defended positions farther down the corridor.

LeMaine kept up a steady barrage of laser fire to make them cower while Heckler and Kellogg dragged the other two onto the bridge.

LeMaine backed away. Taking two injured men with him would slowed the Hellhounds' progress, but LeMaine wasn't about to leave anyone behind.

Nunn, Monk, and Peterman stood guard on the bridge. They formed a defended corridor to the hull breach. As soon as LeMaine stepped in, they closed ranks to protect his retreat.

LeMaine ducked through the breach, halted there, and aimed his weapon in all directions while the others staggered outside. He checked every angle to make sure no Axichis came near him, but the Hellhounds had a much bigger problem now. The *Scagrak* no longer protected them.

Elian bombers hung low in the sky and rained rockets and cannon strikes all over the area. Attack cruisers pelted back and forth. They flattened the Axichis warships lying helpless and immobile on the tarmac.

None of the Axichis ships fought back. From what LeMaine could see, the *Scagrak* was the only warship that even made it off the ground.

Another warship detonated not far away and the pavement rocked beneath LeMaine's feet. Kellogg stumbled under McFarlane's weight.

LeMaine dropped his rifle on its strap and rushed to Kellogg's side. LeMaine wedged himself under McFarlane's other arm and heaved.

Monk and Buca appeared out of the smoke to guard LeMaine. He and Kellogg staggered from one explosion to another until the Thailiv's tangled streets swallowed them.

Chapter 13

LeMaine couldn't see where he was going. Sweat got into his eyes and all Thailiv's streets and corners looked the same.

Nunn and Buca guarded the way ahead for LeMaine and Kellogg to follow them. LeMaine kept his eyes on Nunn at all costs. The smoke cleared enough for LeMaine to see Monk farther along, but other than that, LeMaine might be anywhere.

Buca pushed LeMaine's shoulder to steer him to the right. LeMaine heard the Hellhounds talking, but too much dust and smoke stung LeMaine's eyes. He couldn't see what they were doing.

Buca guided him into an alley and then helped Kellogg lower McFarlane to the ground. Kellogg got to work right away.

LeMaine caught his breath while the rest of the Hellhounds wedged themselves into the alley with him. They were all here, and in a second, Orr, Stivers, Lexington, Porter, Altman, and the rest of the Elian personnel showed up, too.

"You okay, Sir?" Polasek asked.

LeMaine nodded and gasped. "Anyone....down?"

"We lost three in the corridor," Porter replied, "but everyone else is here. Thank you, Captain."

"We aren't home yet." LeMaine ran his wrist across his eyes. His t-shirt was soaked.

Kellogg had stopped working on McFarlane and turned his attention to Gwinn. McFarlane was still conscious and babbling. "Kepler! Where's Kepler? I need Kepler! I can't see!"

Porter went over to him and squeezed McFarlane's shoulder. "It's all right, Sal. You're gonna be all right. You're with us."

McFarlane tried to look everywhere. "Zack? Is that you? I can't see anything. Where's Kepler?"

"Kepler's dead, but another medic is here. He'll work on you. Just stay calm and relax. You're safe."

McFarlane's face twisted. "I can't see, Zack! I'm blind."

"Easy, son," LeMaine told him. "Give us a second to check you out and we might be able to fix the problem."

McFarlane turned his face toward LeMaine's voice without seeing anyone. "Who is that? I don't recognize your voice."

"I'm Captain LeMaine of the Elian Special Forces. Do you remember how you got hurt?"

McFarlane frowned. "Special Forces! How......?"

"He doesn't remember," Porter murmured.

"Keep him calm," Kellogg ordered. "I have to deal with Gwinn before I do anything else."

Porter squatted down next to McFarlane and pressed his hand. LeMaine hauled himself to his feet and did an assessment on the rest of the group.

All the Hellhounds seemed fine. Monk, Lemon, and Peterman were all bleeding, but they were all on their feet. They kept a sharp eye on the surroundings and their weapons handy. None of them complained or asked for medical attention.

Buca stood guard at the head of the alley. Lexington, Orr, and Stivers stayed with him to back him up. The rest of the Elian personnel hung back and eyed the Hellhounds with a mixture of awe and suspicion.

LeMaine grabbed Polasek's wrist and took a look at Polasek's remote. "I gotta get me one of these, Lieutenant."

Polasek chuckled. "I'd offer to let you take my jacket, but I don't think it would fit you."

LeMaine had to grin. His young SIC barely came up to his chin. LeMaine probably wouldn't be able to get Polasek's jacket over one of his own beefy arms.

Explosions were still going off at the landing zone. LeMaine didn't see anyone nearby except Nainians.

"How do we get in touch with Command?" Polasek asked. "The natives must have some communications equipment on this planet."

"It would be nice if we could locate that militia again," LeMaine agreed. "I bet they have communications off planet."

Polasek peeked around Buca to survey the street. "Any ideas?"

"We're going to have our work cut out for us with a group this big. Any Axichis left on this planet will come for us like a moth to the flame."

"So what's the plan? You're in charge here."

"Do me a favor and stop reminding me of that, will you?"

Polasek laughed. "I don't mind as long as I can hide behind you. Just don't let anything happen to you, okay?"

LeMaine joined in the joke. "What's so funny, Sir?" Nunn called out. "Don't leave us hanging."

"Nothing's funny." LeMaine strode back to the three pilots. "You boys hanging tough?"

"You bet, Sir," Lexington replied. "Just point us at the enemy and we're there."

"Good for you. Go stand over there and help Buca in case anyone comes." LeMaine strode deeper into the alley and halted in front of Altman. "You and Porter are in command of these people, aren't you, son?"

"Most of them, Sir," Altman replied. "Some of them belong to Gwinn's and McFarlane's crews."

"You and Porter are in charge of everyone as of now. I want you to assign ten of your frostiest characters to stand guard over this alley. Post your people up there where Buca is and back here to defend both sides. Understand? You people are going to stay here with your wounded while the Hellhounds and I go try to find a way off this planet."

Altman started to say, "Let us come with you, Sir....." but LeMaine cut him off.

"You have your orders, Lieutenant. I can't take you with me. There are too many of you and we're all in hostile territory. Someone would have to stay behind to defend the wounded. The more of you stay, the better chance you all have of getting off this planet alive. Understand?"

Altman straightened up and squared his shoulders. "Yes, Sir. You can count on us."

"Good." LeMaine returned to Kellogg. The medic had turned Gwinn onto his back. "What's the situation, Sergeant?"

"He has a broken nose." Kellogg was fixing the electrolyzer to Gwinn's face. "After I fix that, I'll deal with McFarlane."

Kellogg met LeMaine's eyes and shot him a don't-leave-me-out-of-any-action glance. LeMaine didn't want to wait, but the group wasn't in any immediate danger in this alley.

He made the rounds while he waited. The Hellhounds adjusted their weapons, but without fuel to power these laser rifles, no one could rearm. None of them would have any idea how much firepower they had left before all their weapons became useless.

Kellogg finally helped Gwinn sit up ajg Kellogg propped him sitting against a wall. "Sit tight and don't do anything strenuous for a while."

Kellogg moved over to McFarlane and scanned the lieutenant's head. "What's the story?" LeMaine asked.

"He has some swelling in his brain. I can relieve that, but I can't guarantee it will bring his sight back."

McFarlane burst into tears and started blubbering. Porter grimaced and looked away, but he didn't let go of McFarlane's hand.

Kellogg started working on McFarlane's head. "Keep still, Lieutenant, or I'll have to sedate you."

McFarlane got more and more agitated and started begging. "Please fix it. I have a daughter back home. I'll never get to see her again. I'll never see my wife or the sunset or....."

LeMaine nudged Kellogg and gave him a pointed look. Kellogg put his scanner down, picked up his syringe, and injected something into McFarlane's neck. The young lieutenant fell instantly unconscious and silence descended over the alley.

"Jesus!" Porter muttered. "I never knew he was such a wet dishrag."

"I'll leave you with a few more doses of sedative," Kellogg replied. "You can keep him like this until we come back."

Porter grinned at LeMaine and tried to bite it back. "You can do that?"

"We could do a lot worse if it was a question of everyone's safety." Kellogg started drilling into McFarlane's skull, drained the swelling, and then electrolyzed the hole. "He should be fine, but we won't know if the procedure restored his sight until he regains consciousness."

LeMaine pressed the syringe into Porter's hands along with an ampule of the sedative. "If you have to move suddenly, it will work better for everyone if he's awake and on his feet. Let him regain consciousness, and if he stays calm and cooperative, let him stay that way. If he acts up, put him down. Understand?"

"Yes, Sir. Perfectly."

"Good man." LeMaine squeezed Porter's shoulder. "You and Altman take charge here."

"Yes, Sir. No problem."

LeMaine went back to the Hellhounds. "Anything moving out there, Corporal?" he asked Buca.

"Not a thing. It's all quiet."

LeMaine glanced at Polasek, but checking Polasek's remote wouldn't help anyone right now.

They gathered their weapons, returned to Buca's side at the head of the alley, and peered out at the quiet street. A few Nainians went about their business out there. They hardly paid any attention to the Hellhounds at all.

LeMaine considered going out there and asking one of the civilians to put him in touch with the Thailiv militia. Someone in this town must know where to find them.

He took one step forward when gunfire erupted a few streets away. LeMaine pulled back until he saw the same militia group charge around a corner with Xars in the lead.

The militia skidded into view, spun backward, and exchanged carbine fire with a squad of Axichis advancing from the south.

LeMaine didn't hesitate a second. He opened fire from the corner and the rest of the Hellhounds joined in. Buca took the opposite wall and the other Hellhounds wedged themselves in below both shooters.

The Axichis started out by aiming for the militia. When the Hellhounds joined in, the Axichis tried to fight both flanks at once. The Axichis swiveled toward the alley and the militia cut them down from the other side. The two flanks left the enemy nowhere to run.

Xars held the Axichis bodies at gunpoint and then lowered his carbine when he recognized LeMaine. "Thank you, Captain."

"You don't know how happy I am to see you. We were hoping we would run into you."

"Why?" Xars glanced into the alley. "What are *they* doing here?"

"We freed them from an Axichis warship. We need communications with Command to get out of here. Can you help us?"

"We don't have communications with Command, but I think I know somewhere we can find them. There is a good chance it will mean fighting, though."

"We can handle fighting."

The man cast a critical glance at the laser rifles the Hellhounds were holding. "You'll need more weapons than that. We can get them for you."

"That would be great. Would you have a safe place we can hide these people until someone comes to pick them up? We have a few wounded."

"Follow me, but stay ready. There are Axichis stragglers all over town."

The Hellhounds moved into the open, and in a second, they merged with the Thailiv militia heading down the street. The two groups got jumbled together with everyone guarding everyone else.

Porter and Altman steered their people to the center. The Hellhounds, the three pilots, and the militia arranged themselves around the outside. Two burly corporals hefted McFarlane who was still unconscious, but Gwinn was walking on his own without too much trouble.

LeMaine moved up to Xars's side. "How far away are we?"

"Two miles," Xars growled.

LeMaine bit back the urge to complain. Two miles through a city crawling with Axichis was not his idea of getting to safety, but it was better than hiding in an alley.

The air battle faded farther behind them....or maybe it was over. LeMaine could only hope the Elian Military had destroyed the last traces of Axichis resistance. He and these stragglers could just kick back on Nainia until things settled down, but Hellhound missions rarely turned out that way.

Kellogg dropped back to the men carrying McFarlane and Kellogg worked on the man on the march. LeMaine kept his concentration on everyone else. He didn't have time to worry about one man and McFarlane was in the best possible hands with Kellogg.

Nothing happened until Xars halted at a rundown building. The big Buzath stood guard and pointed his weapon into the lightless basement. "This is it. We can contact Command from here."

LeMaine paused to look back. Ten Elian bombers loomed on the horizon, but they didn't come down to land.

Distant explosions echoed across the landscape, but LeMaine didn't see any Axichis craft at all—no warships, no fighters—nothing. Without the bombers and the noise, no one would know there was a war going on at all.

Altman led his people to the entrance. The lieutenant was just about to duck inside and climb down when Xars grabbed Altman's arm. "Stop!"

"What's up?" LeMaine asked. "You said......"

Xars held up a hand to silence him. "It isn't safe. Something's wrong."

"How can you tell?" Peterman asked. The Hellhounds and some of the other Elian personnel gathered around to listen.

Xars strained his ears to listen and then waved his carbine at the whole crowd. "Back away! Go! Go now!"

Altman tore away from him. "I'm going in. I don't care what you say. We've been walking long enough and you said we'd be safe here." He waved the corporals forward. McFarlane had his eyes open and was showing signs of being able to see.

"NO!" Xars bellowed. He lunged for Altman, and at that moment, the building exploded without warning.

The shockwave slapped LeMaine backward with unspeakable force. Brick, rubble, and debris hurtled in his face and he slammed hard against another building across the street.

He floundered to his feet tasting blood in his mouth. He coughed and tried to blink dust out of his eyes so he could see anyone or anything in the chaos. A giant crater covered half the block where the building had just been standing. Bodies littered the pavement.

LeMaine stumbled from one to the next. Lemon hauled herself up a few feet from him and LeMaine got hold of her jacket so he wouldn't lose her. They staggered forward and LeMaine searched everywhere for the Hellhounds.

Polasek and Heckler came lurching around a corner leaning on each other. Blood streaked Polasek's face and he struggled to support Heckler's much bigger body on his shoulder.

LeMaine guided all three Hellhounds to a protected corner where he first landed after the blast. "Stay here!" he told Polasek. "Make sure you're here when I get back."

Polasek nodded and didn't answer. He was too busy working to unbutton Heckler's jacket.

LeMaine turned back to the havoc laid out before him all over the street. He couldn't figure out why or how the building blew up, but what difference did it make?

He went from body to body. He found Peterman, Monk, and Buca, Xars, and a bunch of Nainian militia members.

LeMaine took them all back to join the others, but the longer he searched, the more his heart sank. He found Porter and McFarlane dead along with at least half their people. This was a disaster and LeMaine didn't even know what caused it.

He circled the crater until he located the rest of the Hellhounds. One of Kellogg's arms lay in bloody shreds from his shoulder. Nunn had ripped open Kellogg's backpack and was working fast to seal the wounds. When LeMaine found them, he saw Orr and Stivers dead just a few paces away.

LeMaine returned to Kellogg's side, but Nunn had already done the job. She and LeMaine helped Kellogg to his feet, picked up Kellogg's kit, and took everything back to the group.

Nunn helped Kellogg check out the rest of the wounded while LeMaine cast a critical eye at the crater. Wondering what happened wouldn't help him.

He squatted down next to Xars, who was dealing with his own injured people. "What now?"

Xars glanced up at LeMaine. "The Axichis....."

A high-pitched scream cut him off, and before anyone could react, ten Axichis fighter craft wheeled over the city slicing lasers in all directions.

Elian attack cruisers hounded the Axichis over Thailiv, but they couldn't stop the destruction. The Axichis fired into buildings and neighborhoods as well as backward to counter the Elian assault.

The Axichis howled past the crater and a whole cloud of Axichis warships descended from the atmosphere right on top of the Hellhounds' position. The Elian bombers already on the planet rounded on the enemy and opened fire.

The two fleets bombarded each other and the city below. More ships from both sides arrived to join in and the situation became all too horribly clear in a split second.

"They aren't using the frequencies!" Peterman yelled.

"They're using them!" Buca hollered back. "The frequencies aren't working anymore. The Axichis must have found a way to counter them."

LeMaine grabbed the nearest person he could reach. "Everybody up! We have to get out of here!"

Half the group supported the other half staggering away from the blast site, but nowhere was safe. Three bombers surrounded a single warship. Axichis fighter craft and Elian attack cruisers whizzed all over the place. The bombers pounded the warship from every side until the thing exploded and smashed into a building packed with Nainians.

Screams and deafening noise ripped through the city as the whole structure detonated in flames. LeMaine veered hard to his left and stumbled over Xars running at his side. "Where can we go? There has to be somewhere!"

"Follow me!" Xars charged from one intersection to another. More ships from both sides crashed, fired, and decimated the city everywhere he went.

Xars entered a wide avenue. It looked like it followed a straight run through the city, but LeMaine didn't want to trust that. The avenue would only leave the group more vulnerable to attack from the air.

Xars darted into a different alley and the crowd herded under cover. People collapsed against the walls gasping for breath. LeMaine did a head count on the Hellhounds. Kellogg looked like shit, but he was on his feet and running on his own now.

Five Nainians and seven other Elians accompanied the Hellhounds. That was all LeMaine had to show for all the people he rescued from the *Scagrak*.

He wouldn't even have that many if he couldn't find a way out of this city and off this planet. He returned to Xars. "What's your plan? Where are you leading us?"

"The militia has a base outside of town. We have communications equipment and weapons....and ships hidden there. We can go there and get everything we need. You can take one of our ships to rejoin the fleet."

"How do we know the base isn't booby trapped like the building?" Peterman asked.

"The Axichis had their own special forces in Thailiv long before you came. They tried to take this planet early in the war, but our militias drove them off. The Axichis landed their own special operatives to track us down and put us out of business. They've been following us for weeks."

"All the more reason they would know about a base outside of town," Polasek pointed out. "We could be walking into another trap."

"They don't know about our base outside of town. We kept it a secret from everyone, including our own people. Only the militia officers and squad leaders know where it is and none of the militia personnel were ever allowed to go there. We kept it hidden in case of a real emergency."

"Well, this is a real emergency," LeMaine added, "and if you're wrong, we're all dead."

"I'll prove it to you. My people and I will enter the base first. If it is booby trapped, we'll die while you stay alive."

"Are you calling Captain LeMaine a coward?" Lemon snarled.

"Zip it, Hellhounds," LeMaine ordered. "I have a better idea. I say we set a trap for the Axichis—if there are any left on this planet to follow us."

Xars cocked his head. "How do you figure?"

"We make for the base. If the Axichis know about you and they suspect you have hidden resources, they'll follow. We can set up a trap to lure them to the base and then spring it on them. We can get rid of them and reach the base at the same time."

"What if they have set up booby traps?" Peterman asked. "How do you plan to avoid those?"

"I just told you—by leading the Axichis into them."

"Wouldn't the Axichis know about their own booby traps?" Nunn asked.

"That's exactly why they would tip us off to where the booby traps are." LeMaine turned back to Xars. "Take us to the base."

Xars stole a peek outside. "The battle is getting heavier....and it's getting closer."

"Let's go." LeMaine started forward. "Polasek, you take Lemon, Nunn, and O'Hara. Hang back here and see if any Axichis come out of the woodwork to follow us."

"When do you want to spring the trap?" Polasek asked.

"Assuming there is one," Heckler growled.

"First make sure there are some Axichis following us."

"And if there are?"

"Then wait until we get near the base. You can signal Peterman through your remotes and we'll set up......."

A subtle noise of falling gravel cut LeMaine off and all the Hellhounds snapped alert. LeMaine shouldered his rifle and the Nainians brought up their carbines.

The squad eased to the end of the alley. LeMaine and Xars surveyed the avenue sweeping their guns everywhere, but there was nothing there.

"They're here!" Xars whispered. "They're keeping us under surveillance."

"Then it's time to give them something to see. Let's move it out. Polasek, take your team to the south. Make it look like we're splitting up and then circle around to flank the Axichis from behind."

"Yes, Sir."

LeMaine squinted toward where the sound came from, but he didn't see anything to tip him off that the Axichis were still there....or that they'd ever been there. Was Xars imagining things?

These Nainians had been patrolling their city a lot longer than the Hellhounds. LeMaine was prepared to gamble on Xars's intelligence. Being overly cautious wouldn't hurt anybody, but dismissing Xars's warning sure might.

LeMaine forced himself to lower his weapon and he motioned for the others to do the same. It took all his resolve to turn his back on the Axichis' hiding place and walk away.

Chapter 14

Peterman nudged LeMaine. "I just got a signal from Polasek. The Axichis are behind us."

"How far?"

"He says the enemy patrol is about five hundred yards behind us. He and the others are trailing about five hundred yards behind *them*. He says for you to signal him when you want him to attack."

LeMaine scanned the terrain ahead as Xars led the fugitives out of Thailiv. The group wound through neighborhoods and finally left the city for the surrounding farmland. Isolated houses dotted the countryside with livestock still grazing in the fields.

"Where's the base?" LeMaine asked. "I don't see anything."

"It's right over....." The words barely left Xars's mouth when a laser hissed past LeMaine's ear. The squad ducked for cover, but the laser wasn't aimed at them. It smashed into a house a hundred yards off.

Kellogg poked his head up. "Where's it coming from?"

Peterman grabbed him and yanked him down as more lasers streaked across the area. They pounded into the ground, ripped up sod, and a few animals exploded. "Get down! The Axichis can hit from anywhere."

"They're bombing the base!" Xars leapt to his feet. "We have to get there before they destroy our ships."

"What about....?" LeMaine began.

Xars was already rallying the rest of his people. "If you want to get off this planet, you better come now!"

Xars didn't wait for LeMaine to reply. LeMaine sprang out of hiding to follow Xars. All the Hellhounds responded, too, but the instant they got into the open field, the Axichis patrol following them opened fire from the bushes.

Lasers zinged all over the place. One of them sliced LeMaine's thigh, but he hardly felt it. He yelled to Peterman, "Signal the rear attack!"

Peterman called into his remote, but LeMaine couldn't hear him over the noise. Axichis lasers rocketed out of Thailiv. LeMaine couldn't even see any warships nearby.

Another house disintegrated to matchsticks. Splintered boards and broken glass twirled through the air and pelted LeMaine's cheeks and eyelids. He squinted on the run trying to see where Xars was going, but LeMaine couldn't see anyone in front of him. He was alone out here with lasers whizzing all around him.

Gunfire split the din coming from behind him. He spun around to face an Axichis patrol crouching where the Hellhounds had just been hiding. The patrol added their lasers to the mayhem and Lexington went down.

The young pilot hit the dirt, flipped over, and struggled to sit up so he could keep shooting. Kellogg darted forward, seized Lexington's hand, and dragged him behind LeMaine. Lexington kept shooting while Kellogg worked on him.

More lasers pelted the neighborhood, destroyed houses, and blasted the place to a hell. Polasek stuck his head out of the bushes and LeMaine spotted Lemon shooting from the trees. The Hellhounds laid into the Axichis from behind until both groups cleared the enemy patrol, but nothing could stop the warships' assault.

Someone grabbed LeMaine's arm. "This way!"

Xars appeared out of the chaos and tugged LeMaine toward the crater where the first house had been. LeMaine didn't see anything there, but he couldn't stay here with the warships tearing the neighborhood apart. He better go find out what Xars wanted to show him.

LeMaine motioned the others forward. Xars led everyone over to the crater, but they had to crouch more than once to avoid getting killed in the process.

Xars approached the hole when four warships thundered out of nowhere. They rained hellfire, not on the cowering squad, but on the land around the crater.

They decimated the area with blasts until, in front of the Hellhounds shocked eyes, a whole section of the landscape caved under the bombardment. That piece of ground split from the farmland and sank to leave acres of countryside lying thirty feet beneath the rest.

"No!" Xars croaked.

LeMaine saw it all in a blink. The Nainian resistance must have stored their emergency equipment and supplies down there. Their secret underground base must have been under that section. Now it lay flattened and wrecked where no one would ever be able to get to it.

LeMaine took hold of Xars's sleeve. "Come on. We have to....."

Another bone-shaking boom cut him off. The Axichis warships directly overhead swiveled to confront ten Elian bombers coming in fast.

Cannon fire erupted from the bombers to tear the Axichis apart, but the Elians' shots barely touched the warships. The Axichis returned fire with countless lasers and one of the bombers exploded directly over the Hellhounds' position.

LeMaine gave Xars one more tug and hauled the Nainian leader away. No one was going anywhere or contacting anyone from here.

The Hellhounds turned in the only direction left—back toward the trees and neighborhoods they'd just come from. More explosions and gunfire crashed and smashed above LeMaine's head. He had to duck to protect himself, but he never stopped running.

"Get under cover!" he yelled to the others. "Get off the field!"

The Nainians, Elians, and Hellhounds bolted for the trees only to run straight into the Axichis patrol waiting there. LeMaine swung his rifle forward to gun them down. He didn't care anymore who or what stood in his way as long as he broke through to safety.

Monk, Heckler, and Buca led the group and saw the threat first. An Axichis laser cut across Heckler's neck and he bellowed in fury.

All three Hellhounds reacted in a flash. They leveled their weapons to destroy the enemy just as a warship laser pelted the ground right on top of its own patrol.

The Axichis never saw it coming and three bodies cartwheeled into the air. The Hellhounds didn't have to fire a shot. They overran the patrol and plunged into the trees.

"Keep going!" LeMaine yelled from the back. "Don't stop!"

The Hellhounds slashed branches out of the way and burst onto an open road behind the woods. They charged down the street and back into the maze of Thailiv's many neighborhoods.

Heckler staggered and Monk caught him. Buca noticed and he and Monk veered to one side. They darted into an abandoned building and the rest of the Hellhounds crowded in after them.

Kellogg went over to Heckler and Heckler roared again when Kellogg started sealing the wound in his neck.

"So much for contacting Command," Polasek gasped.

"If that was our only way of contacting anyone off the planet," Lemon replied, "we're in trouble."

"Turns out your secret emergency base wasn't so secret after all," Nunn added. "Those warships knew exactly where to hit it."

"Can you read the state of the battle outside?" LeMaine asked Polasek.

Polasek glanced at his remote and shrugged. "Nothing is going on that we don't already know about. The bombers are fighting the warships. That doesn't help us. We'd have to wait until the bombers clear the Axichis off the planet. Even then, we don't know if the bombers will land here."

Peterman looked at his remote, too. "The battle is drifting away from Thailiv. The warships are pushing the fleet back into the atmosphere."

"I don't like the sound of that," LeMaine growled. "The warships shouldn't be pushing anybody anywhere."

"So it's true," O'Hara remarked. "The frequencies are no good anymore."

"Maybe not," LeMaine replied, "but that doesn't mean new frequencies won't do the trick. You remember what Lulara said. The Axichis must have modulated their power frequency so our weapons don't work. All we have to do is find the new frequency and we're back in business."

"How do we do that?" Polasek asked. "We don't know which frequencies she used and we have no equipment to figure it out."

"You should be able to figure it out, Lieutenant," O'Hara replied. "You had the frequencies in your array the whole time we were on Toreon."

"They were in my array. I didn't memorize them."

"It doesn't matter what the frequencies *were*," Nunn pointed out. "All that matters is that we find out what they are now."

"Then we need to find some equipment to dial in the new frequencies." LeMaine moved over to the front of the building. "You're right, Polasek. The ships on both sides are moving away."

"What does that tell us?" Peterman asked. "I'm going to go out on a limb and say the Thailiv militia doesn't have another secret base somewhere."

LeMaine glanced over his shoulder. All the other Hellhounds looked at Xars at the same time, but he wouldn't meet any of their eyes. He stared at the floor. That answered Peterman's question more eloquently than words.

Kellogg came over to LeMaine. "Sit down, Sir. I need to seal your leg."

"Huh? What do you mean?"

Kellogg jutted his chin at LeMaine's thigh. "That."

LeMaine glanced down. Blood saturated his whole left pant leg from the laser that sliced deep into the muscle. LeMaine didn't even feel it until now.

He sat down on the floor and extended his leg in front of him while Kellogg bent over the wound. LeMaine was about to say something else to Polasek when searing pain shot through him from his leg. "Aarrgh!" he bellowed. "What the hell are you doing to me?"

"I'm trying to get you back on duty." Kellogg looked up and his bright eyes met LeMaine's. "Unless you want to stay here while the rest of us fight the war. I'm sure Polasek would be delighted to take over."

"Whoa! Hold it right there, buddy!" Polasek howled. "I did NOT say that!"

The other Hellhounds laughed. "Let him finish clearing you for duty, Sir," Peterman replied. "Please. Do it for all of us."

LeMaine gritted his teeth. He wasn't about to stay here while Polasek took over to fight the war. Hell no.

"What do you have in mind for our promising future, Sir?" Nunn asked. "And please tell me it involves killing some Axichis."

"We need to get some new frequencies." LeMaine winced again and then Kellogg put away his tools. "We need to find some way to scan the Axichis fighters while they're under bombardment. We need to read their frequencies and then feed the frequencies back to them the way we did before."

"How do we do that?" Heckler asked.

"The same way we did last time," Monk interjected. "We need fighter craft to get near them."

Everyone spun around to stare at Monk and LeMaine raised his eyebrows. "You hear that, Polasek? You got some competition for the top job. Monk is going to take over after I'm too old to walk anymore."

Monk blushed and looked away. "Stop it, Sir."

"You're brilliant, Monk," O'Hara sneered. "Now we just need to find a way to get some fighter craft."

"There are plenty of ships on this planet," Buca remarked. "We can steal one of them."

"If we're going to bother to steal one of them, we might as well steal a bunch of them," LeMaine added. "We just need to find out where they are."

"Don't forget about getting them on the ground," Nunn pointed out. "They're no good to us if they're in the air and we're stuck down here."

"I know where we can find them."

Everyone turned to look at Xars. He hadn't spoken since the Axichis destroyed the militia's not-so-secret base. LeMaine had stopped thinking about the Thailiv militia leader. LeMaine had thought Xars was down for the count.

"I know a way we can get Axichis fighters down on the ground and get their pilots to deploy. That will leave their fighter craft free for you to steal."

"How?" Nunn asked.

"We launch a preemptive strike."

"With what—carbines and stolen laser rifles?" Heckler rumbled. "You'll excuse me if I say that isn't going to work."

"Not with carbines or stolen laser rifles. With rockets. The Axichis have been trying to suppress the Nainian resistance since they first invaded this planet. The militia will assault them. The Axichis will send their fighters to put us down the way they always do. They'll land the way they always do and send out patrols to hunt us down the way they always do."

"Are you sure that will work?" Polasek asked. "How do we know the Axichis won't abandon Nainia altogether?"

"Xars is right," Peterman replied. "The Axichis spent so many resources keeping this planet before now. They won't abandon it, especially not with the Elian Military on the run."

"How do we set up this strike?" Nunn asked. "And *where* do we set it up?"

"*We* will set up the strike." Xars turned to the other Nainians in the group. He started talking to them in one of the local alien languages even though he was the only Buzath among them.

There were only five Nainians left. LeMaine didn't see how so few would be able to launch a preemptive strike against Axichis warships, but he would just have to trust Xars to pull it off. What other option was there?

The six Nainians had hardly even begun their conversation when the other five besides Xars split off. They took one look outside, set off through the streets, and vanished into the warren of alleys and side neighborhoods. LeMaine would probably never see them again.

"What's going on, Captain?" Lexington asked.

"Good question." LeMaine stood up, but Xars was already moving toward the exit.

"Follow me, all of you." He went outside, looked once up and down the street, and headed in a different direction from his friends.

Xars strolled through town in no particular hurry. He didn't check any of the side avenues to see if the Axichis were nearby.

LeMaine and the Hellhounds checked every corner and doorway. Xars's behavior put LeMaine more on edge than if Xars had acted cautiously, but Xars pretended the whole city was perfectly safe.

He led the Hellhounds to some random intersection. LeMaine didn't recognize the neighborhood. He'd never been here before.

Xars turned to face them all. "We'll set the trap here. You'll need to hide yourselves over there. The Axichis will be able to spot you from the air. You're the only humans on the planet, so try to pretend you're civilians. The Axichis fighter craft will come here and land to search the area for us. They'll post a few guards around their ships, and as soon as the patrols leave their vessels, you'll attack and take the ships off the planet. We won't see each other again." He held out his hand to LeMaine. "It was an honor fighting with you, Captain."

"Thank you. I wish there was some way we could repay you."

"Just go. Go back to Elia and finish this. That's the best thing you can do for us."

"Could you keep these people here?" LeMaine indicated the other Elians in their party. "I'll send someone to pick them up."

"Don't worry about them. They're safe here."

"You are NOT leaving me behind!" Lexington protested. "Haven't I proven myself enough to you by now?"

"Fine, Lexington," LeMaine replied. "You can come."

"Yes!" Lexington high-fived Heckler and then Kellogg. The whole squad beamed at him.

"Hide yourselves now. The attack is coming." Xars walked away and LeMaine motioned the remaining Elians to go with Xars. They vanished into a nearby building, but not without plenty of questioning glances at LeMaine before they left.

LeMaine couldn't help them. He couldn't tell these people what the Nainians planned to do since he didn't know himself.

He believed Xars, though. These Elians would be as safe as or safer with the Thailiv militia than they would be anywhere else.

"What does he mean?" Heckler growled. "How can they mount an attack when there's no one here?"

"They must have their own ways. Let's go, Hellhounds. If this doesn't work, we haven't lost anything."

The squad separated into the surrounding buildings. Some had blown out windows. Others were perfectly intact with a few Nainians peeking out from upstairs.

The Hellhounds concealed themselves as best they could. LeMaine hid with Lexington and Monk in a hollow wreck of a building across the intersection. Nunn, Heckler, and O'Hara took a nice storefront opposite where LeMaine could see them.

Lemon, Kellogg, Peterman, and Buca crouched together behind a broken wall leading to a different alley. Only Polasek went off by himself, entered the doorway of what looked like an apartment block, and flattened himself against the wall out of sight.

The Hellhounds held their breath waiting for....something. LeMaine kept looking around searching for anyone connected to the Thailiv militia, but he didn't see anyone. He only saw a few civilians who had taken an interest in what was going on.

Polasek peeked out, caught LeMaine's eye, and shrugged. How long should they wait? Then Nunn stuck her head up. The intersection remained quiet and deserted. Some preemptive strike this turned out to be.

Without warning, a giant laser blasted for the rooftop of Polasek's apartment building. All the Hellhounds looked up as the beam sliced into the sky. It looked like an awful lot like an Axichis laser cannon, but how could it be?

LeMaine braced himself to fight the enemy until he spotted Nainians scurrying around the big gun. Yes, it really was an Axichis laser cannon. The militia must have stolen it.

They aimed it at an angle from the planet's surface and fired far, far away. A distant boom rumbled across the landscape and a flash exploded in the distance.

The Nainians adjusted their aim before they fired again. Another thump rocked the atmosphere and LeMaine ducked lower in his hiding place. This was it. The Nainians were launching their strike. Nothing would bring the Axichis running like this would.

He knew now exactly what was coming. He had no reason to look out anymore. He caught Lexington's eye and then Monk's. They were both thinking the same thing.

LeMaine huddled there listening to the steady boom of Axichis warships exploding in the distance. Elian weapons might not work against Axichis vessels, but Axichis weapons sure did.

A second later, a shriek of engine noise startled him alert. He looked up to see the Nainians swarming off the roof. Shouts went up from all over. "Run! Get out of the building!"

Civilians poured from doorways and flooded the street. Polasek ran with them as three warships and then a flock of fighter craft blasted across Thailiv. They gunned their lasers straight at the building and the laser cannon exploded.

None of the Nainian gunners were there anymore. They charged downstairs and a few people jumped from windows as the warships opened fire.

Women and children scattered into the neighborhood, but the Thailiv militia halted in the middle of the intersection to turn their carbines upward. They returned fire as the fighter craft tilted through the streets blasting everything to hell.

Polasek raced a block away and took refuge in another alley. A few militia members hit some of the fighter craft and then bolted for cover.

The warships blasted the apartment building to smithereens. Their lasers carved it to pieces until one story after another crumbled to nothing. The warships struck something in the building's interior and then the whole structure imploded, but all the residents had already evacuated.

Dust and rubble rained into a giant mound where the building had been. Fighter craft whizzed off hounding the militia into hiding before the fighters came back to search the area.

LeMaine held his breath. The Axichis must be able to see the Hellhounds hiding here. The Axichis would come straight for the Hellhounds. The patrols wouldn't just walk away and leave their ships unprotected—not with Elian Military personnel in the area of the militia's attack.

He counted down the seconds while the fighter craft descended to land. The warships passed back and forth over the neighborhood, but they didn't leave. Xars didn't plan for warships to search the area, either.

How were the Hellhounds supposed to get off the ground with warships standing guard? They would blow the stolen fighter craft away as soon as the Hellhounds tried to use their weapons to defend themselves.

He seriously considered aborting this mission, but the fighter craft were already setting down in the intersection and deploying their patrols.

Axichis ground troops spread out to search the destroyed apartment building. Then, sure enough, they turned toward the Hellhounds' hiding places. Ten Axichis approached the wall where Lemon, Kellogg, Peterman, and Buca were hiding.

LeMaine didn't get a chance to see if his people realized the danger they were in. Footsteps approached LeMaine's position. Monk stiffened and tightened his grip on his rifle. He compressed his lips and scowled getting ready for the confrontation to blow.

Gunfire erupted right behind LeMaine's head. He and Monk sprang to their feet and opened fire on the Axichis, but the whole patrol had turned their backs to the two men. The Axichis closed ranks to defend themselves against a mob of Nainians advancing into the intersection.

LeMaine's group, Kellogg's group, and Heckler's group all jumped out at the same time and blasted into the Axichis from behind. Polasek joined the Nainians and the four flanks surrounded the enemy.

In a matter of seconds, the party leveled the patrol until no Axichis remained. Xars darted out of the crowd and grabbed LeMaine. "Go! Get on board and get out of here! You don't have time to....."

A catastrophic laser scorched from one of the warships and struck the Nainian position, but the militia didn't run. They pulled out another laser cannon—no, several laser cannons.

The militia set up their guns in the middle of the street and bombarded the warships with devastating fire. All the warships turned to counter the assault. That left the fighter craft free.

"Get on board, Hellhounds!" LeMaine called. "Polasek....."

"Yes, Sir! I'm on it!"

The Hellhounds took off running for the Axichis fighters. LeMaine darted onto one of them and scrambled to get the thing off the ground.

The communications system crackled in his ear. "What was that you were saying about needing readings from a ship under Axichis fire?" Nunn asked. "We're under Axichis fire!"

"Get in the air and take it on the chin while Polasek works his magic," LeMaine told them.

"You hear that, Hellhounds?" Heckler growled. "Take it on the chin."

"Oh, I plan to," Peterman replied. "Big, bad Peterman will protect you all from the enemy while you hide behind my coattails and watch."

O'Hara hooted. "Listen to this! We'll see how your numbers stack up when the shooting starts."

"Is that supposed to be some kind of challenge? You slackers haven't beat me yet and I would love to see you try."

"Buca has beaten you," Nunn pointed out.

"Don't drag me into this," Buca interjected. "I won't be hiding behind the lieutenant's coattails."

"What about it, Peterman?" Polasek asked. "How about you hide behind big, bad Buca and let him protect *you* from the enemy?"

"I won't be hiding behind anyone," Peterman returned. "Besides, I'll have my work cut out for me protecting little old O'Hara."

The squad erupted in laughter. "I'm gonna get you for that one, Lieutenant," O'Hara muttered.

"Bring it on, son."

"Hit it, Hellhounds!" LeMaine ordered. "Locate the enemy and engage. Polasek, you hang back and get us those frequencies."

Kellogg whooped and the Hellhounds punched their throttles. They dodged more shots from the warships, but the militia kept the enemy tied up while the squad launched into the sky.

Chapter 15

L eMaine scanned the atmosphere. Only a handful of Axichis warships and no Elian bombers were anywhere near Nainia anymore. LeMaine looked around for the conflict and spotted an enormous space battle going on between two other Elian planets.

Enormous cannons erupted from the Elian base on Viahiri Prime. They spouted into the whirling mass of ships in orbit over Duciris Major, but the cannon shots only bounced off the Axichis hulls. Whatever the Axichis had done with their power signature, they'd dialed it in so the Elians couldn't damage any Axichis vessel now.

More warships orbited Elia with another devastating battle raging over the planet. The Axichis drove the Elian fleet away from Duciris Major so the Elians had to retreat closer to their home planet. This didn't look good. In fact, it looked catastrophic.

Attack cruisers and Axichis fighters revolved around their larger mother ships. Lasers and cannon blasts flashed in space. A few Elian attack cruisers detonated and then a concussive boom jostled LeMaine's craft when a bomber imploded.

The shockwave interrupted the battle for a second. The commotion died as every ship on the field checked its position and the positions of everyone else. A moment of surreal calm fell over the battle and then everyone piled in with a vengeance.

"Go to town, Hellhounds!" LeMaine ordered.

"Stand back, O'Hara!" Peterman called. "You don't want to skin your elbows."

"I don't hear you counting, Lieutenant."

"I don't hear any of you counting," LeMaine interrupted. "I don't want to hear any talk if you aren't tallying kill count."

Buca plunged into the mix with Monk hot on his heels. These Axichis fighters could damage their own kind, but a few Axichis fighters couldn't turn the tide in Elia's favor.

LeMaine veered into line with Buca and Monk and ran between the enemy toward one of the warships. "Get behind us, Polasek!" LeMaine ordered. "We'll draw their fire so you can read their frequencies."

"Right behind you. Let's go."

Buca and Monk started to pull ahead. They widened their formation, LeMaine slotted between them, and all three swooped close to the warship's sides. LeMaine steered his cruiser's nose close to the giant ship's laser ports.

"Wait for it!" LeMaine ordered. "Now!"

The port opened up and lasers erupted into their grouping. Buca and Monk peeled off to both sides and LeMaine sprinted ahead leaving Polasek exposed.

Lasers danced down his hull and crawled closer to the cockpit, but he veered away just in time. Smoke billowed from his port engine and his cruiser turned several revolutions before he stabilized.

"Beat it back to the rear!" LeMaine ordered. "Hellhounds, close ranks and defend Polasek."

"Little old Polasek needs to wipe his nose ....." O'Hara began.

"Not now, Sergeant!" LeMaine roared. "Just do your job."

Monk and Buca came wheeling around the battle. Kellogg and Heckler got to Polasek first. He limped away from the warship that hit him. Lemon, Peterman, and LeMaine showed up to complete their blockade and then the Axichis fighters pounced.

They whirled out of formation and left off attacking all the Elian bombers. A whole crowd of fighter craft surrounded the Hellhounds in a dense swarm.

Lasers flew thick and fast. LeMaine pivoted his cannons right, left, and back again. He fired as many shots at the enemy as he could, but his lasers couldn't make up for their numbers.

The Axichis charged in to break the squad apart. The enemy rushed the Hellhounds' position scattering lasers in all directions. They tried to carve a path between the Hellhounds and drive them apart.

LeMaine dodged in front of them to close the gap and four fighters mobbed in at once. He took a hellish pounding across his starboard flank until Monk and Nunn broke through to counter the attack.

"Kinda need you to step on it, Lieutenant!" LeMaine called.

"Working on it, Sir!" Polasek replied.

"Work on it a little faster!" Lemon bellowed. "We're getting slaughtered out here!"

Seven fighters revolved around her hammering her with lasers. They wedged her backward to drive a space between her and the other Hellhounds. Her craft twirled in all directions raining cannon shots on every enemy, but she couldn't keep up with them.

She spun to starboard and a laser shattered her port engine. Another laser struck her cockpit and the glass cover cracked. She ripped the ship back to port only to take another blast on the starboard side.

"Sergeant!" LeMaine called, but he couldn't reach her with so many enemy fighters blocking his way. He couldn't even see the warships anymore.

A yell echoed down the communications system. Was that Lemon's cruiser exploding? Monk, Heckler, and Nunn sprinted across the battlefield with fighters swarming all around them. They veered in front of Lemon, pivoted backward, and guarded her against the enemy assault.

The maneuver left just enough time for Peterman and Kellogg to hustle up behind the Axichis and shred them on both sides.

LeMaine broke out of his own firefight searching for Polasek. He hung back the way LeMaine told him to while Buca and O'Hara defended him. The two Hellhounds aimed their cannons outward in both directions, but anyone could see they didn't stand a chance.

More enemy fighter craft seemed to gather from all over. The larger battle must be turning against the Elians.

"Got it!" Polasek cheered. "I got the frequencies!"

"Transmit them to the rest of the squad!" LeMaine ordered.

Polasek didn't answer and the battle became even more chaotic. LeMaine did his best to carve an opening between himself and O'Hara, but the fighters were just too thick. LeMaine faced impossible numbers everywhere he turned. He couldn't defend himself against their lasers.

His heart sank when he spotted even more fighters advancing from Viahiri Prime. How did they get near the planet? No more cannon fire came from the surface. Now nothing stood between the Axichis and Elia itself.

The fighters crept closer to Polasek. LeMaine couldn't let them attack. He punched his throttle, dodged his adversaries, and sprinted for O'Hara's position. LeMaine sent a volley past Polasek's ship and LeMaine skidded to a standstill behind Polasek's tail.

LeMaine didn't dare to ask what was taking Polasek so long. LeMaine could only hope and pray he held out long enough for Polasek to transmit the frequencies. Maybe then someone would survive this battle.

The fighters saw him and the jig was up. They had to notice everyone working so hard to defend this one stricken fighter craft. The Hellhounds couldn't have made it more obvious that this was the most important ship on the field.

The enemy attacked without mercy. They hammered LeMaine and then sprinted past him to lay into Polasek. Buca tried to wheel and help LeMaine out, but too many fighters were already surrounding both of them.

Lasers punched Polasek's starboard wing and the whole wing severed, tilted off, and floated away into space. LeMaine redoubled his efforts, but he couldn't drive the fighters away by himself.

He looked around frantically for any help, but he already knew none would come. He froze and almost doubted his own senses when three Elian bombers rocketed out of the battle heading straight for him.

Actually, they weren't heading straight for him. They were trying to reach Elia and the Hellhounds just happened to be in their way, but LeMaine was never so happy to see them.

Attack cruisers surrounded them and the three bombers plowed their way through the fighters pinning down the Hellhounds.

"Polasek!" LeMaine called. "Do you read?"

No one answered. Polasek's cruiser still showed full power and Polasek's life signs all read normal. What was wrong? Did those last shots knock out Polasek's communications system? If they did, he wouldn't be able to transmit and the whole Elian fleet would be dead in the water.

The Axichis fighters abandoned the Hellhounds to deal with the incoming bombers. The *Lucidity* and the *Excursion* wheeled their cannons to return fire, and this time, the two bombers teamed up. They combined their firepower and destroyed five fighters right off the bat.

"That's what I'm talking about!" Lemon crowed. "*Lucidity*: five. Hellhounds: squat."

"What about us?" a familiar voice asked. Another attack cruiser circled the *Lucidity*. It somersaulted near LeMaine's cockpit and DeYoung grinned down at him.

"Not her again!" Peterman teased.

"Did you miss me, Hellhounds? I don't hear any numbers coming through the system."

"I am gonna whoop your ass, lady," Heckler snarled. "Do you see us out here shooting at them?"

"Coordinate with my crew," DeYoung replied. "It usually takes four cruisers working in tandem to destroy one fighter."

"I like them odds," O'Hara chimed in. "Buca....."

"Let's go." Buca and O'Hara exploded out of the crowd and LeMaine veered to starboard to join them. They only had three ships between them, but a second later, two more cruisers from the *Lucidity* joined in.

Axichis fighters surrounded the *Lucidity* and the *Excursion*. The enemy tried to cut the two ships off from reaching Elia, but the bombers worked in concert now. Every time one of them made a shot, the other ship matched it. They pounded the fighters one after another without missing once. Fighters exploded all over the map.

LeMaine, Buca, and O'Hara synchronized their attack runs and the *Lucidity* cruisers fell into formation. They circled isolated fighters blowing up as many as they could hit.

Now LeMaine understood why the Axichis wanted to separate the Elian ships from each other, but it no longer worked. The Axichis gathered in an arrow formation and dove point first into the Hellhounds. They scattered the Elians, but that only worked to the Hellhounds' advantage.

LeMaine's group rotated to the other side of the battle and saw the Hellhounds lined up in a gauntlet of cannons. *Lucidity* cruisers dotted the ranks. The two sides parted to let the Axichis through and then the Hellhounds unloaded without mercy.

More fighters exploded and LeMaine left the squad to fight them while he turned back to Polasek. His craft sat unmoving and unresponsive where LeMaine left it.

LeMaine sprinted in that direction to make sure Polasek was all right. When LeMaine got near enough, he spotted Polasek working feverishly over the controls inside his craft.

Polasek glanced up and his eyes met LeMaine's. Polasek's lips moved and he went into a flurry of sign language explaining what was wrong. He pointed down at his controls and then held up his hand near his cheek.

He extended his thumb toward his ear and his pinky toward his mouth while he talked. So that confirmed it. Polasek had no communications, which meant the Elian fleet wouldn't be able to use whatever frequencies he worked out.

A dull thud drew LeMaine's attention back to the battle. The *Lucidity* and the *Excursion* no longer picked off fighters here and there. They rotated away from the battle and LeMaine's stomach dropped when he saw more Axichis warships moving in.

They followed the bombers' path trying to reach Elia. The *Lucidity*, the *Excursion*, and the Hellhounds were the only Elian forces standing in the enemy's way.

Colonel Nicholson's deep booming voice came through the communications system. "Target those warships! All ships—defend Elia!"

The Hellhounds stopped shooting fighters to follow the order. The *Lucidity* and the *Excursion* bombers laid into the first warship in line, but without effect. The squad could shoot Axichis fighters all day long. They wouldn't win the war without some other way to defeat the larger, more powerful Axichis warships.

The Hellhounds rocketed out of the battle and closed ranks with the *Lucidity*. At least they were all well clear of Polasek's stricken fighter.

The whole Elian contingent pounded the first warship and left themselves exposed to attack by the others. Lexington pulled up next to LeMaine and the rest of the *Lucidity* cruisers gathered around, too.

They unloaded on the warship and the hull started to buckle. Colonel Nicholson called orders and encouragement down the ranks, but LeMaine couldn't hear him over the noise.

Two more warships flanked the battle line. A laser deflected off the *Excursion's* hull, skidded sideways, and smashed into Lexington's cruiser. It blew in LeMaine's face and someone screamed from farther away.

LeMaine squinted into the barrage of combined lasers and cannon fire. He concentrated everything on targeting the warship in front of him and then the whole thing exploded in his face.

The shockwave caught his cruiser in an avalanche. He tried to see through blinding light and searing heat as the impact hit his ship. It hurled him away and all his controls shut down at once.

Chapter 16

LeMaine swam back to consciousness and cradled his throbbing head. He had to blink several times before he could see well enough to remember where he was.

His fighter craft drifted in space. Every system in the cockpit was dead and nothing responded when he tried to restore power.

More Axichis fighters, Elian attack cruisers, and a confused jumble of debris revolved around him through the stars. Two other stricken fighters wheeled past his cockpit. Nunn gave him a cheery wave and DeYoung shrugged helplessly behind the glass of her own cruiser's cockpit.

That last massive explosion must have deactivated all these ships in the middle of a raging battle. None of them could communicate or do anything.

LeMaine looked around for the rest of his Hellhounds, but the other fighters were too far away for him to see. He also spotted the Elian bombers *Lucidity* and the *Excursion* not too far off, but he couldn't reach them or contact them, either. He was adrift.

He turned the other way trying to read the outcome of the battle and his scalp prickled at what he saw. A towering line of destroyers stood between him and the Elian solar system....and these were NOT the Axichis invaders who attacked his squad.

Cold sweat broke out on LeMaine's palms. He instinctively tightened his grip on his cannon's firing mechanism even though he knew it didn't work anymore. Those ships belonged to the Imoliv race which meant only one thing.

Two solar systems flanked Elia on either side. The Axichis had always been friendly and enjoyed free trade and diplomatic relations with Elia—right up until this traitorous invasion.

The Imoliv on the other side had never allowed diplomatic dialogue. They shunned Elia's repeated attempts to establish some communication between their systems. The Imoliv flatly refused to trade with Elia under any circumstances. The Imoliv wouldn't even explain why.

The Imoliv had always kept a standing fleet of well-armed ships stationed along the buffer zone that separated their system from Elia. The Imoliv had kept their guns trained on Elia at all times as if Elia was arming to destroy the Imoliv at a moment's notice.

The Imoliv maintained such a hostile stance toward Elia that their posture spurred the most development and production of the entire Elian war machine. The Elian Military had prepared itself to fight the Imoliv if the Imoliv ever decided they'd had enough of defending themselves and took the initiative.

The Elian Military would never have been in such a position to defend itself against the Axichis invasion if they hadn't been keeping an eye on the Imoliv all this time.

That was the colossal irony of this whole lunatic situation. The system the Elians had thought were their friends turned out to be their true enemies. The system the Elians thought were their enemies turned out to be a godsend in disguise.

None of that made LeMaine feel better now. The Imoliv had always stood guard on their side of the buffer zone. They'd stayed on their side of the border watching the Axichis throw down on the Elian Military. The Imoliv didn't raise a finger to help the Elians—not that anyone expected them to.

That last blast had flung LeMaine, the Hellhounds, and the two bombers into Imoliv space. All those Elian vessels were behind the Imoliv line—inside the buffer zone.

The Imoliv had crossed into the buffer zone, too. They advanced their line right up to the Elian border and blockaded the Elian spacecraft from reentering their own space.

Would the Imoliv let the Elian craft reenter their own system—assuming the Elian craft could get their engines working? The Imoliv might make the Elians fight their way through—as if these puny Elians could fight the Imoliv defense force.

For some reason, though the Imoliv didn't attack. Did they see that the Elians were stricken and defenseless? They must. The Imoliv must be able to see that none of these fighters had power or functioning weapons systems.

LeMaine could see explosions going off beyond the border. The Elians and the Axichis remained locked in combat inside Elian space, but the Imoliv just sat here doing nothing. They advanced inside the buffer zone to protect the border, but they didn't raise a finger to help Elia.

LeMaine couldn't get out of this fight. He and all the Hellhounds were trapped with nothing to do but wait. His fighter rotated in space. He could see Peterman and Monk not far away, each one enclosed in his own little fishbowl.

They all floated there for at least five minutes before one of the Imoliv destroyers migrated out of the defense line. The ship reversed and then turned around. Its engines flared once and it eased backward, first toward the *Lucidity* and then toward the *Excursion*.

The Imoliv vessel opened its rear hatch and a laser extended from the ship's hull. The laser touched the *Lucidity*, but it didn't damage the bomber. It towed the ship inside the Imoliv vessel's hull and then did the same thing to the *Excursion*.

LeMaine stiffened when the Imoliv ship turned to the Hellhounds' fighters and the nearby attack cruisers, but he could only sit while the Imoliv brought all the Hellhounds and then all of DeYoung's people on board, too.

The laser pulled LeMaine's fighter inside a huge empty cargo hold and the ship banged down on a steel floor. All the other stricken Elian craft sat around the two bombers. None of those ships could even turn their power on.

LeMaine could see all his own people much more clearly now. The Hellhounds left their cockpits one by one. They must be trying to get out of their fighters. LeMaine tried it, but the controls didn't work.

Monk stood up on his pilot's seat and tried to kick his cockpit cover open, but no matter how many times he smashed it, it stayed closed.

Monk flopped down in the seat. All the Hellhounds looked at each other and then at LeMaine, but he couldn't help them. They were the Imoliv's prisoners now. The Imoliv must want something from these Elians. The Imoliv wouldn't leave the Hellhounds down here forever.

He heard banging coming from somewhere, but he couldn't go outside to see what it was. A moment later, a flash of light from the *Lucidity* caught his attention. A laser carved through the bomber's hull and the rear hatch slammed down hard on the floor.

A bunch of Elian security troops stalked out of the ship's flight deck sweeping their carbines right and left. They searched the area around the *Lucidity* until they confirmed that the hold was empty.

They spread through the hold and set up a perimeter around the Elian ships. Then a swarm of mechanics fanned out across the floor and started cutting everyone out of their vessels.

LeMaine hopped to the ground with a relieved sigh. He said, "Thanks," to the mechanic who freed him, but the guy was already going off somewhere else.

DeYoung came over to LeMaine followed by Polasek and Lemon. "Well, Sir, this is a pickle," Polasek observed.

"Forget that. Did you get the frequencies?"

"I got 'em and I copied them into my remote before the communications system went down, but they don't do us much good in here, do they? The question is how do we get them back to Elia."

"The question is how we get out of here in one piece." LeMaine looked all around him.

More Elian personnel kept showing up by the second. The *Excursion* crew had carved their way out of their own ship and the rest of the Hellhounds came over to join LeMaine. DeYoung's pilots were assembling to receive orders from her, too.

"What's the plan, Sir?" Kellogg asked. "Don't tell me we're going to get into a war against the Imoliv, too."

"What are you complaining about?" Peterman asked. "Another war means more wounded for you."

Kellogg turned bright red. "This might come as a surprise to you, Lieutenant, but I don't enjoy seeing people get injured or killed."

"Aawwww!" O'Hara sang. "Big, bad Kellogg has a soft little heart after all!"

"For someone with a soft heart, you sure got yourself a cruel job going around electrolyzing everyone," Nunn observed.

"Would you rather I didn't electrolyze you?" Kellogg asked. "Would you rather I just left you to walk around with broken bones and cuts and rifle wounds to your chests and your guts spilling out? I'm hurt. I thought you Hellhounds knew better."

Peterman squeezed Kellogg's shoulder. "I know you do, son. It was a stupid joke. I'm sorry."

"Come here, you big softy." Heckler hooked his elbow around Kellogg's neck, jerked him into a choke hold, and rubbed his knuckles in Kellogg's curly hair. "You know we love you and can't live without you."

"I can," Lemon muttered.

"Give Kellogg a break," Nunn chimed in. "He's right. If he didn't electrolyze us, someone else would—someone we might not be able to rib as much as we rib him."

"Yeah, that would be terrible," O'Hara agreed. "Sorry, Kellogg."

"I should electrolyze you all just for saying that," Kellogg grumbled.

"I have a better idea," Peterman began. "How about you just.....?"

"Shut it!" LeMaine hissed. "Pull it up, Hellhounds."

Everyone turned around to see what he meant. The Hellhounds stiffened as another group of people exited the *Lucidity*. Colonel Nicholson, Commander Lodge, Captain James Hurst, and most of the *Lucidity's* bridge staff came over to LeMaine's squad.

The Hellhounds and DeYoung's crew moved back to leave a clear path for Colonel Nicholson to reach LeMaine. The colonel extended his hand. "Mission accomplished, Owen. Congratulations."

"Thank you for saying so, Sir, but I don't think this situation calls for congratulations."

Colonel Nicholson grimaced at the surroundings. "No. You're right. It doesn't."

Commander Lodge shook hands with LeMaine, too. "I'm just glad you made it with all your people alive and intact."

"Not quite, Sir. We lost Orr, Stivers, and Lexington—three of the bravest soldiers I've ever had the pleasure to serve with. I'd like to recommend them for posthumous decorations when this is all over.....and we lost quite a few people on Nainia, too."

"I realize that, Owen," Colonel Nicholson replied. "Let's concentrate on the matter at hand before we get into that."

"Yes, Sir. Polasek here worked out a new set of frequencies we can use against the Axichis. We just need to find a way to deploy them."

Captain Hurst stepped forward and held out his hand. "How ya doing, Owen? It's good to see you again."

"You, too, Jimmy. You're keeping well."

Captain Hurst laughed. "I don't have any excuse when I'm sitting behind a desk all the time—not like you. I thought you'd be dead by the time you were thirty and here you are proving us all wrong."

LeMaine had to laugh and he heard the Hellhounds whispering behind him. They would have a field day with this as soon as the brass disappeared.

Colonel Nicholson waved behind him. "You Hellhounds get over to the *Lucidity* and gear up. We don't know what these Imoliv have in mind and I want our best squad ready for anything."

"Yes, Sir," LeMaine replied.

Captain Hurst started to say, "DeYoung, take your crew back to the ship and......" when a deep boom startled everyone. It vibrated the whole Imoliv destroyers.

The command staff turned to see what made the noise and the security troops rushed over to position themselves between the Elian personnel and a sliding panel in the side wall.

The section hissed back to reveal a group of aliens standing in a smallish compartment beyond.

These aliens stood upright and most of them dwarfed LeMaine in height. Their pale, scaly skin, sharply defined cheekbones, and heavily boned brows gave their small, hard eyes a flinty, dangerous look—or that might just have been the way they were eyeing the Elians trapped in their hold.

The Imoliv had arrived to meet their prisoners.

Chapter 17

T he Imoliv sauntered slowly into the ship's hold and looked down their noses at all the Elians milling around.

The *Lucidity* security troops held the Imoliv at constant gunpoint to stop the aliens from approaching the brass, but the Imoliv looked down their noses at the security troops, too.

One dignified male Imoliv stepped forward first. The others stayed slightly behind him, so he must have been their leader or maybe the captain of this destroyer.

LeMaine would never mistake the way this man held his shoulders back, his chin up, and the way his eyes flicked from face to face and person to person. This man was used to wielding authority, not just with his subordinates, but with everyone.

The rest of the group acted the same way, but this man made it especially obvious that he was in charge.

The Imoliv eyed everyone in the hold, turned their attention to the brass, and strode over to Colonel Nicholson, Commander Lodge, and Captain Hurst.

The security troops got in the Imoliv's faces again and three of the soldiers jammed their carbine barrels right into the leader's chest.

He barely glanced at them, even when they shoved him to a stop. They yelled in his face not to take another step or they would shoot him on the spot.

His features betrayed just the slightest hint of annoyance and then his hard eyes darted to the three officers standing behind the troops.

"I'm Colonel Nicholson of the Elian Military Command," Colonel Nicholson began. "What do you mean by taking us as prisoners? This is a serious breach of diplomatic protocol. I demand that you release us at once."

"You're in no position to demand anything from us, Colonel," the Imoliv leader replied in perfect English. "Your ships invaded our territory. That makes you the criminal parties and subject to our reprisals."

"We didn't invade anything," Commander Lodge blurted out. "We were in battle against the Axichis and the explosion threw us into the buffer zone. We never invaded Imoliv territory and it was completely unintentional."

"The buffer zone is on the Imoliv side of the border. Therefore, you invaded Imoliv territory." The Imoliv leader turned his penetrating gaze to all the ships lying around. "At any rate, here you are. It doesn't appear you'll be going anywhere in these ships anyway. You might as well stay here and make yourselves comfortable."

"We can't stay here!" Commander Lodge countered. "We're at war against the Axichis."

The leader raised his eyebrows ever so slightly. "Why are you at war against them? They've been your allies for centuries."

"Not anymore. They invaded us and attacked our planets. We've been fighting to throw them out of our system ever since." Commander Lodge narrowed his eyes at the Imoliv leader. "You should have been able to see that from here. You would have been monitoring the situation in Elia and you did nothing to help us."

Colonel Nicholson held up his hands between Commander Lodge and the Imoliv leader. "Excuse my subordinate here. You can imagine we're all a little disturbed by this turn of events. I think we may be getting off on the wrong foot here. I've told you my name. Would you be so kind as to tell me yours so we can discuss this like rational, civilized individuals?"

He held out his hand to the Imoliv leader. No one in Elia knew much about the Imoliv except that they liked to keep to themselves.

LeMaine didn't know if they used hand-shaking as a form of introduction. The rest of the Elian personnel here would be just as in the dark about Imoliv customs as he was.

The leader glanced down at Colonel Nicholson's hand. Whether he understood the gesture or not, the leader stopped short of wrinkling his nose at it, but he didn't make any move to shake it nor did his expression soften.

"My name.....is Sehiri," he replied. "I am the commander in charge of perimeter defense along our border with Elia. I am personally responsible for ensuring that the Elian Military does not invade Imoliv territory....."

"I already told you we didn't invade!" Commander Lodge cut in again, but Colonel Nicholson stopped him.

Commander Sehiri's eyes flicked in Lodge's direction once and then he scanned the rest of the assembled personnel with his most dismissive glance yet.

"You keep claiming that you didn't invade and yet here you are, on our side of the border, with all these attack vessels armed and prepared for warfare. You claim to be at war against the Axichis and that the last battle flung you into our territory inadvertently, but that could all be a lie. How am I to know you aren't in league with the Axichis? You could have staged this whole episode to get your vessels inside our border to attack us instead."

Commander Lodge flared up and inhaled to launch into another sally about how ridiculous that was, but Colonel Nicholson stopped him again. Nicholson laid his hand on Lodge's arm and gave him a very subtle pull backward to ease Lodge away from Sehiri.

"I beg your pardon," Colonel Nicholson began again. "We never intended to trespass on your territory. Just tell us how we can rectify the situation to your satisfaction. We'll do whatever we can to smooth things over. We don't want any hostility between us and the Imoliv. That's the last thing we want."

Sehiri gave him such a direct, unforgiving stare that anyone could see plain as day that there was already plenty of hostility between the Elians and the Imoliv. It was all on the Imoliv side.

Sehiri didn't soften in the slightest. "There is nothing you can do to rectify the situation. You are already here along with your attack vessels. You can imagine that we have no intention of releasing any of you or your ships. You might turn around and attack us outright or you might return to your own space only to launch another assault on us from there. You might even bring the Axichis with you. No, Colonel. I'm afraid you must all stay here for the time being....."

"For how long?" Commander Lodge demanded. "You can't hold us here forever."

"I am already holding you, my dear Sir," Sehiri replied in his silkiest tone. "I will continue to hold you for as long as I deem it necessary. I suggest you make yourselves comfortable. You aren't going anywhere."

He turned and strode out of the hold. The other Imoliv parted to let him through and then they followed him to the same sliding panel. They stepped into the compartment behind and the panel slid shut.

"This is outrageous!" Commander Lodge fumed as soon as the Imoliv disappeared. "This is a diplomatic outrage! They can't do this to us!"

"Forget all that." Colonel Nicholson turned to LeMaine. "I want your squad armed to the teeth, Owen. Get all your people primed and prepped for battle and then I want to see you and Polasek in private."

"Yes, Sir," LeMaine replied.

Colonel Nicholson turned to DeYoung and Captain Hurst. "Get all your crews on repair duty. I want every last single thing that's wrong with these ships repaired as soon as possible. I want every ship in this hold ready to fly and ready to shoot."

They both said, "Yes, Sir," and the party scattered.

LeMaine gave orders to the Hellhounds to rearm from the *Lucidity*. Then LeMaine pulled Polasek aside and they joined Colonel Nicholson and Commander Lodge in one corner of the hold.

The repair crews hustled around banging, welding, scraping, and tinkering. The noise escalated to the point where the four men had to talk loudly just to make themselves heard. No one could or would overhear them.

Colonel Nicholson started by addressing Polasek. "Lieutenant, I want you to make it your task to load those frequencies onto every ship here. I want all these vessels to be ready to deploy the new frequencies the instant we get out of here."

"Yes, Sir," Polasek replied. "That will take some time, you understand."

"Of course I understand. I also want you to load the frequencies into the communications systems of all these ships. The instant we get out of here, I want all these craft to transmit the frequencies to every other ship in our fleet. I don't want any delay. Do you understand?"

"Yes, Sir. I understand." Polasek cocked his head. "*Does* that mean we're getting out of here, Sir?"

Colonel Nicholson's features hardened and he turned to LeMaine. "As soon as your squad arms up, I want you to start working on a way to escape from this ship. I'll assign another team to inspect this hold, but I doubt Commander Sehiri would have put us in here if there was a way for us to get out."

"No, Sir," LeMaine replied. "I was thinking the same thing."

"I'm glad we think the same. I want your squad on that detail. Get us the hell out of here, Owen. I know you and your squad will be the best men for the job."

"Thank you, Sir. We're on it."

LeMaine and Polasek headed back toward the *Lucidity* while Colonel Nicholson and Commander Lodge stayed where they were with their heads together in deep conversation.

"So you and the Hellhounds get to go out on escape detail while I'm stuck programming a bunch of computers?" Polasek complained. "That's hardly fair."

LeMaine spun around, but he relaxed when he saw Polasek smirking at him. "That's what you get for becoming a communications specialist instead of a hard-assed Marine like Heckler. It could have been worse. You could have been stuck behind a desk on Elia all this time."

"Yeah, that would have been my worst nightmare." Polasek turned his gaze toward the *Lucidity*. "I wonder how bad the damage is. It could take the repair crews quite a while to fix all these ships to the point where I can even carry out the colonel's order."

"Do your best, son." LeMaine bumped Polasek's shoulder and they climbed up into the *Lucidity's* flight deck to meet the other Hellhounds.

LeMaine went over to the weapons locker and took down one carbine after another. Polasek stood back and watched the other Hellhounds gearing up, checking their weapons, adjusting their body armor, and going through their packs to check their supplies.

"Hey!" O'Hara called. "Why isn't Polasek gearing up? You aren't staying behind with the babysitter are you, Lieutenant?"

"You better watch your mouth, Sergeant," Polasek countered. "I might remind you that not just your lives, but the lives of every other Elian on the field are right here." He tapped his remote.

LeMaine checked his, too. "Colonel Nicholson was right. Our remotes can't read anything beyond these walls, which means we'll have to do it the old-fashioned way. Split up into teams— O'Hara, you take Heckler and Monk, Peterman can take Nunn, and Kellogg can take Lemon. Search this hold and report back on any weaknesses, vulnerabilities, or anything else we can exploit. Buca, you come with me."

The teams broke up, Polasek went inside the *Lucidity*, and Buca migrated over to LeMaine's side. Buca shot a glance toward the sliding panel where the Imoliv arrived and departed. "Who were those people?"

LeMaine's head shot up. "You don't know?"

"No. I've never been off my home planet before this campaign."

LeMaine sighed and went back to looking around him. "Sorry about that. Sometimes it seems like you've been with us the whole time. I keep forgetting."

"So who are they?"

"They're the Imoliv. The Elian system is here.....with the Axichis on one side and the Imoliv in the other. Elia is between them.....like this."

LeMaine positioned his hands to show Buca the layout of the three systems. Buca furrowed his brow and cocked his head to listen. He really didn't know—but how could he? He probably hadn't received any education at all.

LeMaine marveled at that because Buca was so astute in every other way.

"We've never established diplomatic relations with the Imoliv," LeMaine went on. "They've always held us at a distance. The Axichis always treated us as their friends, which I guess goes to show that you never really can know what anyone is thinking."

"How do you plan to get out of this hold?" Buca asked.

"If I knew that, I wouldn't be searching the place for a way out. That's why we're doing this. We can't form a plan until we know the layout of the hold and the area outside it."

Buca nodded. "I see."

"Do you have any ideas? If you do, by all means, share them with me. I'm wide open here."

"No, I was just about to say the same thing." Buca scanned the area around him and watched the mechanics for a while. "I was going to say that I couldn't form a plan without knowing what lies beyond these walls."

"Let's find out, then."

LeMaine and Buca went to the sliding panel where the Imoliv entered. Then they searched the rest of the hold. The other teams did the same thing and the squad reassembled near the *Lucidity*.

"This place is locked up tighter than a witch's asshole," O'Hara exclaimed.

"Do you really have to put in those terms?" Peterman asked.

"What terms would you rather I used? It *is* locked up tighter than a witch's asshole."

"Could you maybe use some terms that don't give us all such a vivid picture of your sexual exploits?" Peterman went on. "After all, how do you actually know that a witch's asshole is that tight? It might be extremely loose and soft and easy to break into. Please, Sergeant. Give us all the benefit of your expert experience and research."

The others laughed. "O'Hara is right about one thing," Heckler remarked. "We aren't getting out of here by force—not from the inside. We might need to use the old crowbar trick."

"What is the old crowbar trick?" Buca asked.

"He means we might need to pull a jailbreak by sneaking out of the hold and breaking it from the outside," Nunn explained.

"If we could break it from the outside, we would already be outside the hold," Buca pointed out. "We wouldn't need to break it because we already would have broken it."

"Don't try to confuse them with logic," Lemon interjected. "You might fry one of their circuits—or all of them."

"There might be a way to break the hold," LeMaine suggested. "I mean there might be a way for *us* to break the hold—just our squad. Then, once we're out and running around at large on this ship, we could find a way to release all the other craft."

"All the other craft would have to be operational for that to work," Kellogg chimed in. "Getting out of this hold and getting the craft off the ship won't do squat for anyone if these ships aren't fit to fly anywhere."

"Which is exactly why Colonel Nicholson ordered all these crews to repair their ships to be ready to fly as soon as possible," LeMaine replied. "Now we just have to figure out......"

He broke off when Polasek showed up.

"What are you doing back so soon, Lieutenant?" Peterman asked. "Don't tell me you already saved the world and now you're ready for a lunch break."

"No one will be saving the world anytime soon," Polasek replied. "All the electrical systems on all these ships are fried. I can't upload the frequencies to anyone or anything. They don't even have the power to make repairs."

"But.....they're welding." Lemon pointed across the hold.

"They're using portable equipment with remote battery power," Polasek explained.

Some of the mechanics had been welding and cutting destroyed sections of attack cruisers and fighter craft. Even as the squad watched, other crewmen came over and stopped them from working. Everybody had to conserve the power they had.

"Damn!" Heckler muttered. "That's no good."

"All the more reason we gotta find our way out of this hold," LeMaine replied. "We need these ships repaired and we need them repaired now."

"How can we make repairs without power?" Nunn asked.

"We have power," LeMaine replied. "We're sitting on one of the greatest power sources available. It's all around us. It's what's keeping us confined here. We just need to find a way to tap it."

Chapter 18

LeMaine and the other Hellhounds stood in the very center of the hold staring at the wall.

"Umm....Captain?" Heckler growled. "What exactly are we doing here?"

"We're looking at that sliding panel where the Imoliv came in and out of the hold. It's the only vulnerability in the place. If we're going to crack this thing, we gotta do it here."

"How exactly do you plan to do that?" Nunn asked.

"We have to wait for the Imoliv to come back," LeMaine replied. "They came in and went out through here, which means this door leads to the part of the ship where the Imoliv are controlling this hold. That's the direction we have to go, and since we can't get out any other way, we have to wait for them to open the door from the other side."

"And this helps us.....how?" O'Hara asked. "We could be in here for a hundred years and the Imoliv might not come back. They might leave us down here to exhaust our food and water supplies. They might decide to starve us to death and never show their faces to us again."

"Listen to who's a beaming ball of sunshine," Heckler growled. "Why don't you throw in a few gladiator games and cannibalism, too, while you're at it? Maybe the Imoliv are taking us all back to their homeworld to make us fight each other to the death and then roast us over an open flame and eat us in celebration of our defeat."

"Heckler!" Kellogg exclaimed. "That is the longest speech I've ever heard you make."

"I can make another, longer one when I rip your head open and yell down into the cavernous void where your brain should be."

The others laughed, but LeMaine didn't join in. He had other things on his mind—like getting the hell out of here.

Lemon approached their squad just then coming from the *Lucidity*. She wasn't wearing her body armor or carrying her pack. She wore her normal uniform and nothing else.

"All set, Corporal?" LeMaine asked.

"All set and ready to roll," Lemon replied.

"Where have you been, Lemon?" Nunn asked.

"Wouldn't you like to know," Lemon muttered.

"I would like to know. That's why I asked."

"You all wanted to know how we're going to get out of here," LeMaine told them. "You're about to find out. Lemon here has her disguise suit on under her uniform. The minute the Imoliv come back, she'll disguise herself while they aren't looking, sneak into that compartment with them, and get out onto the ship. Then she'll find a way to release us so the rest of us can get out onto the ship, too."

"And by 'get out onto the ship'," O'Hara went on, "I'm assuming you mean so we can wreak mayhem and havoc on the Imoliv, sabotage their ship, steal their power, and break our people out of here."

"Who's better at wreaking mayhem and havoc than you, champ?" Kellogg teased.

"You got that right," O'Hara replied. "I'm glad someone is finally learning to appreciate my skills and talents."

"We've all had plenty of time to appreciate your mouth," Nunn countered. "What about it, Sir? What do we do once we get out onto the ship?"

"We *don't* wreak mayhem and havoc—not yet," LeMaine replied. "We don't want the Imoliv to even know we're there until after we get all these ships repaired. Our first objective is to divert power to this hold so our people can get to work and get these ships operational again."

"How do we do that?" Nunn asked again.

Kellogg swatted her shoulder. "You heard the man earlier. We won't know how to do it until we see the lay of the land outside. That's first. How many times does he have to say it?"

"All right, all right," Nunn exclaimed. "Keep your panties on."

LeMaine waved Lemon away. "Go do your thing, Sergeant. Make yourself scarce."

"Yes, Sir."

She sauntered off into the crowds of crewmen and mechanics working all over the hold. They couldn't do much without power tools, but they were still hard at it with whatever hand tools they could spare.

"I should have been an expert in disguise," O'Hara mused. "She has such a cool job."

"Don't let her hear you saying that," Kellogg replied.

"You couldn't be an expert in disguise, Sergeant," Peterman cut in. "You couldn't go a day without everyone paying attention to you and laughing at your stupid jokes."

"I could go a day.....max," O'Hara replied and got another laugh from the rest of the squad.

LeMaine watched Lemon out of sight and then turned back to the door. He had no way of knowing when she would come back to the door or what she would look like when she did. She could disguise herself as anything and anyone.

He would probably never see her and the Imoliv sure wouldn't. She might blend in perfectly with the walls so the Imoliv never knew she was there.

"You still didn't answer my question, Sir," O'Hara went on. "The Imoliv might not come back. They might never open that door again. We'd be waiting for ages and never get anywhere."

"Show some respect for the man," Peterman told him. "I'm sure Captain LeMaine has thought of something that you haven't."

"You're right, Sergeant," LeMaine told O'Hara. "I thought of that, too, which is why we aren't waiting around for the Imoliv to decide to come back. We're going to make them come, and when they do, we have to make sure they don't see Lemon."

"How could they see her when she's disguised?" Nunn asked.

LeMaine didn't answer. He turned the other way and watched a crew of mechanics from the *Excursion*. They'd been welding one of the attack cruisers that got damaged in the battle.

At some unspoken signal, the crew left the cruiser, wheeled their welding unit to the nearest wall, and started cutting into it. Sparks flew in all directions and a dazzling flare of light erupted from the wall.

It blasted the welding crew away and the unit exploded. The crew and the unit hurtled backward, slammed onto the floor, and slid a dozen yards before they skidded to a stop.

People came over to help the crew up and study the unit. Black smoke billowed from its circuitry. Other Elian personnel went to inspect the place where they'd tried to weld through the wall. There was nothing there, not even a scratch.

Captain Hurst went over to talk to the crew and then Colonel Nicholson and Commander Lodge came out of the *Lucidity* to see what was going on. The two officers made it halfway across the hold when the panel slid back.

All the Elian personnel froze as the Imoliv stepped out onto the floor. They left the panel open, but the compartment inside appeared just as solid and impenetrable as the rest of the hold.

Sehiri took a few strides onto the floor and paused there to cast his usual dismissive glance around. He took in the scene with Captain Hurst talking to the welding crew, but Sehiri didn't go over there.

He waited way too long and then sauntered leisurely over to Colonel Nicholson and Commander Lodge. "You should not have done that, Colonel. It was unwise. I'm afraid my goodwill has its limits and you have exhausted what was left of it."

"You call keeping us locked up in here goodwill?" Commander Lodge fired back. "What were we supposed to do? We don't even have power to run our life support systems, let alone make repairs."

"And yet you have the power to try to cut through these walls," Sehiri pointed out. "It would appear from my perspective that your people aren't as helpless as you'd have me believe."

"Of course we tried to cut through the walls," Lodge snapped. "Did you really think we would just sit around and wait for you to decide to kill us all? We won't just bow to your whim and do whatever you tell us. We're getting out of here and you can't stop us."

"It would appear that I can." Sehiri turned back to Colonel Nicholson. "The next time one of your people tries to escape from this hold, I will hold you and your fellow officers personally responsible. I will come for you and you will bear the punishment on behalf of all your people. This is your last and only warning, Colonel. My patience is at its end. Do not tempt me any further. If I come back and remove you from this hold and your people continue to defy me, I will work my way down the chain of command one man at a time until you heed my warning. Do not think for an instant that I make these threats idly. You and your people would be wise to cooperate with me."

He let his eyes drag over the whole assembly. All the Elian personnel stood around in breathless silence and took in his every word.

He turned ever so slowly and walked back to the compartment, stepped inside, and the doors slid shut. The rest of the Imoliv party went with him.

LeMaine's eyes followed Sehiri's every move. LeMaine and the rest of the Elian personnel stared at Sehiri and his entourage as the panel slid shut with them inside the compartment. They were alone. There was no one in there with them.

"Do you think she made it?" Nunn whispered as soon as the panel closed.

"Were you watching the compartment while Sehiri was talking to Colonel Nicholson?" Kellogg asked. "I sure wasn't. I bet you anything she made it out."

"We'll find out in an hour." LeMaine tapped his remote and started a countdown timer.

He'd arranged for Lemon to open the panel for him and the other Hellhounds after an hour—assuming she made it out of the hold without getting caught. Now he and the Hellhounds just had to wait for her to carry out her side of the mission.

The rest of the personnel got back to work. LeMaine waved the Hellhounds forward to follow him. They migrated closer to the panel, and when none of the other busy workers bothered them, the squad stopped in front of the door.

Heckler propped his shoulder against the wall, pulled out a toothpick, and stuck it in his mouth. He started chewing it and surveying the people around him as though he'd never seen them before in his life.

Kellogg squatted down, ripped open his backpack, and started going through his medical gear. O'Hara took out his sniper scope, fitted it to the top of his carbine, and started adjusting the sights.

Peterman pulled a notebook and a pencil from his breast pocket and started writing on it. "What do you always keep writing about, Lieutenant?" Nunn asked. "You're always scribbling in that notebook."

"Just observations.....ideas......whatever pops into my head. It's nothing important."

"It must not be if it came out of your head," Kellogg teased.

Peterman only chuckled. "I'm thinking of writing a book on Elian species relations. We've seen a lot on this squad. We know more about all the species living in the Elian system than some experts."

Buca crossed to Kellogg's side, squatted down next to him, rested his elbows on his knees, and peered up at Peterman. "What other species are living in this system? I don't know them. Tell me about them. Tell me what you've learned. I would really like to know."

"Do you know any?" O'Hara asked.

"I know a few," Buca murmured.

"Don't give him a hard time," Peterman countered. "It isn't his fault he didn't get an education. It's a sign of intelligence when a man can admit what he doesn't know." He turned back to Buca. "Well, as you've seen, there are Maczhi, Cezians....."

"Humans," Monk interjected.

"Genius insight, brainless," Nunn interjected. "Buca already knows there are humans here and he can see perfectly well how we act, what we look like, and all our quirks and behaviors. He isn't asking about that."

"Look, man." Peterman squatted down next to Buca, flipped to a new page of his notebook, and started sketching on it. "Here's the Elian solar system here. Here's Axichis territory here and here's the Imoliv system here. Here's Elia, Dyson, Ar'el, Morea, Halira, Aora....."

Peterman drew a quick outline of the Elian solar system and named all the planets one after another, finishing with Ziea, Buca's home planet.

Then Peterman started to explain the cultures, species, and political organization of each planet, starting with the Elian homeworld.

The rest of the Hellhounds fell silent to listen and LeMaine found himself tuning in, too. Peterman went into great detail about each species, their social customs and traditions, and how these affected their relations and standing with every other species, not just on their own planets, but in the wider Elian political community.

LeMaine marveled at what an expert Peterman was on all these subjects. He really did know more than just about all the political scientists working in and for the Elian Assembly. Peterman could have been anything. He could have been a general or a senator or a governor of one of these planets.

Instead, he was here getting shot at by random alien enemies and fighting in the war with the Hellhounds.

The rest of the squad seemed to be coming to the same conclusion about Peterman. None of them interrupted his lecture and none of them smarted off even once. They all took it in with rapt attention just like Buca did.

They got so engrossed in what he was saying that none of them noticed the time ticking away. LeMaine got distracted by the subject, too, until a vibration on his remote caught his attention.

He glanced down. Only five minutes remained before Lemon was supposed to open the panel.

LeMaine went over to Peterman and rested his hand on Peterman's shoulder. "Put the lecture on pause, Professor. You can continue this later after we've wreaked mayhem and havoc."

"I knew it!" O'Hara exclaimed and grabbed his gear.

"Leave your carbines here," LeMaine ordered. "We're doing this quietly. If any Imoliv catch us, shut them up quietly and don't let the others know we're out there."

The Hellhounds stacked their carbines against the wall, but they took their packs with them, surrounded the panel, and flattened themselves to the wall on either side of the opening.

LeMaine glanced down at his remote. Less than one minute remained before the hour ran out. What if something went wrong with Lemon? What if the Imoliv captured her?

The panel swished back. The compartment was empty.

LeMaine and the rest of the squad hustled inside. He glanced back to see several Elian crewmen watching them go, but the ships' personnel had all received orders not to give any sign of what the Hellhounds were doing. The Hellhounds were on their own mission.

Chapter 19

The panel slid closed to lock the Hellhounds into this compartment. Nothing happened for a second and then a different panel slid back on the rear wall. This compartment was really just some kind of antechamber or maybe a decompression block for getting into and out of the hold.

The squad stepped through the rear panel into another large hold, but this one obviously hadn't been set up to confine anybody. Pipes, conduits for wires, and computer components covered every wall and crossed the ceiling.

"What are we doing here, Sir?" Heckler asked.

"We're accessing the ship's power systems. Come on, Monk." LeMaine towed Monk toward some of the computer components and parked him in front of a control station in the corner. "See what you can find out about this ship and where we can feed a power supply into the hold. The rest of you—spread out and make sure no one catches us."

Monk went to work. LeMaine watched him for a few minutes, but since he didn't understand what Monk was doing, LeMaine wandered off to check on the other Hellhounds.

He found Nunn and O'Hara searching some pipes across one wall. Heckler and Buca climbed a scaffolding to search the ceiling.

LeMaine continued toward the back of the hold where he discovered Peterman and Kellogg lying flat on their stomachs on a grille overlooking another vast hold.

LeMaine stretched out next to Peterman. "What's the word?"

Peterman pointed at Imoliv technicians, mechanics, and maintenance crews working around Imoliv fighter craft. "It looks like the Imoliv are arming attack craft and assembling ground troops. They're preparing for war, but they aren't deploying anyone yet. Maybe they're just in a holding pattern until someone decides what to do next."

"Sehiri seems like a reasonable guy," LeMaine remarked. "He probably wants to see if we were telling the truth before he launches a full-scale assault on Elia."

"He has no reason to launch an assault against Elia," Peterman replied. "The war hasn't spilled over to the Imoliv system yet. The Axichis aren't here and no Elian ships are attacking the Imoliv no matter what he says."

"They have a lot of power and equipment down there," Kellogg remarked. "If Monk can't find anything up here, maybe we could go down there to find something."

"We couldn't go down there," Peterman pointed out. "There must be a two hundred crewmen down there."

"We would sneak down," Kellogg suggested. "They would never know we were there."

"We couldn't sneak down there, either," Peterman argued. "It's too risky."

"Lemon could sneak down there," Kellogg went on. "They would never catch her."

"But she doesn't know anything about electronics or ships' power systems," Peterman pointed out. "She could get down there, but then what would she do? She wouldn't be able to figure out the Imoliv's systems well enough to patch it back to the hold, let alone be able to do it without getting caught."

Kellogg shrugged. "True. I didn't think of that."

"If Monk can figure out a way to do it......" LeMaine began, but he stopped when three Imoliv broke away from the rest of the work crews.

The crews had been gathered around one of the control stations adjusting things and discussing something. Now these three men crossed the hold and started climbing a set of stairs leading to the Hellhounds' hiding place.

"Shit!" Kellogg whispered. "They're coming up here!"

"Pull back," LeMaine murmured.

"What if they catch us?" Kellogg asked, but LeMaine didn't have time to answer.

He, Kellogg, and Peterman pushed themselves up and retreated into the snarl of pipes just as the three Imoliv reached the catwalk where the three men had just been lying.

"They're coming this way!" Peterman hissed.

"We have to neutralize them before they find the rest of the squad!" Kellogg insisted. "We have to make sure they don't report us to Sehiri."

"Softly," LeMaine murmured back. "Neutralize them, but do it silently. Don't alert anyone else."

He gestured for Kellogg and Peterman to hide in the pipes while LeMaine went the other way. He found a nook between some conduits opposite them. From here, the three Hellhounds could flank the approaching Imoliv.

The Imoliv didn't see or hear the Hellhounds until all three men pounced on them. Kellogg jumped on one and pulled the man to the ground.

They got into a wrestling match on the floor, and when the second Imoliv spun around to help his friend, Peterman appeared out of nowhere, jumped the second man from behind, and locked a chokehold around his neck.

The third Imoliv had been standing far enough away from them not to get tangled in the confusion. He pulled some kind of handgun from his uniform and raised it to aim at Peterman.

LeMaine lunged for him, seized the guy by the throat with one hand, and grabbed the gun with the other. The guy resisted, his arm swung up, and he fired into the ceiling.

The shot zinged into the pipes, crashed off several of them, and Heckler bellowed from out of sight. The sound echoed through the ship. It sounded way too loud when LeMaine had been trying to do this quietly.

That idea went straight out the window when the Imoliv he was fighting put up a much stiffer fight than LeMaine was expecting. The Imoliv crewman got his gun hand out of LeMaine's grasp, but LeMaine still kept a hold on the guy's neck from behind.

The man struggled for a few seconds and then rotated the gun backward. He fired under his arm and would have gutted LeMaine if he hadn't sprung out of the way just in time.

The shot smashed into another wall of pipes and made a deafening clang. That would definitely bring the Imoliv running.

Kellogg fought his adversary to the ground, dropped the body to one side, and rushed LeMaine's opponent. Kellogg grabbed the guy's gun hand with both of his and wrestled it into the air again, but more shots just kept belching from the weapon.

More shots ricocheted out of nowhere and Kellogg and LeMaine jolted backward to find themselves face to face with a whole squad of armed Imoliv. They wore a different style of uniform than Sehiri and his entourage.

These men looked like security guards and they all opened fire on the three Hellhounds. The security forces even gunned down their own man while they were trying to hit the Hellhounds.

The Imoliv used some kind of phase weapon that LeMaine didn't recognize. One shot blasted Kellogg's shoulder apart. He wheeled away from the fight and toppled to the floor with a shriek of pain.

Peterman still worked to wrench his adversary back and forth in a chokehold. The security guards fired on him, too, but Peterman twisted his victim around and used the Imoliv's body as a shield to protect himself.

That left LeMaine alone and unarmed against all these armed Imoliv. He did the only thing he could do and charged them.

He made it as far as the first guard just as the guy's weapon went off. It had been pointing straight for LeMaine's chest, but he guided it under his own arm so that it pointed behind him.

LeMaine punched the first guard in the face as hard as he could and then shoved the guy into the rest of his squad. LeMaine had no weapons to fight these people, so he would just have to make up for it with sheer batshit lunacy.

He kicked out at the first guard, brought the man to his knees, and yanked the weapon out of his hands. LeMaine turned the weapon on the rest of the squad when, out of nowhere, Buca dropped from the rafters right into the middle of the Imoliv squad.

His weight slammed three guards to the floor and then he whirled among them snapping necks, stabbing his fingers into their eyes and throats, and bringing them down like a demon on a rampage.

The sight electrified LeMaine and he plunged in going berserk. He smashed his weapon into the guards' faces, earned himself a little extra breathing space, and turned the weapon on them.

He gunned down seven of them. Buca got the rest.

Buca finished killing two more Imoliv by rushing one, snatching the man's weapon away, and then stabbing the muzzle full force into the guy's sternum. The impact caved in the barrel and the man went down in the pile of bodies around Buca's ankles.

LeMaine spun around to find Peterman on his feet. The Imoliv he had choked was dead.

Kellogg lay sprawled on the floor writhing in agony. His arm lay from the shredded remains of his shoulder. Only a few scraps of flesh held his arm to the rest of his body.

LeMaine, Buca, and Peterman rushed over to him. LeMaine attacked Kellogg trying to get his backpack off to reach Kellogg's medical supplies, but Kellogg was lying on top of it and moving around too much for LeMaine to free it.

LeMaine leapt up on his knees stripping off his own backpack. "You gotta be quiet, Sergeant! You'll bring the whole pack down on top of us!"

"I'm trying, Sir!" Kellogg croaked through gritted teeth and another agonized groan escaped him.

Peterman started gathering up the security guard's rifles. "It looks like our cover is blown, Sir."

"You can say that again. Let's get back to the...." More gunfire interrupted LeMaine. He cast one glance toward the other hold—the hold all these guards were coming from. "Run! Get out of here! Clear the rest of the squad from the...."

He didn't finish before gunfire smashed into the pipes right by his head. Peterman hesitated just long enough to hold out a rifle to LeMaine, but LeMaine didn't have time to take it before another security squad appeared—a bigger squad this time.

Peterman swung one of his guns around and returned fire. That instant of cover gave LeMaine just enough time to grab Kellogg by his good wrist and haul him into the nearby pipes. Buca appeared at LeMaine's side carrying the backpack that LeMaine just took off.

Peterman stayed behind shooting into the Imoliv squad. LeMaine lost sight of him, but at least the gunfire was still going off on both sides. Peterman was still alive and covering for his squad mates, but for how long?

That sound got farther and farther away. LeMaine slid Kellogg into a hidden corner somewhere deep in the pipes. By that time, all sound of gunfire coming from behind LeMaine had ceased.

Kellogg gave another excruciating half-groan, half-yell of pain when LeMaine let go of him. LeMaine dropped on his knees scrambling to get his pack open. "Be quiet, Sergeant!"

Kellogg only grimaced again. He wouldn't keep quiet. He couldn't. Blood saturated his uniform.

LeMaine glanced behind him to see if the Imoliv were approaching. That was when he noticed a smear of blood leading from the gun battle right to Kellogg. The Imoliv could follow that blood trail straight to LeMaine and his two friends.

LeMaine could only think of one thing. He had to knock Kellogg out—fast. LeMaine had to keep Kellogg quiet and then move him somewhere the Imoliv wouldn't find them. Then he could worry about saving Kellogg's life.

LeMaine scrambled in his pack searching for.....anything. His hand closed around the painkillers and he immediately discarded them. They wouldn't work fast enough.

He kept searching when Buca wrapped both his hands around Kellogg's face, turned Kellogg's eyes to gaze up into his own, and Buca brought his own eyes within inches of Kellogg's nose.

"Look at me, Kellogg," Buca murmured. "Look at me. You're looking into my eyes....."

Kellogg stiffened for a second. He panted hard, but at least he wasn't making any more noise. He gasped as though he might be surprised by something he saw in Buca's eyes....and then Kellogg relaxed all over. He stopped struggling.

LeMaine snatched the bone electrolyzer. It was the only thing he could think of that would do the job quickly enough.

He slapped it onto Kellogg's destroyed shoulder and fired. Kellogg crumpled in Buca's hands. Kellogg's eyes closed and Buca guided the unconscious body onto the floor.

"What did you do to him?" LeMaine whispered.

"It's an old Maczhi fighting trick to distract enemies and animals until you can kill them."

LeMaine resisted the urge to make any comment about old Maczhi fighting tricks. "We have to get him out of here. The blood trail will give us away. We need to move him somewhere else. Then I'll stop the bleeding."

"I'll carry him," Buca offered. "I'm stronger than you are."

LeMaine made a strategic decision not to respond to that, either, except to nod. He zipped up his pack and swung it onto his back.

Buca grabbed Kellogg's good arm and hoisted Kellogg's floppy body onto his shoulder. LeMaine led the way and they worked their way deeper into the pipes where no one would be able to find them.

Chapter 20

Buca lowered Kellogg onto the floor and LeMaine knelt down next to the body. "He's lost a lot of blood. That's a much bigger problem than his shoulder being all torn up like this."

"Where did you learn so much about medicine?" Buca asked.

"I didn't. I just learned the basics. He's the expert. That's why we have to bring him back." LeMaine nodded behind him. "Why don't you go scout around and see what you can see? See if any of the Imoliv are near us.....and see if you can find out what's happening with the rest of the squad."

As if someone read LeMaine's mind, gunfire erupted in the distance. LeMaine wasn't even sure where he and Buca were anymore compared to the hold where they'd left the rest of the Hellhounds.

Buca stood up and left LeMaine alone to patch up Kellogg. LeMaine had his work cut out for him sealing all the torn flesh and then electrolyzing the bone back into place.

He left Kellogg unconscious through the whole process. Then he injected Kellogg with a massive dose of painkillers and waited a few minutes for them to take effect before LeMaine applied the antidote to wake Kellogg up.

Kellogg jolted out of his trance with a yell. LeMaine clapped his hand over Kellogg's mouth. "Quiet, Sergeant! We aren't out of danger yet."

Kellogg jerked right and left. "Where are we? What happened to the....?" He froze and his expression changed when he remembered.

He looked down at his shoulder. Most of his shirt and jacket had been torn to shreds. Blood darkened his whole uniform down to his hips.

"Thank you, Sir," he murmured.

"Forget that, son," LeMaine replied. "Let's get back to the hold and see what the rest of the squad is doing. I sent Buca to see and he hasn't come back."

More gunshots erupted somewhere, but they didn't sound like they were coming from the direction LeMaine thought the hold was.

He helped Kellogg up. Kellogg moved a little stiffly, but he seemed to be all right.

LeMaine inched his way into the pipes and his instincts about where they were turned out to be right. He came to the edge of the pipes and looked out at the same hold where he'd left Monk working at the control station.

Monk wasn't there. A different squad of twenty Imoliv held Peterman, Nunn, and O'Hara at gunpoint. The Imoliv had taken all the Hellhounds' packs. Peterman had been shot three times—once in the thigh, once in the side, and once through the side of his neck.

Nunn scrambled to control the bleeding and O'Hara did his best to help her. Thankfully, the Imoliv didn't stop them from working on Peterman.

Kellogg surged forward to go out there, but LeMaine stopped him. It took a lot to restrain Kellogg, but LeMaine couldn't let him risk getting shot again himself.

LeMaine and Kellogg hid in the pipes and watched as another bunch of Imoliv entered the hold. They were doing their level best to force Heckler to march in front of them. They should have known better.

He put up one hell of a fight and spun backward to attack them. He nearly punched through them to make a run for it before all the Imoliv already inside the hold jumped on him to stop him.

They fought him to the ground, punched and kicked him into submission, and then one of them sprang to his feet straddling Heckler and aiming a handgun right in his face.

"One move and I shoot!" the guard bellowed and Heckler gave it up.

The Imoliv dragged him back to where Nunn and O'Hara were still making a heroic effort to stop Peterman's bleeding.

Blood dripped from Heckler's nose, forehead, scalp, ear, and multiple other wounds all over his body, but he kept stiffening and glaring at the Imoliv like he wanted to attack them again.

"Where's Monk?" Kellogg whispered in LeMaine's ear. "Do you think they caught him already?"

LeMaine shook his head and almost said he didn't know when gunfire exploded from somewhere overhead. Phase shots blasted out of the scaffolding near the ceiling and brought down four Imoliv, including the guy who threatened Heckler.

All the Imoliv raised their weapons to aim at the spot, but they couldn't see anything.

"What the hell is that?!" Kellogg hissed.

"I think I know," LeMaine called back as another volley broke out from the ceiling—in a different place this time. "There's only one person I know who would do something like this and he isn't on the floor. Come on!"

More shots kept ripping out of the scaffolding and bringing down one guard after another. The shots seemed to come from everywhere at once, but LeMaine recognized one thing right away. Whoever was shooting was using the Imoliv's own weapons against them.

That gave LeMaine an idea and he took off toward the second hold—the one with all the Imoliv crewmen working in it. All these security guards came from there. Any reinforcements would come from there, too.

He tried not to run too fast, but Kellogg kept up just fine. "What are we doing here?" Kellogg whispered when LeMaine pulled up at the site of their first fight against the Imoliv.

"We're getting weapons just like Buca did," LeMaine replied. "He stole weapons from the guards and now he's sniping them with their own guns. He's a genius, that boy!"

"You gotta wonder why he's been wasting his life on Ziea all these years when he could have been so much more," Kellogg remarked.

"No one discovered him until he discovered us," LeMaine replied. "We're the first opportunity he's had to show his skills. You go over there....and don't get shot this time."

Kellogg snorted and backed off toward the other wall of pipes opposite LeMaine's hiding place. He wanted to hurry up and get some weapons so he could help the others, but he couldn't rush this.

He and Kellogg were unarmed, unlike the Imoliv. The Imoliv wouldn't hesitate to kill anyone who resisted.....so why hadn't they killed Heckler yet?

LeMaine pushed that thought out of his head and turned his attention to the stairs rising to this hold level. He was right about the Imoliv sending reinforcements.

The battle in the top hold got so hot that another squad of security troops pounded up the stairs on their way to quell the disturbance. It sure sounded like more than one gun was going off up there. Did Monk get away, too? Were he and Buca working together?

LeMaine could only hope so. He had to retreat even farther to make sure the new squad of guards didn't spot him.

He didn't jump right out and attack them this time. He waited until the very last guards drew level with his hiding place and then passed him on their way around the bend.

He pivoted out of hiding just as the last guard turned the corner. LeMaine grabbed him, clamped his hand over the guard's mouth, and hauled the guy back into the pipes. Kellogg did the same thing and took his victim to his own side of the hold.

The guard that LeMaine captured struggled hard. LeMaine almost lost his grip on the guy more than once. Then LeMaine grabbed a handful of the guy's windpipe and ripped it out.

The guy gasped and choked for breath. His hands fell away from LeMaine's arms and the guy grabbed his own throat. That gave LeMaine a split second to snap the guy's neck.

The body wilted to the floor and LeMaine snatched the guard's rifle, stepped over the fallen Imoliv, and approached the open floor. He didn't see Kellogg anywhere or the guard that Kellogg attacked.

LeMaine went over there, but Kellogg wasn't hiding in the other tangle of pipes, either. He'd vanished.

LeMaine couldn't spend any more time hunting for Kellogg. LeMaine retreated back to the same spot to spy on the Hellhounds and their captors.

The Imoliv had subdued Heckler again. The mystery shooter no longer popped off shots from the ceiling. Everything appeared quiet. Nunn and O'Hara had stopped Peterman's bleeding enough that they weren't working on him anymore.

The Imoliv wrestled the four Hellhounds to their feet. Heckler looked worse than Peterman with most of his face bashed in. He limped, hunched his shoulders, and hugged one arm over his stomach as the Imoliv marched him, Nunn, and O'Hara out of the hold.

The Imoliv had to haul Peterman by his arms, but he held his head up and he had his eyes open. He just couldn't walk.

The Imoliv vanished along with the four Hellhounds and the hold fell silent once again.

LeMaine held his breath to listen before he dared to step out. He swept his weapon back and forth to make sure there was no one around. Then he approached the control station where Monk had been working.

LeMaine didn't understand what he was looking at, and a second later, a bang from the scaffolding overhead startled him into jerking up his weapon again.

Buca sprang down from up there and Kellogg sauntered out of the shadows. "Did you find anything on there, Sir?" Kellogg asked. "Is there any sign of Monk?"

"There's no sign of anything that I can figure out." LeMaine turned to Buca. "Please tell me you're a computer expert into the bargain."

"I'm sorry," Buca replied. "I would be lying if I told you that."

"I was joking, son." LeMaine bent over the controls again. "This is definitely reading the whole ship. It shows the layout of all the decks.....and here's the bridge. Sehiri must be there."

"How does that help us?" Kellogg asked. "We couldn't take bridge with just the three of us.....and look. There must be a thousand Imoliv on this ship. No wonder they can afford to send so many security guards after us."

"I was just thinking the same thing," LeMaine replied ."We'll just have to....."

A soft click cut him off as a gun barrel jabbed him right under the ear. "Don't move," a low Imoliv voice murmured. "It would be a pleasure to kill you right here and now."

More armed Imoliv appeared out of nowhere. Actually, they didn't appear out of nowhere. It just seemed that way because LeMaine had been so distracted by the controls.

The Imoliv surrounded the friends and held Buca and Kellogg at gunpoint, too.

"Step away from the controls," the same soft voice told him. "It would be a shame if my crew had to clean your brains off of such delicate electronic equipment."

LeMaine recognized that voice. He backed away from the controls and turned around to find Sehiri standing before him aiming a handgun in LeMaine's face.

Chapter 21

"You see, Captain," Sehiri breezed. "I am not on the bridge of this ship at all. I'm here, standing right in front of you. Do you have anything to say in your own defense?"

"No," LeMaine replied. It was getting a bit late in the game for him to go around apologizing for anything.

"What are you doing here?" Sehiri asked.

"We're trying to find a way to siphon power from your ship into the hold so we can repair our own vessels......but you already knew that."

Sehiri cocked his head to one side and inspected LeMaine closely. "Who are you? You didn't address me when I went into the hold to introduce myself to your officers."

"I'm Captain Owen LeMaine and I'm not senior enough to negotiate with the leader of another population. I'm just a grunt."

Sehiri raised his eyebrows. "I don't know that word....except when it refers to the sound a rutting animal makes. Is that what you'd have me believe you are?"

LeMaine struggled to stop the blood from rushing to his cheeks, but it was too late. "It means I'm a rank-and-file soldier. I'm not top brass like Colonel Nicholson and Commander Lodge. If you want to negotiate with Elian officers, you talk to them."

"So......" Sehiri's eyes skimmed LeMaine's uniform. "Are you not an officer?"

"I am, but I'm not as high as them. I'm just in charge of my own squad—nothing more."

He wasn't thinking and gestured to Kellogg and Buca to make his point. They hardly made up a squad.

"You and your squad must be highly regarded if your officers sent you out here to steal power from us," Sehiri remarked. "Why did they send you and not another group?"

"There was no other group to send. The others are all ships' crews and we're trained for that kind of thing."

Sehiri's eyebrows lifted even higher. "You are? You're trained to steal power from other ships? Are you pirates?"

"No, not that. I didn't mean we were trained to steal power. We're trained to.....well, we execute high-risk, high-value operations not usually assigned to the regular Military. We're Special Forces."

"Ah!" Sehiri murmured. "I understand now."

"Are you going to kill us?" LeMaine asked.

Sehiri inclined his head the other way. "Do you and your men often get killed in the line of duty?"

LeMaine tried to shrug that away. "Often enough. Too often for my taste."

Sehiri squared his shoulders. "I do not plan to kill you, Captain—not just yet, anyway. In the meantime, I must take you back to the hold. I made a pledge to Colonel Nicholson and I would be remiss if I didn't fulfill it."

The other Imoliv shoved Kellogg and Buca forward. More Imoliv moved in from the sides, grabbed LeMaine, and hauled him away with the other two.

Sehiri waited just long enough to make sure the guards didn't lose control of the three Hellhounds. The guards had snatched the three men's weapons as soon as the Imoliv made their appearance. Now LeMaine and his friends were unarmed again and surrounded by deadly aliens.

LeMaine would have liked to fight back. He didn't want to find out what Sehiri had in mind when he got the three men back to the hold, but LeMaine didn't dare to resist. Sehiri had all these armed guards on his side.

They went back through the same compartment. The group reentered the hold and all the Elian personnel turned around to stare.

Another group of Imoliv held the other Hellhounds at gunpoint. Heckler and Peterman lay on the floor while medics scrambled to work on them. The Imoliv didn't interfere with this, either.

That sight alone made LeMaine think Sehiri and the Imoliv weren't as bad as they seemed. Sehiri had done everything and made every move with masterfully measured control. He didn't inflict misery on the rank-and-file soldiers if he didn't have to. When they got hurt, he let them give each other medical treatment.

Monk knelt not far from the rest of the squad. Two guards stood over him in particular. They aimed their guns at the back of his skull while he knelt on the floor with his fingers laced behind his head.

His eyes shot to LeMaine instantly, but neither Monk nor LeMaine said or did any-thing. LeMaine didn't see Lemon anywhere. Was she still at large somewhere on the Imoliv vessel?

Sehiri gestured to his men and they halted LeMaine, Buca, and Kellogg in the middle of the hold. Everyone watched and listened in silence. No one seemed to be working on anything except for the medics.

"Here is the rest of your squad, Colonel," Sehiri breezed to Colonel Nicholson. "We discovered this man....." He indicated Monk. "He had deactivated the protective shields surrounding this hold. You would have been able to cut through the walls and no doubt patch into our carrier's power supply, but don't worry. We've re-established the field now, so this squad's mission to leave the hold was a failure."

"What do you want from us?" Colonel Nicholson snarled. "We'll never stop trying to get out of here."

"I already told you, Colonel," Sehiri returned. "I have no way to corroborate your story that the Axichis attacked you....."

"You can see on your own scans that the Axichis have been attacking Elian planets for days," LeMaine interrupted. "Do you think we staged it that they wiped out our people and destroyed our own cities? I don't see why you keep lying about it."

The words slipped out before LeMaine thought to stop himself. Sehiri turned on him with a much sharper, more hawkish look than he'd ever given Colonel Nicholson or Commander Lodge—or anyone else, including the Hellhounds.

Sehiri gave him a piercing stare and then turned back to Colonel Nicholson as though LeMaine hadn't spoken. "All you had to do was stay in here and cooperate. We would have established whether you were telling the truth. If you were, we would have released you back to your own side of the border. You didn't do that. Now I have no choice but to carry out my threat by removing you, Colonel."

Commander Lodge surged forward. "You can't do that....!"

Lightning quick, one of the Imoliv guards smashed him in the face with the butt of one of their guns. Commander Lodge hit the floor and half a dozen Elian personnel dragged him out of danger.

Sehiri watched the whole incident without moving a muscle. When it ended, he waved his hand at nothing. "I already told you I would do this, but you didn't listen to me. If it happens again, I will remove *him* next." He pointed to Commander Lodge, who lay on the floor flanked by medics. "I will continue working my way down the chain of command for as long as necessary to get you people to cooperate."

He turned and fixed LeMaine in particular with another penetrating stare. LeMaine couldn't imagine why Sehiri took such an interest in him. There were plenty of other officers here more highly ranked than LeMaine.

Sehiri obviously didn't know that, though. Maybe he thought LeMaine was next in line after Commander Lodge.

Sehiri waved to his guards. They strode over to Colonel Nicholson, grabbed him by the elbows, and shoved him forward to follow Sehiri to the compartment. Colonel Nicholson resisted just enough to get near LeMaine before they hauled him away.

"You and Jimmy take over here, Owen," Colonel Nicholson whispered. "Don't let anyone else get taken. Understand?"

LeMaine didn't have time to say anything before the Imoliv forced Colonel Nicholson into the compartment. He twisted in their grasp once to look back before they jerked him around to face forward.

Sehiri stepped into the compartment and turned around to wait for them to bring Colonel Nicholson inside. LeMaine hated to think of what the Imoliv would do to him once they got him out of this hold, but at least they didn't execute him right here on the floor in front of everyone. That would have been disastrous.

The guards marched him into the compartment and they all turned around to stare out at the Elian company. Colonel Nicholson struggled to control his features. Sehiri gazed at everyone in the same serene calm and then his sharp eyes flicked over to LeMaine again.

Their gazes locked. Was Sehiri challenging LeMaine? Why would he when LeMaine just told Sehiri that he wasn't a senior officer here?

LeMaine didn't understand it. He was just turning his mind to what he and Captain Hurst would do, now that they were in charge of this mess.

The Imoliv in the compartment started to relax in anticipation of the panel sliding closed. At that moment, a punishing smash struck the ship from beyond the compartment.

The impact hurled all the Imoliv, Sehiri, and Colonel Nicholson out of the compartment. The same blow hurled everyone else in the hold off their feet. Everyone skidded across the floor and then another crushing blow against the ship's outer hull sent everyone flying through the air.

The ship tipped violently in one direction and everyone, Elian and Imoliv alike, landed all mixed up together against the opposite wall.

More hammer strikes all over the ship sent attack cruisers wheeled off their landing gear, crashing into walls, and then slamming down on top of people. The *Excursion* skidded hard in one direction and almost landed on top of the people floundering on the floor before another blow sent the ship toppling end over end in the other direction.

LeMaine swam through bodies trying to orient himself. He bumped into Monk. "You okay, son?" LeMaine hollered over the noise.

"What's happening?" Monk yelled back.

"We're under attack!" LeMaine looked around—God knows what for. Nothing in here could help him.

Then he spotted Sehiri. LeMaine grabbed him. "Who's attacking? WHO'S AT-TACKING YOUR SHIP?!!"

Sehiri swam back to awareness. He looked dazed like he might have gotten hit in the head. "We were....we were.....well behind the line......"

"Were the Axichis nearby on the Elian side?!!" LeMaine hollered.

"We were....hailing them....."

LeMaine squatted down and got right in Sehiri's face. "We can fight them! My man has frequencies that deactivate Axichis craft. We can help you defeat them, but you have to work with us! We're at war against the same people now! You can't keep us locked up in here. DO YOU UNDERSTAND ME?!!"

LeMaine tried not to shake Sehiri too hard, but he might have done it anyway without meaning to. LeMaine couldn't be sure anymore what he was doing.

He cast one last desperate glance around the hold. More pounding strikes of cannon fire plastered the ship's sides. He had to get out of here.

He bowed down and measured his words with care. "All our craft have been disabled. You have to give us some fighter craft. We can deploy our frequencies against the Axichis, but we need to get out there to do it....or you can take my man to your bridge and do it there. It's up to you....." LeMaine made another split-second decision. "But I'll be going with him. You won't take him alone."

Sehiri nodded once. That was the only acknowledgment LeMaine needed.

He dragged Sehiri out of the confusion, but more booms and crashes kept rocking the ship and making it difficult to stand up.

LeMaine looked around at the Elian personnel trying to drag themselves off the floor. He didn't see Polasek anywhere. That was going to complicate things.

The Hellhounds scrambled toward him. Monk stood up along with Buca. Nunn, Kellogg, and O'Hara appeared out of the confusion and then, amazingly, Lemon turned up wearing her uniform again.

"Sergeant...." LeMaine began.

"Don't worry about it, Sir. Not a problem."

"Did you see any fighter craft on board this ship?" LeMaine asked.

"Yes, Sir. They're all downstairs in the launch bay....if the Imoliv haven't already launched them against the Axichis."

LeMaine turned back to Sehiri. "What do you say? We can cover more enemy targets if you send us out in fighter craft. You know we never attacked the Imoliv. Don't make this worse for your own people by saying we did."

Sehiri gave LeMaine another searching look and then nodded. "Very well, Captain. I'll give you and your squad fighter craft—no one else. I don't know why, but I trust you more than the rest of these people."

LeMaine snorted. "I hear that a lot." He turned to the other Hellhounds. "Where's Polasek?"

Just then, Peterman came over with Polasek at his side. Peterman was standing up and walking around, thank God.

LeMaine frowned at him. "Are you clear for duty, Lieutenant?"

"This happened before the medics said so, but I feel all right."

LeMaine made a face and turned to Kellogg. "What do you say, Sergeant?"

Kellogg shrugged. "He looks all right to me and we don't have time for me to give him a full exam. It isn't like he's going to be any better or worse on the battlefield if he's clear or not. He can see straight enough to fly. That's good enough for me."

"You're in charge here." LeMaine turned back to Sehiri. "Show us where these fighter craft are."

Sehiri glanced back and forth between the squad members. He listened to their conversation with interest. It took him a minute to get past that and catch up to what LeMaine just said.

Sehiri jumped. "Oh, yes! Follow me."

Chapter 22

S ehiri led the way out of the hold. Several Imoliv guards tried to stop the Hellhounds from going with him, but more strikes from outside kept tilting the floor up and back in all directions.

The group staggered to the compartment and the panel slid shut leaving the Hellhounds alone with Sehiri. It would have been the perfect time to smash his ugly face in, but LeMaine had other things on his mind.

"Is this the first aggression the Axichis have ever shown the Imoliv?" he asked as soon as the door shut.

"We've never had any dealings with the Axichis before—aggressive or otherwise," Sehiri replied. "Elia has always stood between us and the Axichis. We've always been satisfied that the Axichis dealt with Elia and left us alone."

"So the Axichis never made diplomatic overtures to the Imoliv?" Peterman asked. "That's strange."

"We never considered the Axichis a threat—not the way we viewed Elia a threat," Sehiri went on. "We share a border with Elia. Elia seemed a much more immediate concern."

LeMaine faced front. "It looks like the Axichis took everybody in."

"Now it's time to give those bastards some payback," Heckler growled and turned to Polasek. "Do you still have the frequencies, Lieutenant?"

"Right here." Polasek tapped his wrist. "I powered down my remote when we first got into the hold just in case. I didn't want to run out of juice in case I got a chance to transfer the frequencies to another craft."

"Save the detailed explanation for another time," Heckler growled.

LeMaine turned to Lemon. "Did you notice anything strange outside the ship? Did you get a chance to check any of the Imoliv's systems?"

"Why are you asking her?" Sehiri asked.

"Never mind," LeMaine began and almost asked Sehiri where to go, but just then, the rear panel opened.

Sehiri stepped forward to lead everyone, but Lemon got there first. "This way, Sir." She strode in front and all the Hellhounds followed her. They all forgot Sehiri was here.

She turned off into a stairwell, passed through the second hold that LeMaine had spied on earlier with Kellogg and Peterman, and down another flight of stairs to an even lower hold.

Imoliv fighter craft launch chutes lined the hold by the hundreds. Half of the craft had already launched. The rest sat in their chutes waiting to deploy.

Even then, when the Hellhounds reached the threshold, more catastrophic gunfire plastered the hull right underneath them. The hold rocked and everyone pitched over each other.

"Mount up!" LeMaine yelled over the noise. "Get in the air and get those frequencies deployed to every ship in range!"

Yells answered him as the Hellhounds struggled to right themselves. Then everyone took off running, including LeMaine.

He forgot to say anything to Sehiri, but he figured later that it probably worked out for the best. LeMaine couldn't exactly thank Sehiri for this. Sehiri's decision to let the squad go was all about saving his own ass. Sehiri still held hundreds of Elian personnel locked up in that hold—not to mention whatever Sehiri still planned to do with Colonel Nicholson.

LeMaine raced to the nearest fighter that didn't already have someone in it. He put his foot on the ladder leading to the cockpit and the cockpit cover opened automatically. He just hoped the controls wouldn't be too foreign.

He lowered himself into the seat, pulled on the helmet that lay resting on the cushion, and the cover closed on top of him. All the controls blinked on.

"This seems pretty straightforward," Nunn remarked.

"It better be or we're all screwed," Lemon added.

"How are those frequencies looking, Lieutenant?" LeMaine asked.

"All loaded up and ready to deploy," Polasek replied. "We just gotta get out there."

"Here we go!" O'Hara yelled. "Holy shit! This thing is launching all by itself! Yeee-haw!!"

He gave a wild whoop as his fighter rocketed down the chute and then all the others took off at the same time.

LeMaine's fighter slammed him back in the seat. He had to fight the G force to keep his hands on the steering cradle. It reacted instantaneously to his slightest move. He could control the helm, the throttle, and the weapons system from here.

A chart of the surrounding space blipped up on the dashboard in front of him. He caught one fleeting view of a raging battle going on between the Axichis and the Imoliv before his fighter erupted out of the ship's hold.

The Hellhounds plunged into the mayhem along with at least a hundred other Imoliv craft all battling to the death against Axichis fighter craft. The Imoliv soared in coordinated formations hammering the Axichis with their phase weapons, but they produced no more effect than Elian cannons.

The Axichis had crossed the buffer zone and invaded Imoliv space. The Elian defensive line remained in position on the other side of the border.

LeMaine didn't have time to wonder if the Elian Military had been communicating with the Imoliv about the captured ships, but the Elians didn't dare to cross the border to fight the Axichis. The Elians stayed where they were and watched.

That might have looked heartless to the outside observer, but the Elian Military couldn't afford to get into a shooting war against the Imoliv at a time like this. That was exactly what would have happened if even one Elian ship crossed the border.

It had already happened by accident. The Military wouldn't let it happen on purpose. Elia had enough to worry about from the Axichis.

LeMaine plowed into the fight targeting any Axichis craft he could lay his eyes on. "Do it, Polasek!" he roared. "Deploy the frequencies now....and transmit them to the Elian fleet."

No one answered him. LeMaine tried to spot Polasek in the confusion, but so many shots sizzled back and forth that he couldn't see a thing. He couldn't even tell which Imoliv fighters belonged to the Hellhounds and which were being piloted by Imoliv.

LeMaine wheeled back the other way and gunned his engines. Fighter craft zoomed all around him. Axichis fighters traded shots with Imoliv fighters. Axichis lasers collided with Imoliv phase cannons and exploded in massive fireballs that obscured the field even more.

"Polasek!!" LeMaine roared. "Polasek, where are you?! Answer me!!"

Nothing.

"I don't see him, Sir," Nunn called.

"That's impossible!" LeMaine countered. "He was with us two seconds ago. Spread out and find him."

"I'm a little busy here!!" O'Hara yelled from somewhere. "These assholes don't like to lose."

"Polasek!!" LeMaine bellowed again.

He gave it up when he still got no answer. There had to be another way—a better way.

He retreated out of the battle and turned his attention to the controls. He ran a few quick scans on the Imoliv fighters and isolated the ones with human life signs. Buca was going into one of his crazy suicide plunges and giving the Axichis fighters a rough time.

LeMaine counted up the human pilots on the field. They were all there. He just couldn't tell which one was Polasek or why he failed to respond.

LeMaine had to go back into the chaos to track down each member of his squad. He passed Nunn, Kellogg, and Lemon. Then LeMaine went near O'Hara and got into an unholy firefight against ten Axichis fighters who were all ganging up on O'Hara.

It took LeMaine a while to fight his way out of the weeds. He trained his ship toward Polasek, but right then, the Imoliv destroyer the squad just escaped started firing its phase cannons into the battle targeting Axichis warships.

The Imoliv phase weapon smashed into the Axichis' sides and detonated outward. These shots put the Imoliv fighter craft in more danger than the Axichis. The Imoliv fired dozens of times before someone on the bridge woke up to the fact.

LeMaine dodged as many of those cannon shots as he could until one struck too close. It slapped his fighter out of control and he rolled the rest of the way to where Polasek hovered.

He sat in his cockpit looking down at something. He didn't look up nor did he fly around. He definitely wasn't deploying the frequencies.

"What's the problem, Lieutenant?" LeMaine asked.

Polasek didn't respond. He didn't look up—not until LeMaine soared right across the fighter's nose.

Polasek glanced up and his expression changed when he saw LeMaine. Polasek's mouth moved and he pointed down at his controls, but no sound came through LeMaine's helmet. Was Polasek's fighter malfunctioning—again? Did he get hit or something?

Something must have happened to stop him from deploying the frequencies. LeMaine tried to think what to do about it. He couldn't exactly take Polasek on board in the middle of a battle.

LeMaine glanced back toward the Elian line. All he had to do was get Polasek back to Elia. The Military would know what to do with the frequencies—hopefully.

"Hellhounds—converge on Polasek!" LeMaine called to the others. "Form a defensive line to guard Polasek's retreat."

"What's wrong, Sir?" Kellogg asked. "He should have deployed the frequencies by now."

"He must be having some malfunction," LeMaine replied. "He can't communicate with anyone. I'm transmitting his coordinates. Work your way over here and give him some cover to fall back to the Elian side."

"You got it," Heckler replied and his fighter wheeled out of the confusion heading for the spot LeMaine indicated.

LeMaine got Polasek's attention again and pointed toward the Elian barricade. Polasek frowned and said something else. He didn't look too keen to go over there.

Polasek pointed at his fighter, then at the other Imoliv pilots fighting everyone, and LeMaine got the message. The Elians would think an Imoliv fighter was trying to cross the line.

LeMaine nodded and pulled his own craft into a reverse spiral. Nunn, O'Hara, Heckler, and Lemon showed up to defend Polasek and he turned away to follow LeMaine.

LeMaine veered hard and took off in a fast sprint down the Elian blockade. He opened a channel to the *Barracuda,* one of the biggest Elian bombers on the block.

"Bomber *Barracuda,* this is Captain Owen LeMaine on a mission for Colonel Elias Nicholson. We are on board Imoliv fighter craft bringing new frequencies to use against the Axichis. I request permission to cross the border escorting my pilot into Elian space so he can transmit the frequencies to the rest of the Elian fleet."

A clear male voice answered him through the same channel. "Unknown Imoliv fighter craft, pull away from the border now. I repeat pull away from the border now or we will interpret your actions as a hostile threat to your sovereign territory. Do not approach your border or we will open fire."

LeMaine cocked his ear. "Is that you, Simon—Simon Morgenstern? It's Owen LeMaine. We served in the Rexorana Campaign. Don't you remember? We're crossing in Imoliv fighter craft. My communications expert has a new set of frequencies you can use against the Axichis. The Imoliv gave us these craft so we could deploy the frequencies."

"Unknown Imoliv fighter craft—move away from the border or we will open fire. Your proximity and flight path are an open violation of our territorial rights. Pull away from the border now. This is your last warning."

"Bastards!" Heckler growled. "They won't listen to reason."

"We're under fire!" Lemon yelled.

LeMaine turned back to the bigger problem at hand. The Axichis noticed the Hellhounds gathered around that one fighter craft. Whether the Axichis understood Polasek's importance or not didn't matter.

They broke off fighting the Imoliv and the Axichis came swooping in to pound the Hellhounds with brutal fire. The Hellhounds returned it as best they could, but the Imoliv phase cannons couldn't damage the Axichis any better than Elian weapons.

The Axichis came in fast and hot laying down sweeping carpets of lasers. They tried to hit Polasek, but Nunn and Kellogg darted in front of him and took the brunt of the assault on their own craft.

"I'm hit!" Nunn yelled. "My weapons system is shutting down. I'm down to one cannon!"

"There has to be a way to deploy those frequencies!" Peterman yelled. "There has to be a way to transfer them to one of our own craft."

LeMaine didn't see how and he had bigger fish to fry. He swerved into the path of five Axichis fighters, unloaded on them, and finally distracted them away from Polasek.

He took LeMaine's advice and retreated back toward the Elian blockade. He must not have heard the warning not to approach the line.

More Axichis rocketed into the area trying to hit Polasek, and when they couldn't reach him, they went to work trying to destroy the Hellhounds. At the same instant, all the Imoliv pilots in the air came after the Axichis from the Imoliv side.

The Imoliv pilots hammered the Axichis away from the Imoliv system, which pushed the whole battle closer to the Elian blockade. Elian bombers kept announcing their intention to shoot if anyone crossed the border, but it was already too late.

The Axichis wheeled in for another pass and lasers struck Monk's fighter. The engine exploded. "I'm out of control!" he hollered. "This ship won't fly straight!"

He swerved dangerously close to the Elian blockade and then another Axichis laser hit his other engine.

He gave a roar of fright as his fighter blasted across the line. He barely squeezed past the *Barracuda* before the bomber opened fire.

Monk's fighter vanished in a hail of cannon explosions. LeMaine turned back to try to help Monk, but LeMaine couldn't do that without crossing the line himself.

He hovered between one rock and another and then another explosion went off right behind him. The Imoliv had opened fire on the Axichis again and the fireball flung Nunn and Heckler over the line into Elian space.

In a split second, all the Axichis dove in firing at once. LeMaine whipped around trying to defend himself, but his phase cannons didn't work against the Axichis.

Lasers danced over his cockpit cover and brutal fire pounded his fighter all over. He couldn't even see the people shooting at him.

The next second he burst out of the confusion and wheeled through the stars. His stomach dropped when he saw where he was.

The entire battle—the Hellhounds, the Axichis, the Imoliv fighter pilots—the whole jumbled soup had moved back to the Elian side, but this turned out to be so much worse than LeMaine feared.

The Axichis still wheeled everywhere striking any Elian and Imoliv target they could hit. The Elians trained all their firepower on the Imoliv fighter craft.

LeMaine couldn't for the life of him figure out why the *Barracuda* didn't respond to his message or why the bomber's gunners didn't see human and Maczhi life signs on board.

Anyone could see that the Axichis were the ones who drove these Imoliv fighters into Elian space. The *Barracuda's* officers could see that just as well as Sehiri could see that the Axichis were at war against Elia. None of this made any sense.

He took another plastering of cannon fire on his left side coming from bomber *Thunderclap*. He gunned his engines trying to get away from her and the same ship struck him in the tail. She stalked him down.

The rest of the Elian line broke apart—at least it looked that way from where he sat. Bombers moved through the system hunting down every Imoliv fighter that crossed the border.

LeMaine turned a revolution over the planet Ar'el, but he steered away when he got too close to the cities. He didn't want any gunfire putting innocent people in danger.

He came around the other side of the planet and tried to sprint into open space, only to run into a trap set up between the *Matriarch* and the *Paradox*. They closed him from either side and struck him back and forth between them.

He tried one last time to call out to them, but he got no response. In his last, most desperate act, he turns his phase cannons on his own people and the *Thunderclap* smacked him hard from behind.

The blow sent him reeling head over heel and then the *Barracuda* took out his starboard engine. His fighter somersaulted wildly while he wrestled to bring the controls back into line. He righted the ship for an instant and then another brutal smash took out his port engine.

His fighter pivoted over in the air and he caught sight of one of Ar'el's moons. Its name was Kathopra and low, scrubby steppes covered it from one polar ice cap to the other. It wasn't hospitable enough for anyone to settle on, but at least it had a breathable atmosphere.

He barely got a look at it before another cruel bombardment shattered his cockpit cover. The glass exploded in his face and something very hard knocked him out.

Chapter 23

LeMaine dragged his head up against the irresistible urge to pass out again. His head pounded and he tasted blood in his mouth. He could barely see the countryside around him, but at least he was on the ground. He wasn't in battle anymore—against anyone.

His vision blurred and he struggled to pull it back into focus, but at that moment, hands started patting him down. "Captain!" someone yelled. "Captain LeMaine! Look at me!"

LeMaine dragged his head up with an almighty effort and found himself looking at Kellogg. Nunn was with him and so was Monk.

LeMaine's head flopped again. "You shouldn't be down here."

"We didn't exactly have a choice, did we?" Monk grumbled. "Those cocksuckers shot us down in our own space."

"They didn't know what they were doing," Kellogg replied. "All they saw was Imoliv fighters crossing the border. The bombers were probably under orders to shoot any Imoliv craft that crossed no matter what it was. Come on, Monk. Lift him out of here. I need to check his head."

"You can see what kind of condition his head is in," Nunn countered, but no one answered—or maybe LeMaine just passed out at that moment and didn't hear the rest of their conversation.

Monk wrapped his arms around LeMaine's chest and heaved him out of the cockpit. LeMaine blacked out again, and when he woke up, he was lying on the ground looking up at the sky—or he would have been if Kellogg's face hadn't been in the way.

"Am I dead?" LeMaine groaned. "Please say I am."

Kellogg grinned at him. "You aren't. Sorry. Better luck next time."

"Damn it," LeMaine growled. "And I tried so hard that time."

Nunn laughed. "I think he's gonna be okay."

O'Hara stuck his head over Nunn's shoulder. "How is he?"

"He'll be fine when I finish with him," Kellogg replied. "Where are the lieutenants?"

"Lieutenants?" LeMaine asked. "Are they both here?"

"They're here and Polasek's remote is intact with the frequencies still on it," Nunn told him. "He says he got hit with a stray phase blast when he first launched and it took out his communication system."

"That's just our luck," Monk added. "What do we do now, Sir?"

"At least wait until I fix his brain before you go asking him strategy questions like that," Kellogg interrupted.

LeMaine struggled to follow their conversation. Only one thing stuck out at him. Both Polasek and Peterman were on this moon.....and so were Monk, Nunn, Kellogg, and O'Hara. Were all the Hellhounds here, too?

Kellogg kept working on him and LeMaine's mind slowly started to clear. He went over the battle one step at a time.

"You're clear, Sir," Kellogg told him. "You can get up now."

He pulled LeMaine into a sitting position, but LeMaine didn't feel like getting up and Kellogg didn't tell him to. Being cleared for duty didn't necessarily mean he was ready to hit the decks running.

He squinted at the landscape which was as inhospitable as he could possibly hope. A biting, bitter wind blasted over the scrub. He didn't see one trace of civilization anywhere because this moon didn't have any.

The Hellhounds gathered around him talking. In a few minutes, Polasek and Peterman showed up with Buca, Heckler, and Lemon. Everyone was here—unfortunately.

"How's it going, Sir?" Peterman asked.

"It would be going better if I had a nice juicy steak and a glass of red wine about now," LeMaine replied. "Where's the service, I ask you?"

That got a laugh out of everyone. "We better find some shelter," Heckler growled. "This moon has a short solar cycle. It will be night soon and it's bound to get cold."

"You're right, Corporal," LeMaine replied and got to his feet. "Did anybody see anything promising when they were walking around earlier?"

"There are some rocks over there with some caves in them." Lemon pointed to the west. "It isn't much, but it's better than bunking down out here in the wind."

"All right. Let's go."

The squad set off and LeMaine sidled over to Polasek on their way to the rocks in question. "I hear you got hit as soon as you deployed your fighter."

"Yes, Sir. Sorry about that. I did what I could."

"Don't apologize. Shit happens. I don't care about anything as long as you still have the frequencies."

Polasek smirked and then bit it back. "I'm guessing you do care about a few other things besides that."

"Don't give me any lip," LeMaine fired back. "I gotta spend the night rough with these smart-asses."

Polasek laughed. "So do I. What do you want to bet we can beat them down when it comes to wisecracking?"

"I heard that!" O'Hara yelled over. "You better be careful what you wish for, Lieutenant."

"Is that supposed to be a challenge, Sergeant?" Polasek returned. "I bet you anything you want that Captain LeMaine, Lieutenant Peterman, and I can beat down all the rest of you slackers put together."

Howls of excited glee broke out amongst the rest of the squad. "What are we wagering?" Heckler asked.

"What do you kids want to play for?" LeMaine asked.

The rest of the squad put their heads together to discuss what they should ask for as a reward if they won the Great Wisecracking Smackdown that was going to take place as soon as the squad made it to the rocks. They never once considered they might lose.

"What should we ask for?" Polasek asked LeMaine on the side.

"Did you really have to lay down that challenge?" LeMaine countered. "Are you sure we can beat them?"

"It doesn't make much difference who wins. We're gonna need something pretty spectacular to take our minds off *this.*" Polasek made a face at the landscape.

The wind had picked up if that was even possible. It shrieked across the Kathopra getting colder by the second. Flecks of ice swirled in it and it sliced right through LeMaine's fatigues.

"You're right, Lieutenant," he replied. "You're a genius."

"You're gonna have to carry our team," Polasek told him. "You're the best at wising off. Peterman and I will back you up, but you're our anchorman."

LeMaine had to laugh. He had to admit that Polasek was right. This contest would be fun—a hell of a lot funner than spending the night on this moon would be without something to take everyone's mind off their circumstances.

Peterman came over to them jotting in his notebook. "What are you chronicling for your book now, Lieutenant?" Polasek asked.

"I'm taking notes on this crash along with the date. I keep a diary of my deployments, so I'll need to record this one."

"Did you see anything in the other fighters after you all landed?" LeMaine asked. "I'm sorry I didn't ask earlier. Did you all get shot down?"

"Not all. Monk got shot down and then Kellogg's fighter took damage," Polasek replied. "The rest came down to land to see how you and Monk were doing."

"And before you ask," Peterman interjected, "None of them had any rations or water or emergency supplies on board. The Imoliv aren't very well prepared for battle."

"Or at least not for their pilots to get shot down on enemy moons," Polasek finished.

"That's going to make tonight even more challenging," LeMaine remarked and the other two nodded.

The squad approached the rocks and Lemon squeezed through a crack between two massive boulders. The other Hellhounds did the same, though it took a while and a whole lot of trash talk before Monk and Heckler managed to wedge their big bodies through the opening.

LeMaine didn't fare much better, but getting inside the cave turned out to be a massive relief. The walls completely cut the wind, which was turning into a gale-force ice storm as the Kathopra darkened with approaching night.

The cave also turned out to be pitch dark. The only light came through the narrow slit opening. That would disappear as soon as the Kathopra turned away from the sun.

"Anybody got any way to light a fire?" Nunn asked.

"And keep it going?" Lemon added.

A sudden flare of light erupted in the darkness to reveal Heckler squatting in the middle of the floor. He placed the flare between all the assembled Hellhounds, forced himself outside, and came back with an armload of scrub. The wind had dried it to tinder.

He laid the branches on top of the flare and they caught fire. Light and heat spread through the cave and the others started to relax.

"Thanks, Heckler," Kellogg exclaimed. "This is banging."

"Anytime, my friends, anytime," Heckler rumbled. "It's the least I can do for my homeboys and girls."

O'Hara squatted down and extended his hands to the flames. "It sure would be nice to have something to eat right now."

"Why don't you go out and hunt something?" Nunn suggested.

O'Hara snorted. "This moon doesn't have any native animals for me to hunt."

"You wouldn't be able to move fast enough to catch them anyway," Polasek added. "You might be able to watch them through your scope, but that's about it."

Monk burst out laughing. "Let the burns begin!"

The others guffawed loudly and everyone gathered around. Polasek and Peterman started grinning. LeMaine tried not to get too invested in the outcome, but he also prepared himself to take as much ribbing as anybody. He would be the crew's first target.

Kellogg kicked things off. "Did I ever tell you about the time Lieutenant Peterman tried to check a book out of the library?"

"Why do you enjoy saying cruel things about each other?" Buca asked. "Why do you find it so funny to insult each other and to be insulted by each other?"

The others snickered, but right at that moment, another scream of wind tore past the cave opening. The crack in the rocks made a high-pitched, eerily human sound like the dying wail of some creature meeting its end.

Everyone turned around to stare at the crack. The wind kept moaning and shrieking outside. The weather was getting worse.

"That doesn't sound good," Lemon murmured.

"Who knows how long we'll be stuck down here before we get out of here," Monk added.

"We have five operational fighter craft," Peterman pointed out.

"But as soon as we launch them, the Elian Military will see us as a threat again," LeMaine pointed out. "Even sending out a mayday call could be seen as a threat. It could bring the whole Military down here to attack us again."

"How do we get off this moon, then?" O'Hara asked. "We can't be stuck here. I have my cousin's bar mitzvah next Saturday."

A few people chuckled and then they started laughing. "You are such a toad, O'Hara," Kellogg chided. "All you care about is your baklava and your pickled pig's feet."

O'Hara sighed heavily and stared down into the flames. "I could sure use some baklava right about now. I wouldn't mind a nice fat, juicy slice of marmalade pie, either."

"Marmalade pie! Yuck!" Heckler roared. "Tell me you don't actually eat that shit."

"He'll eat anything you wave in front of him," Nunn returned. "If we get stuck here long enough, he'll probably wind up chewing on that scrub out there."

"That scrub did look mighty tasty," O'Hara replied and made everyone laugh again.

LeMaine laughed along with them and then caught Polasek looking sidelong in his direction. LeMaine decided not to meet that glance and stared into the fire instead.

He already knew the obstacles keeping the crew from leaving this Kathopra, not to mention all the other obstacles stopping them from delivering the frequencies to the rest of the Elian fleet.

He could take one night not to think about it. All those problems would still be waiting for him in the morning. He could let his crew enjoy this one night of carefree laughter, jokes, and relative comfort.

The hard part would start tomorrow. The task of staying alive on this moon would take center stage. Hunger, cold, and hardship would kill everyone's good mood. Then all anyone would care about would be where their next meal was going to come from.

No one would be laughing and enjoying each other's company then. They better enjoy it while it lasted.

Chapter 24

The Hellhounds sat around the fire. Heckler had kept the squad supplied with scrub all night long to keep everyone warm. He'd been going in and out all morning bringing in more until he piled up a huge stack by the cave door.

"One of us will need to stay in here around the clock to keep the fire going," he told LeMaine. "I suggest we take it in watches. That way, when someone gets too cold outside, they can come in here and warm up while the next person goes out."

"Good idea," LeMaine replied. "You've been going out there all morning keeping the rest of us toasty. You take the first watch."

Heckler's eyebrows flew up. "Seriously?"

"Of course. You've been going out there all night and none of the rest of us have gone out once. You deserve a break."

Heckler turned bright red. "Thank you, Sir."

"Of course.....and from now on, we'll take turns gathering firewood, too. I don't want you losing sleep like you did last night."

Heckler gulped and looked away. "Thank you, Sir."

LeMaine clapped him on the shoulder and pushed him toward the fire. "Sit down, take a load off, and maybe catch forty winks. We're going out to see what we can see. I'll send one of the others back when it's time to change the watch, but even then, I want you to catch up on sleep. I don't want you going out there when you're fatigued. Is that clear, Corporal?"

"Yes, Sir," Heckler growled.

"Good man. Go lie down. The rest of you Hellhounds saddle up and let's go explore this place."

"What are we looking for, Sir?" Nunn asked.

"Anything," LeMaine replied. "Anything at all."

The squad filed out of the cave. The wind had died since last night. Cold, steel-grey skies covered everything this morning—the same as yesterday.

Enough wind still remained that the whole squad hunched their shoulders, pulled their fatigues up around their ears, and narrowed their eyes at the hostile landscape.

They set off across the countryside, but no one talked or joked around. LeMaine didn't feel like it, either. He felt naked without his pack of supplies and a carbine. The Hellhounds had left Sehiri's destroyer with just the clothes on their backs.

The only Hellhound who had been wearing his backpack when the Axichis attacked the Imoliv had been Kellogg. He wore his pack loaded with medical supplies and that was it. He'd already saved LeMaine's life once. How long would those supplies last before he exhausted them all?

That would leave the squad dangerously exposed to injury, sickness, and death, all of which would become progressively more likely the longer the squad stayed on this Kathopra.

LeMaine tried not to let dark thoughts get the better of him, but it was pretty hard not to with the frigid, barren landscape staring him in the face every single second.

He decided on that walk not to spend too much time exploring this place. If he and his squad didn't find some useable resources, he would keep them in the cave where they could at least stay warm. He wouldn't weaken them by sending them out to search for supplies that weren't there.

He also decided to set up one of the operational Imoliv fighter craft to send out a mayday call to the Elian Military. He might not get a response, but he could at least try.

He might even get a hostile response. The Military might send another Special forces squad down here to apprehend the crashed Imoliv pilots.

That would be the absolute best possible scenario that LeMaine could hope for. He would love nothing better than to get taken into custody by another squad of the Elian Special Forces. That would be a dream come true.

He drifted off into a fantasy about the other squad taking him and the Hellhounds back to Elia, giving them all the hot soup, medical care, and comfortable beds they could ask for.

Then the Hellhounds could stay at Command for a few months to debrief about everything that happened. Command could take the frequencies and fight the war while LeMaine stayed behind the front lines.

That was never going to happen. The Hellhounds didn't roll that way. They were always on the front lines even when there was no front line or when everyone else wanted to deny that there was a front line. That was the Hellhound creed—the front line or nowhere.

Kellogg startled him out of his dream world. "Captain!" Kellogg hissed. "We got company!"

All the Hellhounds ducked and crawled on their bellies as Kellogg waved them to the top of a gentle rise in the landscape. The squad peered over the top to see what Kellogg was talking about.

LeMaine stiffened when he saw four Imoliv pilots huddled down at the bottom of the rise. Two of their fighter craft lay flattened and wrecked not far away. One other looked somewhat operational, but that was it.

These four men hadn't taken refuge anywhere, probably because there was nowhere nearby for them to take refuge. They were too far away from the rocks to have discovered the cave that kept the Hellhounds so protected from the weather.

That could only mean one thing. These men must have spent last night in the open and they looked it.

Their pale scaly skin looked even paler. All of them shook violently as they cowered together with no protection whatsoever. None of them looked armed, either. Their fighter craft—the one that survived that last battle—didn't contain any supplies.

LeMaine reminded himself to have a hard talk with Sehiri if LeMaine ever had the misfortune to meet that toffy-nosed snot ever again. He was leaving his men woefully undersupplied and unprepared. That was no way to command a military force.

"What are they doing here?" Nunn murmured.

"Freezing to death," Peterman replied and he started to stand up.

Monk grabbed him. "Don't, Lieutenant! They could be hostile."

"Of course they're hostile," Peterman replied. "They're Imoliv. They've been isolated from Elia for thousands of years. You can't expect them to be friendly, but I sure as hell won't leave them down there to freeze. Jesus Christ! It's bad enough they've spent one night in the open. I'm not letting them do it again. Come on, Captain."

LeMaine stood up. He didn't look forward to going down there and dealing with these Imoliv pilots, but he agreed with Peterman. It was the only humane thing to do.

"This is a bad idea," O'Hara breathed.

"Maybe it is," LeMaine replied. "Stay here. Polasek, you take charge in case anything happens."

"Yes, Sir," Polasek replied.

The other Hellhounds stayed flattened out of sight while Peterman and LeMaine straightened up on top of the rise.

The Imoliv pilots jolted to high alert at the very first sight of the strangers. All four of the pilots sprang to their feet, backed away, and crowded together. They glanced behind them and moved toward their craft.

LeMaine raised his hands in surrender to show he wasn't armed and Peterman copied him. "Here we go," Peterman murmured and started walking down the hill.

The pilots scrambled to come up with some way to protect themselves. They held a hasty conversation with each other. One of them turned to the fighter craft and tried to climb into it, but since he didn't have a ladder to get up there, he couldn't get off the ground.

He tried to put his foot on the landing gear, but his friends pulled him down.

LeMaine stopped Peterman halfway down the hill. "We don't want to hurt you!" he called out. "We want to help you! We're unarmed. We just want to help you! We have a cave over that hill. We have a fire. You can come and get warm. You don't have to spend another night out here in the ice and wind. Come on. What do you say?"

The pilots held another rapid exchange of whispered conversation. Then one of them turned away, boosted his friend up to the fighter's cockpit, and the guy started working furiously to get the cover open.

"Don't come any closer!" another yelled. "We'll arm this fighter and shoot if you try anything."

"You can see we aren't here to try anything!" LeMaine called back. "If you launch that fighter, the whole Elian Military will come down here to shoot you out of the sky. We crashed fighting the Axichis alongside you. We don't want to be your enemies. We're all in serious trouble here and we're bound to be in a whole lot more of it the longer we stay here! We can help you. Come with us. You can get warm in our cave. No one will harm you. I'm a captain in the Elian Military. You have my word that you'll be perfectly safe—as safe as any of us can be on this moon. Don't throw your lives away by staying out here to freeze."

The pilot kept clawing at the cockpit cover, but he couldn't get it open. The other two kept glaring at LeMaine and Peterman in black, murderous hatred. LeMaine distinctly heard one of them telling the others to hurry.

"Well, Lieutenant," LeMaine murmured to Peterman out of the side of his mouth. "I gave it my best shot. Maybe you can convince them."

"I couldn't have said it any better myself. If they didn't listen to what you just said, there's nothing I could say to convince them."

"That isn't what I want to hear, Lieutenant. You're the Command negotiator on this squad. You're supposed to be the expert here."

Peterman chuckled low and all the Imoliv pilots snapped their eyes in his direction to glare at him. This wasn't looking good at all.

"So what do we do next?" LeMaine asked. "Should we just retreat? I don't like leaving them here."

The pilot that had been trying to get the cockpit cover opened gave it up. The man holding him up dropped him to the ground and all four of them narrowed their eyes at LeMaine and Peterman. So they couldn't even get their fighter open, which meant their threats to shoot him were totally hollow. These men were defenseless—just as defenseless as the Hellhounds if not more so.

"I guess we just back off to that hilltop and wait and watch," Peterman suggested. "Maybe they'll come to their senses if we just stick around. They're bound to get desperate eventually. Maybe they'll get desperate enough to accept your offer."

"Yeah, see, the only problem with that is that we would have to stay out here. I don't want to stress our people any more than they already are by keeping them out in the cold longer than necessary."

"I guess we could fall back to the cave and come around to check on them every now and then." Peterman squinted at the horizon. "We aren't getting any searching done standing out here talking to them. Taking them in means more mouths to feed."

"Yeah, I got that." LeMaine glanced over his shoulder. The other Hellhounds crouched behind the hill watching his every move.

He turned back to the pilots and took a deep breath to launch once again into another plea for them to see reason and accept his help. He really did not want to walk away from people in as much trouble as they obviously were.

He straightened up to say what he had to say when a dull boom echoed from way up in the sky. Everyone present looked up as two Elian bombers and three Axichis battleships drifted out of the cloud cover.

They weren't close enough to see people on this moon. Those ships probably didn't even realize the crew was down here. The two sides were much too busy fighting each other.

They traded shots, drifted over the Kathopra, and started to migrate away. They would pass out of sight any second now and leave the crew just as stranded as before.

Without warning, the Axichis burst into a rush of speed, surrounded the Elians with laser fire, and one of the bombers' engines burst into flames. The Elians returned fire, but they couldn't do any damage.

The bomber halted and then the Axichis struck the bomber's other engine. That one exploded and debris and burning gas plummeted through the moon's atmosphere.

"Get down!" LeMaine yelled and tackled Peterman out of the way.

Chapter 25

LeMaine grabbed Peterman and pulled him back toward the hilltop as the damaged bomber started to list to one side. The Axichis doubled down their attack on that one ship and bombarded her with lasers. The ship struggled to correct her attitude and groaned deeper into Kathopra's atmosphere.

"She's going down right on top of us!" LeMaine roared. "Fall back! Get out of the way!"

He shoved Peterman toward the hill. All the Hellhounds sprang to their feet, but at that moment, the Axichis hit the coupling point holding the bomber's burning engine to the rest of the ship's housing. The engine split off and dropped like a stone.

The Imoliv pilots didn't see the approaching disaster until it was too late. The engine smashed into the fighter craft they'd just been trying to break into.

The ship detonated with a shuddering boom and flattened all four pilots to the ground. The flash of burning plasma and flying scrap pelted LeMaine in the face and then the shockwave knocked him flat on his back.

He dragged himself up trying to see through the smoke. The fighter rippled in flame. The four pilots lay scattered on the ground.

The Hellhounds ran up to him right then. Kellogg tried to draw LeMaine back toward the hill, but he shook Kellogg off and approached the four bodies. He couldn't leave them out here, not if any of them were still alive and especially not if any of them were injured.

He flipped the first pilot onto his back. Blood and burns covered his head, back, and arms. He'd had his back to the fighter when it exploded. Blood dripped from his nose and leaked out of the corners of his closed eyes.

"He's still breathing," he told Kellogg. "We gotta help them."

LeMaine turned around just as the other pilots started picking themselves up off the ground. The same burns and bloody patches covered all of them.

The first one curled his lip in a menacing snarl. "Get away from him! Don't you dare touch him, Elian scum!"

"We're trying to help him," Kellogg replied. "I'm a medic. He could be dying. I can help him."

Just then, Buca came over and bent over the unconscious man. "I will take him back to the cave....."

The pilot lunged for Buca and shoved him away hard. "Don't touch him, you filthy alien scum!"

The Imoliv pilot spun the other way baring his teeth and hissing at LeMaine and Kellogg, but at that moment, the wounded bomber plummeted through the atmosphere and smashed into the moon not far away.

It crashed far enough away not to put any of the Hellhounds in danger, but the impact threw everyone off their feet.

Kellogg, LeMaine, and Buca all fell next to the unconscious Imoliv pilot. The other guy toppled and hit the dirt.

At the same instant, two Axichis warships veered out of the atmosphere heading for the crashed bomber. The Axichis must have spotted the party on the ground because the enemy swerved hard and came straight for the stranded group.

The warships unleashed their lasers on the moon and tore up the ground all around where the fighter still sat burning away.

"Come on!" LeMaine yelled. "Let's get out of here!"

He tried to pick up the unconscious man, but Buca got there first, heaved the body onto his shoulder, and took off running at high speed toward the hillside.

The other Hellhounds surrounded the three remaining Imoliv. LeMaine grabbed the guy who had just been threatening the squad. "Come on!"

LeMaine seized him by his shoulders and hoisted him to his feet as Axichis lasers torched the ground all over the place.

The pilot struggled and tried to wrench himself out of LeMaine's grasp. "Get away from me! Don't you dare touch me!"

"Shut up!!" LeMaine roared. "Do you want to die out here?!"

The pilot gave an almighty jerk and tore himself out of LeMaine's grasp, but right at that moment, a stray laser sliced through the pilot's leg and he buckled with a hair-raising shriek.

LeMaine spun back and almost lost his head to another laser zipping past him. He dodged it, grabbed the pilot's wrist, and LeMaine strapped the man's arm over his shoulder.

LeMaine strained every muscle to the breaking point hauling the guy out of range. The pilot's leg dangled by a thin scrap of muscle.

The Axichis warships wheeled off into the sky and came back for another pass, but more Elian bombers showed up before the Axichis could reenter the atmosphere.

The ships got into another brutal battle overhead as the Hellhounds made their escape. Monk and O'Hara grabbed a pilot each. O'Hara's pilot seemed to be running on his own legs. He staggered a lot and O'Hara had to hold him up more than once, but at least the guy could support himself.

The other was unconscious, too. Monk flung the body over his shoulder. LeMaine didn't even know if the pilot was alive or not.

The squad raced over the hilltop and back onto flat open ground. The battle kept raging overhead with cannon fire, lasers, and explosions going off all the time.

Polasek dropped back to LeMaine's side. "Should we check these guys now?"

LeMaine made a quick assessment of the situation. Kellogg ran at Buca's side trying to work on the first patient, but it didn't work out too well while they both tried to run away from the battle.

The man LeMaine was carrying kept shrieking in his ear every time LeMaine took a step. LeMaine couldn't concentrate with that noise. He wanted to stop, but he didn't dare to.

"The battle could spill over down here again," he decided. "Keep moving. We'll check them in the cave."

Almost as if his words made it happen, another Axichis battleship hit an Elian bomber and the bomber thundered lower into the atmosphere. Stray fire on both sides kept pelting the moon.

"Keep moving!!" LeMaine yelled to his squad. "Take these guys back to the cave!"

No one turned around or argued. They just ran for it as more debris and lasers struck the ground. Most of it stayed far enough away not to put the squad in danger, but the battle kept moving around every other second. This stuff could hit someone without warning.

The Hellhounds charged to the cave and dragged the four injured pilots inside. The noise of their entrance woke up Heckler, who had been curled up asleep by the fire like

LeMaine told him to. "What the hell is going on?" he growled as he peeled himself off the floor.

LeMaine lowered his patient into a corner and dropped on one knee. "We gotta stop the bleeding."

He had no supplies and Kellogg was already working on the two unconscious pilots. LeMaine didn't want to interrupt him.

LeMaine grabbed the only spare fabric he could find—the torn-off bloody rag of the pilot's pants. It covered the severed stump of the guy's leg, which hung by one tendon, but at least it was still attached. LeMaine didn't have to carry a severed leg through that battle.

LeMaine ripped the guy's pants away, twisted the scrap of fabric around the stump, and cinched it tight, which made the pilot scream again. "Get away from me! Get your hands off me, you filthy alien!"

"Keep quiet," LeMaine snapped. "I'm saving your miserable life, you ungrateful piece of shit."

The pilot clamped his lips shut barely holding himself together. LeMaine pulled himself together with an effort. He couldn't go losing his temper with these people.

"Just keep still. My medic will fix your leg, but he has to help your friends first. We aren't your enemies. The Axichis are."

The pilot looked away, but at least he didn't try to stop LeMaine from knotting the tourniquet. The bleeding slowed and LeMaine did an assessment of the rest of his body.

"How is he?" Kellogg called over.

"He's all right. None of the burns are bleeding too badly. I don't think he's bleeding from anywhere else and the laser cauterized most of the stump. He should be stable until you're ready to deal with him."

"Good," Kellogg replied. "I need you to help me over here. Come on. Hurry up."

LeMaine gave his pilot one last glance and went over to kneel next to the guy Kellogg was working on. The pilot couldn't have been worse unless he'd already been dead.

He'd taken a laser shot to the chest and the wound gaped open with the guy's shattered ribs, heart, and torn lungs hanging out. Blood poured from everywhere, especially the severed aorta.

Kellogg pinched it off while he tried to tear into his pack at the same time. "Here. Hold this," he told LeMaine.

He nodded at his bloody fingers clamped on the guy's aorta. LeMaine moved in, pinched off the tear, and Kellogg went to work ripping his pack open at high speed.

"How's that guy doing, Monk?" Kellogg called over.

"I can't tell. He's out cold....but he doesn't seem to be bleeding anywhere. He's just covered in burns."

"He could have brain damage. Here. Take my scanner....." Kellogg tossed his scanner across the cave. "Scan his head and see if you can locate any brain damage. No, I changed my mind. You come over here and hold this, Monk. Captain, you go check out that guy."

"Yes, Sir," LeMaine replied and traded places with Monk. Monk pinched off the aorta, handed LeMaine the scanner, and LeMaine went to examine the other unconscious pilot.

He passed the scanner back and forth across the pilot's head. "I don't see anything. All brain activity is reading as normal....and none of his organs are damaged, either."

"He probably just got knocked out," Kellogg decided. "Use the smelling salts and see if you can revive him. Hold this, Monk."

Kellogg handed Monk a clamp to hold while Kellogg dove up to his elbows into his patient's chest.

"What are you doing?" the first pilot asked from where LeMaine had left him.

"You can see what I'm doing," Kellogg snapped over his shoulder. "Captain, give that dude over there an exam."

LeMaine tried the smelling salts, but they didn't do anything, so he crossed to the fourth pilot. He appeared the least injured of the four, but he remained cowering back against the wall and recoiled when LeMaine went near him.

"Don't worry, son," LeMaine told him. "I'm not gonna hurt you. I just want to see if you're injured anywhere."

"Leave him alone!" the first pilot snapped. "I swear, if you do anything to him....."

"You can see I'm not doing anything to him." LeMaine held up the scanner. "If you care about him so much, you would want me to check him out to make sure he's okay."

"What's your problem, anyway?" Heckler growled. "Elians have never been your enemies. You might show a little gratitude."

"Elia has made diplomatic overtures to Imoliv for generations," Peterman added. "The Imoliv have always rejected our best efforts to establish ties, but the Imoliv have never acted aggressively toward Elia, either." He cocked his head at the pilot with the severed leg. This was the only one of the two conscious pilots who would talk to anyone. "Why are your people so hostile toward Elia? Why is it so important that none of us touch you or your comrades?"

"Filthy alien scum!" the pilot spat and shot a death glare at LeMaine. "You keep away from him."

"Is he your friend?" LeMaine asked. "I understand wanting to protect your friends. We're all friends here, and if any filthy alien scum came near them, I would threaten them, too."

"He's my brother, you rotten piece of trash!" the first pilot blurted out. "I swear, if you do anything to him....."

LeMaine raised his eyebrows. "Your brother!" He looked back and forth between them. "You don't look alike. Anyway, he doesn't have any other injuries besides the burns....." LeMaine pointed the scanner at the first pilot. "Neither do you. See? I didn't hurt him and I didn't touch you."

The pilot turned away and glared at the wall instead.

"What's your name, son?" LeMaine asked. "It looks like you boys are here for the foreseeable future. You can't go back out there and it will take some time for Kellogg to take care of your friend here. I'm sorry we don't have any food....."

"We don't take food that's been poisoned by the hands of aliens!" the pilot fired back.

"Jesus!" Nunn exclaimed. "You got some mouth on you, boy, talking to the captain like that. You better watch it. The captain is too nice to smack you silly for insulting him, but we sure as hell aren't."

"Take it easy," LeMaine told her. "That isn't helping anything."

"They obviously have some cultural taboo against contact with outsiders," Peterman remarked. "That explains why they don't want diplomatic relations with us."

"That didn't stop Sehiri from talking to us...and his guards from beating us up," Polasek pointed out. "None of them acted like they had a problem being around us filthy alien scum."

"It does explain why they kept us isolated in the hold and didn't let us out," Nunn went on. "It also explains why Sehiri was so resistant to believing us when we said we didn't mean to invade Imoliv territory."

LeMaine turned back to the first pilot. "Just tell me your name so I don't have to start calling you, 'Hey, you'."

O'Hara laughed. "Or they might have a cultural tradition of putting the family name first, in which case you'd be calling him, 'You, Hey', instead."

The others exploded with laughter. "That was very good, Sergeant," Peterman ex-claimed. "That was one of your best jokes yet."

LeMaine couldn't help joining in, but when the first pilot didn't respond, LeMaine turned to the other guy—the first pilot's brother. "What's your name, son?"

The second brother's eyes darted around the cave and then he mumbled under his breath, "Galo."

"Thank you for confiding in me, Galo," LeMaine went on. "Maybe you'd be so kind as to tell me your brother's name, since I'm too filthy for him to tell me."

"His name is...." Galo began.

The brother snapped, "Don't you say a word!"

"Be quiet, Lutov," Galo murmured low. "You've done enough damage already." His eyes shot up to meet LeMaine's for the first time. "He's scared. We've never met any aliens before."

"I am not scared!" Lutov bellowed, but his eyes sure darted around the cave like he was.

"It will be all right," Galo told him. "You can see these people don't mean us any harm. Look. Their medic is taking care of Sindra and he'll take care of you, too, just as soon as he can. Now sit quietly."

He said the last few words with just that little extra bite that made Lutov shut his mouth. He jerked his head away and looked at the wall, but he made sure to follow that order.

LeMaine raised his eyebrows watching this exchange. The way the brothers had been acting just a minute ago made him think Galo was the younger brother and Lutov was trying to protect him from danger.

Now LeMaine saw a completely different dynamic developing between them. It sure was looking like the other way around.

Chapter 26

Galo glanced up at LeMaine again. Galo didn't look so submissive and cowering now. He just seemed quiet and reserved. Maybe that was why he didn't say anything earlier.

"Thank you for bringing us here, Captain," he went on in a smooth, calm voice. "We're very grateful. Please excuse my brother."

"Don't mention it." LeMaine waved to the people behind him. "These are my Hellhounds. We're Elian Special Forces. We were in battle against the Axichis when we got blown over the border into Imoliv territory. We have frequencies that deactivate Axichis fighter craft. We were trying to deploy them when we got shot down here."

Galo cocked his head to one side. "Is that what you were doing? I wondered why you were flying Imoliv craft."

"Sehiri gave them to us. We were hoping to deploy the frequencies to help both Elia and Imoliv, but enemy fire disabled my lieutenant's craft. It was just plain bad luck."

Galo snorted softly, but he stopped himself from actually smiling. "It looks like bad luck all around."

"You got that right," Heckler growled. "Someone better go out and get some more firewood while we're standing around jacking our jaws. If you're serious about me not doing it, Captain, you'd best assign someone else to do it instead."

"You aren't doing it. Sit down, Corporal." LeMaine scanned face the room. Kellogg was still slaving away over his patient with help from Monk. Sindra. Galo said the unconscious patient's name was Sindra.

LeMaine waved to the rest of the squad. "Lemon, you and O'Hara go gather another big stack of firewood. Don't stop until you have enough to get us through another night on this rock. Polasek, you take Nunn, Peterman, and Buca and go back to exploring this place. Stay away from any downed Imoliv fighter craft, either ours or theirs. See what you can find, but make sure you're back by dark."

"Yes, Sir." Polasek stood up. "Let's go, Hellhounds."

The Hellhounds left the cave leaving Kellogg, Monk, and Heckler alone with the LeMaine and the four Imoliv pilots. Lutov kept glaring at everyone while Galo sat quietly watching and listening to everything.

Kellogg took a second to glance over his shoulder. He was still armpit-deep in blood and gore. "You might want to give him some painkillers," he told LeMaine. "That may be why he's so agitated. Give him something to take the edge off. It might calm him down."

"Good idea." LeMaine crossed to Kellogg's pack, fished out the painkillers, and took them back to Lutov, but when he got near the young pilot, LeMaine hesitated.

He held out the syringe for Lutov to see. "Would you like me to give you some painkillers, son? I won't do it if you don't want me to."

Lutov didn't say anything. He refused even to look at LeMaine.

Galo spoke up again. "I'm sorry, Captain. I'll give it to him if you don't mind."

He stood up, took the syringe out of LeMaine's hand, squatted down next to his brother, injected the painkillers into Lutov's arm, and handed back the syringe. "Thank you."

LeMaine eyed the young man more closely. "You should probably have some, too. Those burns don't look so good."

"I can wait until your medic finishes with the rest of these men."

LeMaine raised his eyebrows again. "Are you in command of this group, son?"

Galo returned to his place and sat down. "I'm not in command of anything. Sindra is our commanding officer."

"Him?" LeMaine spun around to stare at the man with his chest lying open.

"We belong to the Special Operations Corps," Galo went on. "Our team was on a mission to infiltrate Elia and find out....."

"Don't, Galo!" Lutov blurted out. "You can't tell them anything!"

"It's a little late for that now, I'm afraid," Galo murmured. "Our lives are in these people's hands. They might as well know everything."

"Why were you infiltrating Elia?" LeMaine asked.

"Our people have been monitoring the war ever since it started. I heard you say before that Sehiri denied that you were at war against the Axichis, but that was a lie. Our people have been keeping track of the Axichis invasion to make sure it didn't come too close to our border."

"So why infiltrate?" LeMaine asked. "You could see everything from your side of the border."

"We wanted to find out if the Axichis had designs on Imoliv, too. Our plan was to penetrate areas of Elian space the Axichis had already secured under their control. We were supposed to capture an Axichis prisoner—preferably an officer—and interrogate him to see if the Axichis were preparing to invade Imoliv after the Elian Military broke down too far to stop them."

LeMaine snorted and went back over to the fire just as Lemon and O'Hara returned with armloads of wood. They left just as quickly.

LeMaine sat down between Heckler and Kellogg where Kellogg would be able to tell LeMaine if Kellogg needed any help with Sindra.

"I think that last battle pretty much proved the point, didn't it?" LeMaine told Gola. "The Axichis crossed your border and attacked Sehiri's ship outright. We were on board at the time."

Gola stared down into the flames. "I know."

LeMaine studied the young man for another minute. LeMaine had to figure this kid out. "Why don't you come over here and get warm, son? You don't have to sit over there in the cold."

Galo's eyes shot up again. They locked on LeMaine with unusual intensity. LeMaine couldn't remember meeting anyone like this before except maybe Buca himself.

"Thank you for offering, Captain," Galo finally replied. "The cold feels good on my burns. The heat makes them hurt."

"You're welcome to any painkillers you want," Kellogg added over his shoulder. "We got plenty."

"You might need them for something more important than my burns." Galo turned to his brother and said something in their own language. Lutov didn't reply, but he did seem to soften somewhat.

The group sat in silence for a while. Only Kellogg broke that silence by giving occasional orders to Monk, clanking his tools, and cursing every now and then.

Galo and Lutov watched the procedure for an hour until Kellogg finally sat back on his heels, ran his sweaty, blood-splattered forehead across his shoulder, and sighed. "Phew! It's done. He's stabilized. I just have to close him up."

He pulled two blood transfusions out of his pack and gave them both to Sindra.

"How many of those do you have left, Sergeant?" Heckler asked.

"Two more and I'll probably use them on Lutov. We're gonna need to be careful after this, Sir," Kellogg told LeMaine. "We're going to need to make extra sure no one gets injured. That would be worse than going without food."

"I understand, son," LeMaine replied. "If Polasek and the others don't find anything, we'll just stick to this cave. We'll make one more foray to send out a distress call from one of the functional Imoliv fighter craft and set up some kind of system to capture the snow and ice for water. Other than that, we'll just stay under cover."

"Do you mind if I make a suggestion, Sir?" Heckler growled.

"Go right ahead, son," LeMaine replied. "Four heads are better than one. What do you have?"

"I was going to suggest that, if no one responds to the distress call, that we send out a pilot in one of your functional fighter craft. We can plan their trajectory to avoid the fighting. Hell, they can avoid the Elian Military altogether since they seem all trigger-happy about shooting us down. We could send someone out to reach a civilian outpost or some other colony. Then that pilot could alert the authorities that we're here and organize a rescue for us. The Military is likely to listen to one of us in person more than they're likely to respond to any distress call...and it beats the shit out of sitting around waiting for doomsday if you catch my drift, Captain."

"It's a good suggestion, Corporal," LeMaine replied. "We'll do it your way."

"I'm just saying," Heckler went on. "I don't know nothing, but I just thought....."

"Anytime you have any suggestions, let me hear them," LeMaine replied. "We're all this boat together. We might as well all have something to say about how we're gonna do things."

"You're still in charge, Sir," Monk chimed in. "No one else wants the job."

LeMaine laughed and then became aware of Galo and Lutov listening to their conversation. Kellogg finished fusing Sindra's ribs and then sealing up his chest, shooting him full of antibiotics, and then Kellogg stood up straight, stretched his back and shoulders, and groaned. "All right, Lutov. Let's see what we have here."

Lutov stiffened when Kellogg went near him, but Galo laid his hand on his brother's arm. "Let him fix your leg."

Kellogg hesitated until Galo moved over to sit right next to Lutov. Galo tightened his grip on Lutov's arm and then nodded at Kellogg. "Please, Sir. He won't interfere with your work."

"You don't have to call me that," Kellogg replied and dragged his pack over to Lutov's side. "What rank are you boys?"

"Sindra is a lieutenant," Galo replied. "The rest of us are....." He said some word in his own language. "We're all the same rank."

"Did you really plan to carry out a mission inside the Elian system?" Monk asked. "How did you manage to do that without getting caught? You'd be the only Imoliv around. Everyone would recognize you."

"Not to mention your brother's hatred of filthy alien scum like us," Heckler growled. "You'd be surrounded by them."

"We weren't supposed to make contact with any Elians," Galo explained. "As I said, our objective was to get into Axichis-controlled areas of Elia. That way, we would only have contact with the Axichis we captured. Besides, Tavon is a master of disguise."

"You mean......" Kellogg's eyes darted to the last man still sprawled across the floor. "Him?"

As if by magic, Lemon and O'Hara came back just then and the conversation died. Galo kept a firm hold on his brother while Kellogg repaired his leg and gave Lutov another dose of painkillers.

Kellogg finished with Lutov's leg and cleared him for active duty, but the young man didn't move from his place.

Then Kellogg went through the room treating all the pilots' burns. That took an age, and by the time he finished spraying the new skin solution on all their charred and raw skin, he'd used up his whole supply.

He packed up his kit and returned to the fire. "I'm beat. I'm gonna pass out for a while, Sir."

"Good idea, son," LeMaine replied. "Take Heckler with you."

"Are you nuts?" Heckler growled. "I couldn't sleep now if you hit me over the head with a hammer."

"Don't tempt me," Monk replied and made Heckler and Kellogg laugh.

Kellogg started to stretch out on the floor by the fire.

"Aren't you going to help Tavon?" Galo asked.

"There isn't a lot I can do except wait for him to come around," Kellogg replied. "We've already checked that he isn't suffering from any brain injury and all his other organs are working. He should come around soon....."

The words barely got out of his mouth before Tavon started to stir. He blinked and then opened his eyes completely. He picked up his head and his eyes darted around the room before he saw the Elians sitting nearby.

Lemon and O'Hara squatted down by the fire. "That should be enough wood to get us through the night, Sir," Lemon began.

"Good job, you two," LeMaine replied. "You did real good."

"We're gonna need it," O'Hara added. "It's getting cold out there already. Night comes early on this rock."

"Did you see Polasek and the others out there?" LeMaine asked.

"We didn't see shit," Lemon replied. "They were nowhere in sight."

"That's no good," LeMaine mused. "They should have come back by now."

"Unless they found something," Monk interjected.

"You boys better come sit by the fire and get warm," LeMaine told the three Imoliv pilots. "Don't be strangers."

Chapter 27

None of the Imoliv pilots responded to LeMaine's second invitation for them to join the squad around the fire. Tavon and Lutov probably wouldn't have come at all if Galo hadn't gotten to his feet, crossed to the fire, and squatted down. He made sure to leave an extra space between himself and O'Hara.

O'Hara beamed at him with that huge, cheeky, cheery grin of his. No way could Galo interpret that as hostility.

LeMaine knew all of O'Hara's grins too well to mistake that one for a grin of fake delight. O'Hara couldn't be more pleased that this alien stranger was keeping his distance. The whole thing thrilled O'Hara no end.

"Sorry we don't have any food to share, You Hey," O'Hara teased. "If we'd known you were coming, we would have baked you a cake."

Galo frowned. "A what?"

The other Hellhounds burst out laughing. "His name is Galo," LeMaine cut in. "That's Lutov, that's Tavon, and this over here is their commanding officer, Sindra." He turned back to Galo. "This is Brien O'Hara....."

"Don't listen to a word he says," Lemon added. "He's so full of shit he can't even taste his food anymore."

"I can so!" O'Hara countered. "Why do you think I'm so hungry all the time?"

LeMaine finished laughing and then pointed out all the other Hellhounds and introduced them to Galo. Kellogg waved from the floor when his turn came.

Galo frowned at them all. "I won't remember any of that."

"You can just call O'Hara, 'shit-for-brains'....." Lemon began.

"You better be careful," O'Hara warned. "Just wait until I come up with a name for you."

"I would love to see you try," Lemon growled back.

"As you can see," LeMaine told Galo, "we keep it pretty casual around here. I don't know what kind of protocol you're used to in your team....."

"Nothing like this." Galo kept frowning at everyone. "Do you really let them speak to each other like this?"

"It isn't really a question of letting them," LeMaine began, but just then, Polasek, Peterman, and Nunn returned.

LeMaine got to his feet as soon as Polasek entered the cave. "Anything? Where's Buca?"

"He's coming. He just went back to scout around the Imoliv pilots' crafts to make sure there was no one else out there we might have missed."

Polasek broke off as Buca stepped into the cave. "It's all clear and the snow is starting," he reported.

"I have a plastic insulating sheet in my pack, Sir," Kellogg suggested. "We could rig that up to catch the snow."

"Great. Buca, you and Nunn go set it up. See if you can find a depression in these rocks that will catch any melted snow at the bottom."

Kellogg sat up long enough to fish the sheet out of his pack. He handed it to Buca and Buca and Nunn left.

Polasek's group came over to the fire. "There isn't shit out there, Sir—excuse my French."

"That isn't French, Lieutenant," O'Hara called out, but everyone ignored him.

"We searched, but there aren't any living things on this rock except us and the scrub."

"Thanks for trying, son," LeMaine replied.

"That settles it," Heckler replied. "We'll have to send someone out."

"Not yet," LeMaine countered. "First, we send a distress call. Monk, you take O'Hara back to your Imoliv fighter craft. Set up a distress call on repeat with a homing signal to come and find us. Be sure to tell them we're hiding in the caves and give them a description of the rock formation. We'll send it out overnight. If we don't hear from anyone, then we'll send out a pilot."

"The question is who's gonna be the lucky sucker to fly an Imoliv vessel off this moon," Kellogg chimed in. "We can't send out one of these guys. Whoever it is, the Military needs to be able to read a human life sign on board."

"The plan is for the Military to never see the fighter in question," LeMaine replied. "Ideally, the Military will be too preoccupied fighting the Axichis to notice our pilot getting away."

"That's asking a lot considering the Military was right on top of this moon earlier today," Heckler pointed out.

"This was your idea!" LeMaine fired back. "You were the one who suggested sending someone out. Now you're telling me it's a bad idea?"

"I suggested sending someone out no matter where the Elian Military is," Heckler replied. "I say we fly straight through the battle if we have to. It's better than staying here and we've flown through worse."

"How many fighters do we have—working ones, I mean?" LeMaine asked.

"Seven," Polasek replied. "Not enough for all of us."

"The fighters can carry two," Galo cut in.

Everyone turned around to stare at him. "They do?"

"They're designed to," Galo replied. "They don't usually, but if we divide up our numbers so two lighter pilots fly together, it should work."

"I sure as hell hope you're right," Lemon countered.

"I'll prove it to you," Galo went on. "I'll fly with Lutov. That way...."

"That way, you can both get your asses shot off at the same time," O'Hara chimed in, but no one laughed this time.

"If I'm lying, my brother and I will die," Galo told everyone. "I'm telling the truth. I wouldn't risk my life and my brother's life just to deceive you." He glanced around and his gaze stopped on LeMaine. "You believe me, don't you, Captain?"

"Of course I do, son. What can you tell me about Sindra? Will he be hostile when he wakes up?"

"Sindra is a good man. He won't be hostile, not when I explain to him what you've done for us—especially him."

"We just have one problem," Nunn added. "Everyone in this system wants to kill us. As soon as we leave Kathopra in one of those fighters, everyone will start shooting at us including our own."

"That's why I suggested launching when the battle is somewhere else," Heckler replied. "And only one person goes out—an Elian. No offense to you men, but it has to be one of us."

"No, I think Galo is right," LeMaine replied. "It would work better if we all went at once. We can defend each other that way."

Silence answered him, and in that brief pause, Sindra regained consciousness.

Galo went over to him. "These Elians brought us to their shelter, Sir. Their medic saved your life."

Kellogg rested his hand on Sindra's shoulder. "Stay where you are for now, man. You got your chest blown out. You need to wait for the seals to solidify."

Sindra glanced around taking in the whole scene. Then he nodded at LeMaine. "I remember you. Thank you for helping us."

LeMaine glanced over at Lutov. He hadn't said a word since Galo told him to be quiet.

"Are you sure we aren't too filthy alien scum for you to spend the night with?" LeMaine asked.

"We expected we might have some contact with Elians when we came on this mission. I was prepared for them to be something less than the horrible monsters we've all been taught to believe they are."

"That's me—a horrible monster," O'Hara replied and made a face. He wiggled his fingers around and made grunting noises.

"Stand down, Sergeant," LeMaine told him. "Stow it for three minutes, will you?"

"Three minutes. Copy that." O'Hara scowled at his remote and pretended to start a timer.

Lemon groaned and LeMaine turned back to Sindra. "We can't move until you're healthy enough to travel."

Just then, Monk and Peterman came back. "The signal's all set, Sir," Monk announced.

"Excellent. We'll just wait until morning and see if we get any response."

The Hellhounds gathered around the fire and now there wasn't space for anyone to keep their distance. They packed in shoulder to shoulder with the Imoliv pilots. Only Lutov remained outside the circle.

Sindra stayed lying down in the same place, but Monk and LeMaine sat apart from each other so the heat could reach Sindra.

"It's a shame the Imoliv are so hostile toward Elians," Peterman remarked. "We could be working together to defeat the Axichis."

"Maybe that will change once we get off this moon and deploy the frequencies," Kellogg replied.

"I don't think so," Galo murmured. "It will take generations to undo all we've been taught about aliens. The Imoliv will never accept Elia as an ally."

"You never know," Peterman countered. "A war can change a lot, especially when former enemies work together to defeat a common threat. Look at us. We're sitting here talking. That never would have happened if we hadn't all been shot down here."

LeMaine glanced over at Lutov, but no one mentioned him. If he changed his attitude after Kellogg fixed his leg, Lutov didn't show it. He made no effort to join the conversation.

Buca startled everyone by joining the conversation and addressing the Imoliv pilots. "Tell us more about your society. We're all interested to learn your ways." His eyes flicked to his squad mates. "At least, I am."

"So am I," Peterman added. "Please. We would all love to hear. Why did your people develop such an aversion to interaction with outsiders?"

"There's a legend among our people about an alien population pretending to befriend us," Galo began. "They established diplomatic ties with our people. They sent traders and senators and businesspeople. They built markets and ports. Enclaves of their kind came to live in our system. Then they betrayed us, attacked us from within, and sparked a war that nearly wiped out our population. The invaders planned to enslave us all and nearly succeeded. It took many years to eliminate all the infiltrators and then to rebuild our society. We bolstered our defenses and created protocols for contact with anyone who tried to establish relations with us. That was many generations ago. Since then, the anti-alien prejudice has only gotten stronger. Now any contact with an alien is strictly taboo."

"That makes sense," Peterman remarked. "I don't blame you for taking precautions."

"There is a growing movement to reverse the trend," Sindra interjected. "It's still a fringe movement and its members are hunted by the Police and hounded out of society, but nothing can stop it from growing. The movement seeks to make contact with outsiders, to bring in fresh trade with other species, and to open the borders to understanding with other cultures. I hope it succeeds."

"That's blasphemy!" Lutov blurted out. They were the first words he'd spoken since Galo ordered him to remain silent. "It's heresy! It's forbidden!"

Sindra only glanced at him. "I've given the best years of my life to the Imoliv cause. I've been wounded in the line of duty defending our borders....and now this alien has just saved my life. I think I've earned the right to state my opinion."

None of his men answered him.

Sindra waited for his words to sink in and then he glanced up at LeMaine. "It would be an honor to work with your squad, but I might suggest that, instead of flying away from the battle, we fly instead for Imoliv territory."

"You're on drugs!" Lemon blurted out.

"We're closer to Imoliv territory," Peterman pointed out. "If the battle is still too close, then we can get across the border quickly before the Military attacks us again."

"And get taken prisoner by the Imoliv and thrown back in the same hold?" Monk countered. "No, thank you."

"We have one ace up our sleeves," LeMaine pointed out. "Even if the Imoliv do recapture us and lock us up again, these men can take the frequencies to their leadership. The Imoliv can deploy the frequencies against the Axichis....."

"That will help the Imoliv," Nunn pointed out. "It won't help Elia."

"Anything that weakens the Axichis helps Elia," LeMaine replied. "What difference does it make who deploys the frequencies as long as they get deployed? Anyway, even if the Military had the frequencies and could use them freely, I would still want to give them to the Imoliv. I wouldn't want to leave the Imoliv defenseless against the Axichis. We should all be helping each other out as much as we can."

"If you don't mind me saying so, Sir," Polasek cut in, "the frequencies wouldn't just go to the Imoliv. The minute someone deploys the frequencies, they'll get transmitted to everyone on the field no matter which side they're on—including the Axichis."

Heckler snorted. "They won't do the Axichis any good, Lieutenant."

"That's my point," Polasek went on. "Either way, Elia will get them, too. Even if we get retaken by Sehiri and he throws us in the hold, these men can deliver the frequencies to Sehiri and he can deploy them. Mission accomplished."

"Why not just deploy the frequencies yourself the minute you get in the air?" Nunn asked. "You have them in your remote. You just need a functioning fighter craft to deploy them."

"That could work," Polasek replied, "but the Imoliv might not understand what they're receiving. They might not understand about re-transmitting the frequencies or how to attack the Axichis once the frequencies do get deployed. They would need some-one to explain all of that to them. They don't have an open line of communication with any Elian vessel, so what better way than for these men to do it—or for us to do it in person?"

LeMaine rubbed his chin for a minute and then shrugged. "All of you lie down and get some sleep. We have a long, cold night in front of us. We can think it over and discuss it in the morning. We might get rescued before then anyway." He noticed Sindra listening to him. "Excuse me, Lieutenant. I didn't mean to step on your toes."

"I think it will work best if the four of us come under your command from now on, Captain," Sindra replied. "You're senior to us all. Consider us your subordinates until we get out of this mess."

"If that's what you want, I'd be honored to have you. Now get some sleep, Lieutenant. You need to get your strength back."

Chapter 28

L eMaine put the last of the firewood on the fire and glanced up as Buca reentered the cave. "Any luck?"

Buca shook his head. "The signal is still running and there's no sign of anyone out there—from any army. There's also nothing on the fighter's logs to indicate that anyone has responded."

"Damn it," LeMaine muttered and looked back down into the flames.

"What's for breakfast?" Nunn asked. "I'm going for a nice fluffy omelet with crisp asparagus and cheese."

"I'll take the blueberry waffles with whipped cream, walnuts, and a big steaming cappuccino," O'Hara chimed in. "And throw in four slices of bacon—no, make it five."

"I'll take the rib-eye steak—extra rare," Heckler rumbled. "Add a side of huevos rancheros and a cup of black coffee."

"What are you talking about?" Galo asked.

"Food," O'Hara replied. "It's always food when we get stranded anywhere. It helps take our minds off how hungry we are."

Galo frowned. "I would think that would make the hunger worse."

"But it keeps our spirits up," Nunn pointed out. "It helps us imagine what we're going to eat when we get out of this nightmare."

"This is hardly a nightmare," Peterman interjected. "The Gelmyke Campaign was way worse."

"Don't even talk about that!" Heckler fired back.

"Do you really have to bring that up?" Lemon snapped. "We were talking about food."

Peterman turned back to Galo. "You see? Stick with food. No one will argue."

"I wouldn't mind a kelniri nugurilia rulrill and a serving of inzeron vaitania and an ice-cold rodeaturn cubos," Tavon chimed in.

"You'll have to prepare it yourself," Kellogg told him. "They don't serve that at this hotel."

The others all laughed. Kellogg bent over Sindra, checked the seals on his chest, and cleared him for duty. "Thank you, Kellogg," Sindra exclaimed.

"You bet, man. It was my pleasure."

"I told you he enjoys it," Peterman called across the cave. "Don't bother denying it any longer, Sergeant. You just can't get enough of all that blood all over you."

Kellogg made a face. "You better not be taking the piss out of me, Lieutenant. I might be tempted to scramble your brain the next time you pass out. Then you wouldn't be able to remember what you were writing that book about."

Everyone laughed. The Imoliv pilots watched the Hellhounds talking back and forth while everyone got up, gathered what little gear they still had, and headed for the exit.

LeMaine stepped outside and squinted up at the cloudy sky.

"I don't hear the battle," Nunn remarked.

"That doesn't mean anything," Heckler replied. "It might be out of range of our hearing."

"Let's go over to the fighter craft and use the scanners to see." LeMaine waved to the four Imoliv pilots.

Lutov had gone back to being totally silent. He let the others do the talking, especially Galo and Sindra, who had become downright friendly toward the Hellhounds.

"You men come with us," LeMaine told Sindra. "If we're really gonna do this thing and fly out of here, we'll need you with us."

"We might not need to fly toward Imoliv territory," Polasek pointed out. "I might be able to deploy the frequencies as soon as we get in the air."

"No, I've been thinking and I think we should wait," LeMaine replied. "I think we should go to Imoliv territory without deploying the frequencies."

"You mean.....*not* deploy the frequencies....on purpose?" Peterman exclaimed. "Why? Isn't that the whole objective of this trip—to broadcast the frequencies to the whole Elian Military?"

"I've been thinking about our conversation last night," LeMaine replied. "How much better do you think it would be if the frequencies came from the Imoliv? Us delivering the frequencies to the Imoliv could be the turning point in Imoliv-Elian relations. Today could be the day when our people actually make friends with each other. We could be about to usher in a new era of positive diplomatic and trade relations between our two systems. Don't you think that's worth a small delay?"

"If we do it that way," Monk pointed out, "we should have just given the frequencies to Sehiri while we were still on his ship. He could have deployed the frequencies from there. We never would have had to get shot down on this moon and we wouldn't have to risk our asses getting off it."

"You're right," LeMaine replied. "It would have been better to do it that way, but we didn't think of it at the time and he probably wouldn't have listened to us anyway. I was more concerned with getting the frequencies to the Elian Military, but there are wider concerns now. Elia isn't the only system in danger. The Imoliv are in danger, too. They need these frequencies as much as we do."

The two squads arrived at the Hellhounds' last remaining fighters just then and Sindra approached the first one. "So how do you want to do this?"

"We mount up in these fighters," LeMaine replied. "We put two pilots to a craft where necessary and fight our way across the border into Imoliv territory."

"We should transfer the frequencies to all seven fighters before we lift off," Polasek suggested. "That will increase the odds of someone getting the frequencies over the line.....in case we do wind up flying into the battle."

LeMaine waved at Sindra. "Load up and check the scanners. See how close the battle is to us."

Sindra scrambled up the side of one of the craft. He didn't need to use a ladder. He wedged his feet against the ship's outer hull. LeMaine didn't see Sindra stepping on anything in particular, but he must have known a lot more about these fighters than LeMaine did.

LeMaine took a split second to wonder why Sindra didn't climb up his fighter the last time when these pilots had been threatening to blow LeMaine and Peterman away. Then something clicked in LeMaine's mind.

Sindra had been the one yelling threats at LeMaine. Lutov had been the one trying to get the craft's cockpit cover open while Sindra confronted the filthy alien scum. Sindra must not have taught his young subordinate this climbing trick.

Sindra popped the fighter's cockpit cover and lowered himself into his seat. Galo came over to LeMaine while they waited for Sindra to fiddle with the controls.

"Thank you again, Captain," Galo exclaimed. "Thank you for everything. I never imagined an Elian could be as kind and considerate as you have been. I'm grateful that we met you and that you helped us. I hope things change between our peoples....." He shot a glance over his shoulder at his brother. "Despite what prejudices some people still might hold."

"It was my pleasure to meet you, too, son." LeMaine shook Galo's hand. "When you get home, I hope you'll tell your people that the hostility and prejudice is completely one-sided. Elia would like nothing better than to call the Imoliv our friends—just as we do."

"Good news, Captain," Sindra called down from the cockpit. "The battle is directly between us and the Imoliv border. There are fifteen Imoliv destroyers inside the Elian system. The Imoliv are fighting the Elians and leaving the Axichis to do as they please."

Heckler groaned. "Spectacular."

"I'm sure you can make it worse than that if you really try," O'Hara called up to the cockpit. "Come on. You can do it."

"That settles it." LeMaine pointed at his people. "Galo, you take Lutov like you suggested. Tanov, you fly with Sindra. That leaves five craft for us Hellhounds. Lemon, you fly with O'Hara...."

"Aw, hell no!" Lemon roared. "Why don't you just shoot me in the head right now and get it over with?"

O'Hara rubbed his hands and chortled with glee. "This is my chance to finally drive Lemon around the bend."

"You son of a bitch!" Lemon snarled. "I'm gonna kill you, I swear to Christ!"

"You two are the smallest," LeMaine went on. "Peterman and Polasek, you two double up...."

"And try not to solve the world's problems while you're together in the same cockpit," Nunn teased. "Save it until after your craft is on the ground."

"Nunn, you fly with Buca....."

"Yes!!" Nunn pumped her fist in triumph and Buca broke into a very rare grin.

"Aw, come on, Sir!" Lemon complained. "Why can't I fly with Buca?"

"Because Nunn and O'Hara in the same cockpit would be the captain's worst living nightmare," Peterman remarked. "None of the rest of us would ever be able to get their sass out of our ears."

Lemon turned away with another agonized groan. "This is so wrong in so many ways."

Nunn beamed at Buca. "So.....you and me...."

"Yes," he replied. "Why is that so special?"

"Because you're such a badass in the air, man," Polasek told him. "She thinks some of your mojo will rub off on her."

Buca frowned. "Mojo? What's that?"

"He means your magic," O'Hara replied. "He means your special je ne sais quoi."

Buca frowned even more deeply. "What does that mean?"

"It means, 'I don't know what'," Peterman explained and the other Hellhounds laughed. "No really. That's what it means...because he doesn't know what he means."

Gola frowned at LeMaine. "Is it always like this?"

"Non-freakin'-stop," LeMaine replied and had to laugh. He heard that a lot about the Hellhounds constantly mouthing off, to him, to each other, and to anyone else who came within range.

Sindra jumped down just then. "It's looking pretty hot up there."

"All the more reason for us to stick together," LeMaine told him. "Take your people and double up in your craft. We'll go with you and...."

"And may the best pilot win," Nunn finished.

"That isn't what I was about to say, Sergeant," LeMaine fired back.

"But you meant it, didn't you?" O'Hara asked. "That is the basic gist of what you were trying to imply—that we would throw down and kick some ass on our way across the line. Am I right or am I right?"

"Whose ass did you plan to kick, Sergeant?" Peterman asked. "The Imoliv's or the Military's?"

"The basic gist of what I was trying to imply," LeMaine interrupted, "was for us all to do our best and get through the battle alive. Load up, Polasek, and transfer the frequencies to all the other fighters—but don't deploy them. Just get across the line and we'll take it from there."

"Thank you again, Captain." Sindra stepped forward to shake LeMaine's hand. "I hope we're both still alive to talk about this when it's over."

"I hope so, too, Lieutenant. God's speed....and may the best pilot win."

The Hellhounds exploded in laughter and scampered off to their craft. Monk was too big to fly with anyone else, so that left LeMaine and Heckler to fly together. LeMaine wasn't even sure if the little fighter could get off the ground with the two of them in it.

"You better fly this crate, Sir," Heckler told him on their way to their ship.

"No, thanks, Corporal," LeMaine returned. "You're the better pilot."

Heckler whipped around in a hurry. "I am not!"

"Sure you are. Besides, I might decide to take it easy on the Military attack cruisers that get in our way. Go on, son. Show me how it's done."

Heckler turned bright red, but when it came time to get into the cockpit, he moved fast and sure with expert efficiency.

He sat down in the seat. The second position behind the pilot's main position was so small that LeMaine had to cram himself in. That must be why he didn't notice the second seat before. It could hardly be called a seat at all.

The smaller pilots didn't have that problem. Nunn, Lemon, and Polasek slipped right in behind Buca, O'Hara, and Peterman.

Heckler and LeMaine put on their helmets and the Hellhounds' talk came through LeMaine's headset to his ears, but he didn't hear Lemon cursing or O'Hara giving her grief while they went through all their systems checks. LeMaine should have known they would be all business when the shit went down.

LeMaine tried to concentrate on his own checks, but he got distracted by the scans of the battle. It was as bad as Sindra said. In fact, it was worse than he said.

The Elian Military had been on the ropes before. Fighting the Imoliv was the last thing they needed.

The Axichis took advantage of the conflict to fly around both fleets. The Axichis fired their lasers at Elian and Imoliv targets. Every ship they hit wheeled away to defend themselves, only to get sucked back into the conflict by more shots from the other side. This couldn't go on.

"Ready when you give the word, Sir," Heckler announced.

"Are all you Hellhounds ready to rock and roll?" LeMaine asked.

They all called back that they were ready. He checked the four Imoliv pilots and Sindra nodded through his cockpit cover.

"Hit it," LeMaine ordered and Heckler shot off the ground at skull-crushing speed. He rocketed away from Kathopra with Buca, Peterman, and O'Hara right on his tail.

"Coming in fast!" Heckler called. "Get ready to lay down some lead, Sir!"

"Ready," LeMaine replied.

"Light it up!" Heckler ordered and LeMaine opened fire as Heckler and the others plowed headlong into the battle.

Chapter 29

LeMaine opened fire on the battle as Heckler punched the Imoliv fighter craft's throttle to the wall. The Axichis were closest on this side. They gave LeMaine plenty of targets, but this craft's phase cannons didn't damage them.

They retreated from Heckler's speed, though. The Axichis battleships had to get out of the way to prevent Heckler from colliding with them and LeMaine's fighter streaked through the battle.

LeMaine concentrated his cannons to the front. He did his best not to hit any Elian craft, but Heckler was flying too fast to give LeMaine even an instant to direct his fire.

LeMaine didn't want to hit any Imoliv, either, but he wound up hitting ships from both sides. He smacked them out of the way and Heckler squeaked through just as more Imoliv fighter craft came screaming out of nowhere.

"Call 'em off!" Monk yelled to Sindra and Galo. "Can't you contact your own people and tell them it's you?"

"They should be able to see their own craft," Peterman remarked, but at that moment, the incoming Imoliv opened fire.

LeMaine took an instant to realize that the Imoliv pilots were shooting at something behind him. Heckler tried to dodge around their shots. "Fire, Sir!" he roared and LeMaine's fingers tightened on the cannon controls without him even thinking about it.

He spattered the Imoliv with phase shots, only for Heckler to come face to face with a dozen enormous Imoliv destroyers.

They towered over the tiny craft and someone up there must have seen that there were humans flying these ships.

The destroyers opened fire and a brutal phase blast struck LeMaine's ship right in front of Heckler's seat. "Cocksuckers!" he roared and yanked the fighter away.

LeMaine fired at the destroyers, but they were way too big for him to do any damage. Heckler wheeled back toward the Elian line only to take another brutal pounding from the Elian bombers. Elian attack cruisers whizzed through the battle unloading on any Imoliv craft in sight, including the Hellhounds.

No one on the Elian side noticed or cared that five of these Imoliv fighters were being piloted by humans. LeMaine didn't waste time trying to tell them.

"Bring it back around!" he told Heckler. "We gotta get through to the Imoliv side. Don't screw around with these idiots!"

"There are a few destroyers standing the way in case you hadn't noticed!" Heckler bellowed back.

"I noticed! Get over there! Come on! Quit playing around!"

"You call this playing?!" Heckler thundered, but he did as LeMaine said and swung the fighter around to face the Imoliv defensive line.

Imoliv fighters swarmed all around the ship. LeMaine scrambled between the scanners and the cannon controls trying to see who was who.

He could pick out the craft being piloted by humans, but he couldn't distinguish which fighters belonged to the Imoliv pilots he'd met on Kathopra. Heckler erupted onto the field gunning his engines to the limit. LeMaine did his best to shoot across the craft in his path. He didn't want to hit anyone, especially not those four pilots.

A second later, Heckler exploded through the cloud of fighters and broke for the Imoliv line. The destroyers stood there blocking the way with all their guns aimed toward the Elian side.

"Don't try to fight them!" LeMaine yelled. "Get behind them and break for the border!"

Heckler bellowed some indistinct roar of frustration and protest, but he still obeyed. He sprinted into another wild loop and started weaving in and out of the Imoliv line. The destroyers couldn't hit him or didn't try as long as he stayed too close to their ships.

"Follow us, Hellhounds!" LeMaine ordered. "Use the destroyers as cover and make for the Imoliv side."

The Hellhounds raced away from the battle following Heckler's trail. Elian attack cruisers and Imoliv fighters dogged them every step of the way. The Elian craft got too close to the destroyers and the Imoliv opened fire on the Elians.

The Military dropped back under the assault and left the Imoliv fighter craft to go after the crew instead. LeMaine heard Sindra and the others talking to their people in their own language, but it didn't do any good. Which one of these destroyers belonged to Sehiri? LeMaine didn't have time to check.

Heckler took a crackling shot of cannon fire across his bow and LeMaine spun around to return fire on the Imoliv fighters. They were gaining on him.

Heckler hurtled to the end of the Imoliv line and broke hard to port. The border lay ahead, but more destroyers stood guard on the other side. "Are you sure this is what you want?" Heckler growled under his breath. "We'll be flying straight into their guns."

He slowed, and at that moment, two more fighters screamed past the wings on both sides. Sindra and Galo tore away from the battle putting on speed for their home territory. "Keep up with us, Heckler!" Sindra called and then he started talking to his people in their own language again.

Heckler throttled forward, but much more slowly. The other Hellhounds pulled alongside. The squad crept a little closer to the border, but they didn't cross it.

Sidra and Galo crossed and buzzed in front of the Imoliv barricade for a while. Conversation chattered back and forth between the destroyers and the Imoliv craft, but the destroyers didn't act hostile toward their own anymore. What was Sindra saying to them?

He finally turned back and called, "Come on, Captain! It's all right. They've given assurance that they won't fire on any of you. Sehiri will take you back on board his ship."

"I can't flippin' wait," Heckler muttered.

He eased forward and the other Hellhounds inched a little closer to the Imoliv line. LeMaine couldn't tell which one of these ships belonged to Sehiri—not that it mattered.

He almost asked Sindra where to go and what to do when one of the destroyers pulled out of position, rotated backward, and opened a panel into its hold—an empty hold. The *Excursion*, the *Lucidity*, and all their Elian crewmen and personnel were no longer in there.

"Where are all the people Sehiri was holding as prisoners?" LeMaine demanded.

"I don't know," Sindra replied. "Come inside. We can talk to him and he can explain everything."

LeMaine hesitated to go anywhere near Sehiri or his destroyer, but at least he knew about the frequencies. He'd listened to LeMaine about that when the Axichis attacked. Sehiri might be reasonable about the Hellhounds fighting their way back to the Imoliv side.

"What do we do, Sir?" Lemon asked. "Are we really going back in there?"

"Yes," LeMaine replied. "Land on the floor. We'll discuss this with Sehiri and see what happens. Go on, Heckler. No need to stand around on the doormat."

"Doormat! Huh!" Heckler snarled and steered the fighter closer.

He drifted into the hold and set down. The other Hellhounds landed near him and then Sindra and Galo landed their craft, too.

LeMaine didn't need anyone to draw him a picture of why Sehiri didn't let the Hellhounds bring their fighters back into the launch chutes where they belonged. It sure looked to LeMaine like he and the Hellhounds were prisoners again.

The panel slid shut and boomed into place. The fighter's controls read the hold repressurizing. The squad could disembark.

All the Hellhounds stayed where they were until Sindra, Tavon, Galo, and Lutov all popped their cockpit covers and climbed down to the floor. Sindra signaled LeMaine and the others to do the same.

LeMaine jumped down to join them. "Now what? Where is everyone?"

"Sehiri is a very busy man," Sindra explained. "He may have to stay on the bridge and monitor the battle before he comes down here to talk to us."

"Great," Heckler growled.

The other Hellhounds gathered around talking. "How long do we have to stay down here?" Lemon asked.

"It's better than Kathopra, isn't it?" Peterman remarked. "At least we're comfortable here."

"We aren't comfortable because we don't have any food," O'Hara pointed out.

"That's what *you're* here for, champ," Peterman countered. "You can tell us all about what you're going to have for lunch, now that we got breakfast out of the way."

Laughter answered him, but it died soon enough when nothing happened. The squad was trapped on this ship—again.

"Any ideas on what they plan to do?" Peterman asked Sindra. "Did they give you any clues when you were talking to them just now?"

"They sounded reasonable enough," Sindra replied. "They said they would take a look at the frequencies and then decide what to do about them."

"We did NOT just fight our way over here for them to completely ignore us," Lemon spat.

"Keep your hair on," LeMaine ordered. "We don't know anything yet."

"I'm taking a load off." O'Hara went back over to his fighter and sat down on the landing gear. "I'm exhausted after my hard morning's work."

"Now you just need something to put in your mouth so you don't bore us all with your jokes," Kellogg suggested.

Nunn laughed and took a breath to chime in when a different panel slid back across the hold. It was the same one Sehiri used to enter and exit the last time he held Elian personnel captive in here.

He came out of the compartment accompanied by a bunch of his armed security guards. "He sure has a lot of guards," Nunn remarked. "Maybe his entire crew is made up of nothing but security guards."

"And fighter pilots," Heckler added. "Maybe he runs the ship by himself."

Sehiri sauntered over to the group. Sindra took a few steps forward and started talking to Sehiri in his own language. Sindra talked fast like he was trying to explain all this.

Sehiri didn't look at Sindra for a long time. Sehiri kept his eyes locked only on LeMaine.

Sindra kept trying to explain while the others stood around in awkward silence. Sehiri barely glanced at Sindra, said something in his own language, and immediately went back to staring at LeMaine.

Sindra's expression drained off his face and he shot LeMaine a look that LeMaine couldn't read. Was it terror, disappointment, or just distress?

"I'll do what I can, Captain," Sindra murmured. "Just try to....."

Sehiri snapped something short and commanding in his own language. Sindra shut his mouth immediately. Then he and the other four pilots hustled away to the compartment, entered it, and the panel closed behind them. It reopened a second later. It was empty. The pilots were all gone.

"Captain," Sehiri breezed in his most nonchalant tone. "We meet again."

"Sadly," Polasek muttered behind LeMaine's back.

Sehiri's eyes darted in that direction, and for the first time, his icy calm expression slipped ever so slightly. He'd probably never been insulted before in his life.

"You heard Sindra explain why we came back here," LeMaine began. "You know we came to help the Imoliv cause—not to undermine it."

"We have no cause except to defend our own territory," Sehiri replied.

"And yet, here you are, inside Elian space shooting up Elian ships," LeMaine replied. "That doesn't sound like a very defensive position to me. I would be very surprised if any Elian vessel has ever fired on any Imoliv vessel at all in this conflict except on Imoliv vessels that crossed the border into our territory. The Imoliv are the aggressors here."

"You've taken your hatred of other species too far," Peterman chimed in. "It isn't enough anymore that you stay in your own system and keep your people isolated. Now you have to go hunting the filthy alien scum in their own territory and kill them for no reason. Elia has never done anything but extend the hand of friendship to Imoliv. Now you're basically ensuring that the Axichis will destroyed us. What do you think will happen then? The Axichis will come after you and Elia won't be there to help you....which is what we're trying to do now.....but you already knew that because your own pilots just told you so."

Sehiri raised his eyebrows at Peterman. "Who is this man, Captain? He speaks rather freely for a subordinate."

"This is Lieutenant Stuart Peterman. He's the Command negotiator on our squad. He's empowered to speak on Command's behalf in our dealings with other populations. You'd be wise to listen to him."

"But then again," Nunn interjected, "no one ever accused you of being that."

"Quite the contrary," Polasek added.

Sehiri's eyes darted from one person to another. He obviously wasn't used to being spoken to like this and he didn't react right away.

He finally decided to concentrate on LeMaine. "Very well, Captain. I will consider your embassy and I will look into this matter of the frequencies."

"I already told you about the frequencies," LeMaine countered. "Why did you give us fighter craft in the first place if you didn't believe me then?"

"Because he's a raving idiot," Heckler growled.

"With a head too big for his shoulders," Lemon added.

Sehiri chose to ignore the other Hellhounds. "I believed you and gave you fighter craft, but you did not deploy these frequencies. How am I to know you didn't invent them to get off this ship?"

"Our communications officer took a hit that disabled his communications system," Peterman replied. "He couldn't deploy them."

Sehiri pretended not to hear. "I'm afraid I must keep you confined while I investigate this matter. You must understand that I can't keep you and your people together—not after the disaster last time. I will look into this and decide what to do shortly."

He waved to his guards, retreated to the compartment, and left.

The guards surrounded the Hellhounds—two per Hellhound except for Monk and Heckler. The guards posted four of their number around each of those men.

The guards escorted the squad to the compartment and steered one person into it at a time. The panel kept swishing back and forth as each Hellhound vanished onto the ship and didn't reappear.

The guards held LeMaine back until last. He didn't tell his people to cooperate with these jokers. LeMaine didn't plan to, either.

He was starting to seriously regret ever trying to open a doorway between Elia and Imoliv. Galo tried to warn him that the prejudice would be too strong. Now LeMaine found out just how strong it was. The forces of isolation and resentment were too deeply entrenched in Imoliv society.

The guards escorted LeMaine into the compartment, out the other side, and down a different corridor than the one Lemon used to show the Hellhounds out of the hold. The guards didn't rough him up the way he expected. That made a pleasant surprise.

They stopped thirty yards down the hall and turned to what LeMaine first mistook for a blank wall. Another panel slid back to reveal an opening the size of a closet. It couldn't have been more than three feet square.

The guards pushed LeMaine into it and the panel slid shut. The compartment gave him just enough room to turn around and face the spot where he'd just entered. He was all alone in here—a prisoner once again.

Chapter 30

LeMaine rested his aching forehead against the cold steel wall in front of him. He'd been standing up for hours—days maybe. Exhaustion wore down his resolve. He couldn't stay standing a second longer.

This compartment didn't give him enough space to sit down on the floor or to assume any other position. His knees banged the walls if he even tried to bend them, but he had no choice.

His legs buckled and he slumped, but at that instant, a metal shelf slid out of the wall behind him. It slid out exactly at the level of his thighs and he wound up sitting down on that instead of hitting the floor.

He crumpled there, too drained even to think about how this compartment worked or how it knew that he needed to sit down right then.

He leaned his back and head against the wall behind him, and miraculously, the whole compartment tipped backward.

It angled so that he reclined in a comfortable position—or as comfortable as he possibly could be considering this makeshift seat had no padding. The shelf he'd been sitting on retracted so he could lie flat. It wasn't the most inviting bed he'd ever slept in, but at least he was lying down at last.

He must have fallen asleep because he woke up hours later. He felt better except that he was now starving hungry. He hadn't eaten since he left the *Lucidity* on his way to Nainia. He and his squad had been on the run ever since.

He tried to sit up, and without him even thinking about it, the compartment righted itself. It tipped up straight and the shelf extended again so that he sat in the right position.

A different shelf slid out of the wall right in front of him. A panel opened above it and a plate of food appeared in front of him.

He was too grateful to question how or why or where it came from. He attacked the food and wolfed it down his throat without even chewing it. He had no way of knowing when or even if he would ever get any more.

The food made him dizzy and sleepy again. He leaned back and the seat re-positioned itself in the most comfortable position for him. All he needed was a pillow and blanket. Then he'd be set.

Now he could consider how the Imoliv did all this. The wall that produced that food for him was the same wall the guards used to put him in here. That wall wasn't thick enough to contain any machinery, any storage space for the food, or even the dish itself.

He spent a long time thinking about it and puzzling over the construction of this cell. He'd never seen anything like it. He spent the hours of incarceration examining every part of it and trying to figure out a way to escape.

When he got tired of sitting, he stood up and the shelf on which he'd been sitting vanished inside the wall. He tested it out by sitting down four or five more times just to make sure the shelf reappeared exactly when he wanted it to. It did.

He went back to examining the panel the food came out of. It didn't respond the same way. He could prod and pry at the panel all he liked, but it didn't open nor did it produce any more food.

He was just turning to study the back wall when the front panel slid back. LeMaine spun around and stared out at the corridor the guards used to bring him here. Sehiri stood there waiting for him.

LeMaine glanced up and down the corridor. It was empty. Sehiri was alone and he wasn't wearing that dismissive, superior expression anymore.

"Captain," he began in his smoothest tone. "I'd like a word with you if you don't mind."

"Are you sure it's safe for you to be in my presence without your guards?" LeMaine sneered. "How do you know I won't attack you—like last time?"

"I think we can dispense with all that." Sehiri waved toward the corridor. "Walk with me. I want to talk to you."

LeMaine didn't move for a second. He really didn't want to talk to Sehiri, but what the hell did LeMaine have to lose? He stepped out and the panel shut behind him. LeMaine didn't want to trust that. Sehiri would only put him back in there after this was over.

Sehiri sauntered slowly down the corridor so LeMaine had no trouble keeping up with him.

"I've looked into this matter of the frequencies," Sehiri began.

"What is there to look into?" LeMaine demanded. "Sindra already told you everything about them."

"I wanted to talk to you about them in person."

LeMaine scowled at the side of Sehiri's head. "Why are you taking such an interest in me? You have Colonel Nicholson, Commander Lodge, and Captain Hurst somewhere on this ship, don't you? You could ask them anything you wanted to know."

"I prefer to talk to you. I have a strong ability to sense when a person is being sincere with me. I don't trust any of those men you just mentioned. Colonel Nicholson and Commander Lodge are too high up in the chain of command. They have a political agenda that makes me mistrust them."

LeMaine didn't know what to say to that. He couldn't disagree.

His main complaint against Colonel Nicholson and Commander Lodge was their disturbing tendency to bring politics into their dealings with him.

They couldn't just let him do his job without adding some political considerations, most of which didn't bear on him or the Hellhounds at all. In fact, that was his only complaint against them.

"What do you want from me?" he finally asked. "I've already told you everything I know."

"Not everything." Sehiri stopped in the middle of the corridor. It was still totally deserted. There wasn't a single security guard as far as the eye could see. Sehiri and LeMaine were completely alone.

"I want you to tell me what you've seen and experienced with these frequencies," Sehiri went on. "What do they do? How do they do it? How did you come across them? How do you know for certain that they work? Tell me everything—really everything this time. Don't leave anything out."

LeMaine hesitated again. How could he explain absolutely everything about the frequencies? The story of the frequencies started with Lulara, and for that, he had to go all the way back to Ziea.

He found himself pouring out the whole story—how he and the Hellhounds had landed on Ziea looking for a lost diplomat, how Buca had joined the squad, and how they'd discovered Lulara working with the Cezians.

Then he told about crashing on Iumia, Lulara dying, and how she gave LeMaine the frequencies and thanked Buca with her dying breath.

The story got easier after that. LeMaine described how the Hellhounds had used the old frequencies in battle against the Axichis and how the frequencies failed to work before Polasek worked out this new set.

"We haven't had a chance to use them yet. You're right about that," LeMaine told Sehiri. "I can't absolutely guarantee that this set of frequencies will work against the Axichis, but isn't it at least worth trying? What do you have to lose?"

Sehiri remained silent through the whole story. When LeMaine finished, Sehiri remained silent for another long moment before he turned aside.

He went back to sauntering down the corridor like he had all the time in the world. He acted like the Axichis weren't knocking down the Imoliv's door right now, not to mention wiping the floor with Elia right across the street.

LeMaine resisted the urge to tell Sehiri to hurry the hell up and make up his damn mind already. LeMaine wanted to get back to Elia and do whatever he was going to do to help the war effort. He didn't want to fart around on this destroyer having these civil conversations with someone who was just toying with him.

Sehiri took a long time to answer before he said, "I believe you, Captain."

"So....are you going to use them?" LeMaine asked.

Sehiri turned aside to enter a large room packed to the rafters with electronic equipment. An enormous screen covered one wall. It displayed the ongoing battle raging across the border in Elia. This had to be the Imoliv destroyer's bridge.

Sehiri's staff worked on all the controls and monitored the battle. They reported to another tall Imoliv who fired orders back and forth. He seemed to be coordinating the Imoliv fighter craft and the destroyers' responses to everything the Elian Military did.

Sehiri strolled up a sloped ramp to the bridge's top tier. LeMaine turned to follow him and realized a second later that the four pilots were all standing there in a line. They pulled themselves up at attention when Sehiri arrived.

"These men have all told me about what you did for them on Kathopra," Sehiri told LeMaine. "They've also told me that you willingly withheld these frequencies from your own people. They say you brought the frequencies to Imoliv so we could deploy the frequencies ourselves. These men say you did that on the long chance that Imoliv would see Elia as a friend and possibly bridge the gap toward relations between our peoples."

"That's right," LeMaine replied and then frowned at the four pilots, especially Lutov. "Did they *all* say that?"

"Yes," Sehiri replied. "That is what I had to investigate before I could release you from your confinement cell. I had to question these men and make sure that they all told the same story. I didn't want to make the decision based on the word of one or a few."

"So....." LeMaine surveyed the pilots again. He still found it difficult to believe that Lutov actually told the truth about why LeMaine returned to Imoliv territory.

"I believe you brought the frequencies here intending to offer this gesture of goodwill to the Imoliv people," Sehiri went on. "I didn't want to believe it, but the evidence leaves me now choice but to accept that it is the case. I have therefore decided to accept this gift in the spirit with which you offered it. I will deploy the frequencies and let the chips fall where they may."

LeMaine's heart leapt. "Great! So....what do you want me to do? Your fleet is so much more powerful than ours. We've been fighting the Axichis by the skin of our teeth for so long."

"That's obvious." Sehiri waved to the pilots. "You're all dismissed."

The three other pilots gave LeMaine pleading looks before they left the bridge. Lutov didn't look at LeMaine at all.

Sehiri took a few steps to his right and then paced back. He didn't seem in any big hurry to deploy the frequencies.

"So...." LeMaine began again. "Are you going to use them?"

"Not yet. I have a plan, Captain, and for that, I need you and your team."

"Why? We can't do anything you can't do."

"On the contrary. You are Elian and your entire team is Elian....except for this Maczhi you mentioned. That's neither here nor there. I want you to liaise with your people for me."

LeMaine frowned. "Liaise....how?"

"There are over two hundred Elians on board this destroyer, including the three officers you mentioned before—Nicholson, Lodge, and Hurst. None of them trust me and I would lose face if I told them myself what I plan to do. I want you to talk to them, explain my plan, and convince them to get involved. They in turn will aid us in our campaign against the Axichis."

"How could they?" LeMaine asked. "They have two bombers and a bunch of attack cruisers, none of which are operational."

"My maintenance crews have repaired those ships. They're all perfectly functional. We just need the Elian personnel to man them."

LeMaine's jaw hit the floor. "You....repaired them? You...." He blinked and then shut his eyes shaking his head fast. "I don't get this at all."

"That hold you saw when you first entered this ship is only one of many. We separated the Elian personnel from their ships and isolated the Elian personnel in a different part of this destroyer. My maintenance crews repaired all the Elian craft. It wasn't difficult. Elian technology isn't that sophisticated, but we need Elian personnel to fly those ships into battle against the Axichis."

LeMaine shut his mouth with difficulty. "So....what am I supposed to say to Nicholson, Lodge, and Hurst?"

"You'll tell them that we'll deploy the frequencies in a way that allows the Imoliv and Elian Militaries to work together to neutralize the Axichis, but we must coordinate our assault. We need to launch as many ships as possible that are already prepared to use the frequencies with no delay. There *will* be a delay between when the Imoliv deploy the frequencies and when the wider Elian Military receives them. There will be a further delay before the Elian Military understands what they're receiving and how to use them."

LeMaine made a face. "Yeah. I realize all that."

"I will see to it that the *Excursion,* the *Lucidity,* and all their attack cruisers have the frequencies already loaded onto their systems ready to use the instant they launch. Those vessels will work in tandem with the Imoliv defense force to spring a surprise attack on the Axichis. That is why I've kept the Elian ships and their crews on board this long—so we could use them to defeat the Axichis."

LeMaine decided not to address that one. He was too thrilled by Sehiri's proposal.

"Naturally, the Elian personnel will hear all of this much better from you than they will from me," Sehiri finished, "which is why I need you to liaise with them."

LeMaine frowned to himself considering the whole plan. "Yeah. I can see your point now."

"Once you and your personnel are ready to fly, we will arrange our attack."

"What about....?" LeMaine's gaze drifted back to the battle between the Imoliv and the Elians. "What about *them?*"

"Word has already gone out to the rest of the Imoliv defense force that we will be arranging a joint campaign with the Elian Military. This battle is just for show. The Imoliv have adjusted the wavelength of their phase cannons so they no longer do any damage to Elian craft. You can understand that we need to convince the Axichis right up until the last moment that the Elians and the Imoliv are fighting each other. You can already see the Axichis losing interest in defending themselves against either fleet."

LeMaine followed Sehiri's gaze back to the screen and saw that Sehiri was right. The two fleets continued to trade shots. Elian attack cruisers and Imoliv fighters revolved around each other in the chaos.

They hammered each other with punishing fire, but the Imoliv no longer took as much care about hitting vulnerable targets. They seemed more interested in just harassing the Elian cruisers and making the cruisers attack the fighters in return.

The strategy worked. Fewer Axichis swooped around. Those that did didn't take as much of an interest in getting involved. They just watched or, in some cases, just hovered nearby with their noses pointed somewhere else.

More and more Axichis fighters broke off to different parts of the Elian system. Some even retreated as far as the Elian-Axichis border. The battle didn't mean anything to them anymore, now that Elia and Imoliv were fighting each other instead of the Axichis.

"Idiots!" LeMaine whispered.

"You see?" Sehiri asked. "It's the perfect time to strike, but we must act quickly and we must keep it quiet. We can't go transmitting the frequencies to the entire Elian fleet before we spring our trap. The Elians wouldn't be able to resist using the frequencies beforehand."

"So when do you want me to get started? Just tell me where the Elian crews are—oh, and you have to release my squad."

"They've already been released, Captain. They're downstairs with the rest of your people. They're just waiting for you to join them."

Chapter 31

The panel slid back to reveal a hold packed with Elians. All the *Excursion, Lucidity,* and attack cruiser crews were in here.

LeMaine froze in the compartment with Sehiri at his side. Everyone out on the hold floor stopped what they were doing to stare at him standing shoulder to shoulder with their enemy.

The Hellhounds occupied a place to one side. The hold didn't look right without the two destroyers and all the damaged attack craft.

Peterman was talking to Colonel Nicholson and Polasek was talking to Lieutenant DeYoung and Captain Hurst. No one moved, breathed, or made a sound as LeMaine stepped out of the compartment, onto the floor, and the panel swished shut behind him while Sehiri remained inside.

Everyone mobbed LeMaine the instant the panel shut. People surrounded him all talking at once. The Hellhounds elbowed forward trying to shove everyone else aside. LeMaine couldn't hear a thing over the noise.

Monk grabbed him, yanked him away from the crowd, and straight-armed everyone out of the way. Monk dragged LeMaine over to Colonel Nicholson and Monk gave the rest of the personnel such threatening looks that they started to back off.

The Hellhounds kept talking to LeMaine a mile a minute. "We thought you were dead, Sir!" O'Hara announced.

"We did not, you dimwit!" Lemon smacked O'Hara on the back of the head. "No one thought the captain was dead!"

"Where have you been, Sir?" Nunn asked. "We've been in here for days...or it seems like it. No one knew where you were. None of the Imoliv would tell us anything and none of the Elians knew anything, either."

"I'm all right...." LeMaine began, but the other Hellhounds cut him off.

"Are you hurt?" Kellogg asked. "Did they interrogate you or anything?"

"I'm okay," LeMaine replied. "I'm just tired."

"Come over here and sit down, Owen." Colonel Nicholson steered LeMaine toward the hold's back wall and pushed him down on a crate.

LeMaine didn't recognize the crate. It must have come from the Imoliv. Everyone in the hold looked calm and well fed. LeMaine didn't see any extra goods, but the Imoliv must have been giving the Elian crews food and all the other supplies they needed.

Now that LeMaine actually got into this hold, he realized the monumental task in front of him. These people had been living right under each other's feet ever since the Imoliv captured them.

He would never be able to talk to Colonel Nicholson, Commander Lodge, and Captain Hurst in private here. The job of informing all the Elian personnel here would be astronomically more difficult.

Colonel Nicholson pulled up another crate and sat down. He didn't look like he'd been through any brutal interrogation or torture at the hands of his Imoliv captors, either.

Sehiri didn't actually say he'd hurt Nicholson if he didn't cooperate. Sehiri just said he'd remove Nicholson—which he did. Sehiri removed Nicholson from the rest of the Elian captives. That was all. Now he was back and he was just fine.

He leaned close to LeMaine. "What's the story out there, Owen? The Hellhounds say the Imoliv are assaulting the Elian Military inside Elian space. I swear, if I ever get out of here, I'll never rest until I finish off every last rotten one of them."

"You might want to belay that for a little while longer, Sir," LeMaine told him.

"Why should I? They're out there weakening our fleet when the Axichis are already overrunning our system. If we go down, it will be thanks to the Imoliv and their traitorous interference. At least they had the decency not to pretend to be our friends all these years. They must have been planning this from the start. They must have been biding their time before they strengthened their forces enough to strike at our weakest moment."

LeMaine couldn't listen to this. He straightened up and looked around. "Where are Russel and Jimmy?"

"They're over there getting ready to hand out the evening meal. The Imoliv give us food, blankets, medical supplies, toilet facilities—everything we need. The only thing we're missing is separate houses to live in. Otherwise, we might as well be on vacation here."

He laughed at his own joke, but LeMaine couldn't join in. He wanted to get this over with so he could stop carrying it around on his chest. It was turning into an intolerable burden.

"I need you to bring Russel and Jimmy back over here….after they finish what they're doing." LeMaine started to stand up. The Hellhounds hovered nearby—not close enough that they could overhear his conversation with Colonel Nicholson, but close enough to help him if he needed it.

Buca gave LeMaine a particularly piercing look when LeMaine turned around. He could just imagine how they would react when they heard the news.

"If you want to talk to those two, you might as well do it now," Colonel Nicholson replied. "This business of distributing food takes hours and they don't even do the work. They just stand guard to make sure everyone keeps order and no fights break out—but they never do. Wait here. I'll go get them."

Colonel Nicholson bustled off into the crowd and LeMaine got a sinking feeling of dread in the pit of his stomach. This was it. He was going to have to explain this plan to someone now. God only knew how he was going to do that.

No wonder Sehiri asked LeMaine to do it. No one in their right mind would want to explain to the Elians that the Imoliv had completely flipped the script and now wanted to mount a joint surprise attack on the Axichis.

That was the whole point, wasn't it? No one would believe it, especially not the Axichis. The Imoliv had played their hand to the letter. It was the most perfect setup in history.

While LeMaine sat there trying to decide what in the world he could say to these men to explain anything, Buca came up to him. "Is everything all right, Captain?"

"Sure," LeMaine husked. "Everything's swell."

"Swell?" Buca asked. "What does that mean?"

Peterman rolled in behind Buca followed by Polasek. "What's going on?" Peterman asked. "You look pale. Are we in danger? Are the Imoliv planning to execute us?"

"They better not be after we handed them the frequencies on a silver platter," Polasek muttered.

Nunn, Kellogg, O'Hara, and Lemon showed up next. "Are we mobilizing, Sir?" Lemon asked. "Just point us toward the guns we're supposed to use and we'll throw down on these bitches."

"Just don't ask us to fly any Imoliv fighter craft again," Kellogg remarked. "Those things are cursed."

"Maybe they're only cursed for filthy alien scum like you," Nunn teased.

"Don't start shooting your mouths off," O'Hara interjected. "You can all see the captain's bent about something. It must be bad. What's the problem, Sir? Just tell us. We can take it."

LeMaine cringed, and just when he thought his nightmare couldn't get any worse, Colonel Nicholson returned with Commander Lodge and Captain Hurst. "You Hellhounds go get your grub," Captain Hurst told them. "We'll talk to Captain LeMaine and then you can have him back."

"No!" LeMaine forced himself to stand up. "Stick around, Hellhounds. You should hear this, too."

Their eyes widened. "I knew it!" Lemon murmured. "We are throwing down, aren't we? Who are we fighting now, Sir? Please tell me it's the Imoliv."

LeMaine took a deep breath. He tried to look at all of them at once, but that was impossible. He would have liked to tell the Hellhounds first, but he couldn't do that with three officers standing right in front of him.

He turned to face Nicholson, Lodge, and Hurst. "Sehiri believes that we brought the frequencies here as a show of goodwill between Elia and the Imoliv."

"It's about time he came to his senses," Peterman remarked. "God knows he had those four pilots telling him so."

LeMaine shrugged. "I guess I can't blame him for taking precautions. Anyway, he wants to mount a joint operation between us and the Imoliv. He's repaired the *Excursion*, the *Lucidity,* and all our attack craft. He's proposing that we deploy the frequencies in a joint surprise attack against the Axichis. The Imoliv are out there staging a battle between themselves and the Elians to throw the Axichis off their guard. The Axichis are falling for it hook, line, and sinker. They'll never see it coming."

The three officers gaped at him in slack-jawed shock—just like LeMaine expected them to. None of them said a word for a second.

"So that's how it is," LeMaine finished. "Sehiri didn't think you'd be able to hear it from him, so he asked me to liaise for him. He also doesn't want to transmit the frequencies to the rest of the Elian fleet beforehand because he thinks they'll be just desperate enough to jump the gun and blow our wad ahead of time."

Still no one moved or spoke. This was turning into one of most awkward moments of LeMaine's life.

"What do you think?" he finally asked. "Our ships are waiting for us in another hold. We just have to....."

As if by magic, one huge wall of the hold slid aside to reveal the hold next door. The whole Elian assembly gasped in amazement when they saw the *Excursion*, the *Lucidity*, and all their attack cruisers shining in perfect condition.

Excited talk rippled through the hold as everyone streamed into the other room on their way to their ships. The mechanics surrounded all those vessels exclaiming and marveling that the two ships and all the cruisers had been repaired so quickly and so expertly.

"Is this really happening?" Colonel Nicholson husked.

"It's really happening," LeMaine replied, "which means you boys need to get all your crews up to snuff in a big, big hurry. I don't know when Sehiri plans to launch this attack, but we need to be ready when the word comes down. You need to run your crews through all their attack patterns, all their drills, and get them familiar with any improvements the Imoliv might have made to your ships."

Captain Hurst shut his mouth with a click. "This is....this is astounding."

"It looks to me like Sehiri has been playing hard to get," LeMaine replied. "He's been holding us at arm's length until we showed our hand—which we did."

"You did, Owen." Colonel Nicholson shook himself back to his senses and grabbed LeMaine's hand. "You did this, Owen. You're the best we have. There's no question about it." He waved to Lodge and Hurst. "Tell him."

Captain Hurst nodded. "Of course you're the best. Everyone says so."

"We've been saying that for years," Polasek interjected.

"Damn right," Lemon added. "Captain LeMaine all the way."

LeMaine blushed and waved them away. "You Hellhounds get your food and then arm up in the *Lucidity*. We'll be going out in.....well, we'll be going out in something and I don't want to get shot down anywhere without a full pack of supplies."

"Yes, Sir," Peterman replied. "Let's roll, Hellhounds."

They went off toward where the food had been handed out. There was no one over there anymore. LeMaine watched them go and his heart brimmed with affection for them. They were the best—not him.

He thought for a second that it might not be the best idea to release these people on a food supply intended for two hundred crewmen.

Then he thought better of it. The Hellhounds had been living hard for a long time. They deserved to enjoy themselves before they went back into a shit storm that would make everything else pale in comparison.

"We need to discuss this further, Owen," Colonel Nicholson was saying. "We need to know the Imoliv's attack plans, how many vessels they'll be sending over to Elia—every detail they can tell us. We need to alert our people to be ready...."

"We aren't alerting anyone," LeMaine interrupted. "No one on the Elian side can know about this until the attack is already underway. That's the whole idea—that it takes everyone by surprise."

"We can't leave your people in the dark," Commander Lodge chimed in. "We can't leave them unprepared."

"If the Axichis see the Elian Military preparing for any kind of campaign, the Axichis will realize we're planning something and the whole campaign will be over before it starts. Besides, I don't think any of us can communicate with Elia from inside here anyway."

"This is highly out of order, Owen," Colonel Nicholson snarled. "I don't like it."

"We're at war, Sir," LeMaine replied. "We have a powerful, shrewd, and generous ally who's willing to help us drive our enemies out of our system. It's in the Imoliv's interest to defeat the Axichis now. If they don't, the Axichis will overrun Elia and go after the Imoliv next. Trusting Sehiri and playing this his way is our best bet. I'm sorry I can't call that a recommendation. It's just the way we're doing it."

Colonel Nicholson frowned at him and then sighed. "All right, Owen. You've never steered us wrong before." He turned his flinty gaze to the ships in the other hold. There are enough attack cruisers for everyone now. "I was worried we'd be short the next time we went into battle. Come on, Jimmy. Let's go see the ship and then we can inform the crews."

LeMaine watched them walk off toward the *Lucidity*. LeMaine could just imagine the reaction they would get when they informed the crew exactly what they were about to do.

LeMaine didn't want to be around for that, so he headed over to the food tables to join the Hellhounds. They'd already gotten their meals and settled down together at one of the tables. They had the place to themselves.

LeMaine wedged himself in between Peterman and Kellogg. "Are you eating anything?" O'Hara asked. "This stuff is fantastic."

"I'll get there eventually."

"You must be hungry," Heckler growled. "I'll never believe you aren't after that run of trouble we just had."

"The Imoliv fed me pretty well while I was locked up," LeMaine replied.

"What was it like?" Nunn asked.

"Long," LeMaine replied. "I thought it would last forever."

"So what's the deal?" Monk asked. "I guess we're going out in the same cruisers we had when we came in."

"Actually, I was thinking of asking Sehiri to give us Imoliv fighter craft—just us Hellhounds—not the other pilots."

"Why just us?" Buca asked. "If there's a reason Imoliv fighters are better for us, then they must be better for everyone. Do you think phase cannons are better?"

"It doesn't matter what weapon we use as long as the frequencies work," Polasek replied. "That can't be the reason."

"I was just thinking," LeMaine went on. "We can get across the border in Imoliv fighters and make it look like we're reinforcing the Imoliv fleet that's already inside the Elian system. That will be one squad at least already across the line with the frequencies ready to deploy. It will be one less delay. If we strike fast and hot, we can make a dent in the Axichis before the Imoliv even launch."

"Wouldn't that defeat the purpose of the surprise attack?" Kellogg asked. "Isn't the whole idea that we all strike at once?"

"Yes, but think about it," LeMaine replied. "If the Imoliv and our crews attack at the same time, they still have to cross the border and travel to the Axichis before our people can strike the first blow. Now picture this. We're already inside the Elian system all mixed up with the regular Imoliv fleet—which, by the way, will also have the frequencies loaded and ready to deploy. We all pounce on the Axichis and get them on the ropes. Then the Imoliv defensive line charges across the border, the *Excursion* and *Lucidity* crews launch, and we all pile in. It makes the attack faster because we're already there."

"I guess that could work," Heckler replied.

"Do you see a problem with it?" LeMaine asked. "Any of you?"

"I see a problem with it," O'Hara replied. "I see a problem that we don't get to smash in those bastards' faces while we're at it. I'd really like to make them pay for invading us.

Using fighter craft doesn't have the same satisfying crunch of bone if you know what I mean."

"We're eating here, man!" Monk exclaimed. "Can you save the crunch of bone for another time?"

The others laughed and LeMaine joined in. Spending time with his favorite people reminded him how hungry he was. He went to the buffet, helped himself, and returned to his seat.

"Now that's what I'm talking about!" O'Hara crowed when he saw LeMaine's plate. "Finally, a man who knows how to eat. You need to put some meat on your bones, Captain."

"There's nothing wrong with him," Monk countered.

"Except that he's too old to be our CO," Lemon remarked. "They better not be thinking of replacing you, Sir."

"They won't," LeMaine replied. "I'm the only one crazy enough to hang out with you critters."

More laughter broke out and then everybody started talking at the same time. Conversation flew back and forth across the table about the upcoming campaign.

LeMaine took it all in while he ate. He tried not to interject his opinions too much. He didn't want to skew the outcome by anticipating something that couldn't be anticipated.

Chapter 32

LeMaine lowered himself into the seat of his Imoliv fighter craft. Sehiri had been very receptive to LeMaine's idea of sneaking the Hellhounds back inside Elia and embedding the squad amongst the Imoliv fleet.

LeMaine went over the controls. He was getting used to them by now. He double-checked the frequencies. They were ready to deploy the instant the battle started. It wouldn't start just yet, though.

He had to struggle to stop his heart from racing. If this worked, the Elians and the Imoliv would drive the Axichis out of Elia today—right now. The war would be over in a matter of minutes.

What happened between Elia and the Imoliv after that would be totally out of LeMaine's hands, but at least he did his part to make it unfold in a positive direction.

He doubted Elia could be on less than favorable terms with the Imoliv after this. The Imoliv might continue to be isolationist and xenophobic, but they couldn't stay outright hostile toward Elia—not after they worked together to defeat a common threat to both their systems.

Hell, he might even get to see Sindra, Galo, and Tavon again. LeMaine didn't really give a damn if he ever saw Lutov again, but if he did, he wouldn't begrudge the kid. Lutov was just spouting what he'd been taught. Maybe there was hope for the kid yet.

A signal went off on the fighter craft's controls and brought LeMaine back to the present. He had a job to do before Elia and the Imoliv could decide whether to be friends or just neighbors.

"Let's move out, Hellhounds," he ordered. "Nice and easy."

He fired up his engines and the squad launched from Sehiri's destroyer. The squad kept it nice and easy and quiet—no swooping or diving or shooting—not yet.

The Imoliv defensive line stood guard over the boundary to stop anyone from crossing into the Imoliv system. None of those ships paid any attention to more Imoliv fighter craft gliding forward to join the rest of the Imoliv fleet.

The Hellhounds floated into position with the Imoliv defense force. Hundreds of fighter craft hovered around the larger destroyers.

The Elian Military stood off in a threatening formation. They kept their defenses in readiness for another Imoliv assault.

The Military looked pretty ragged and threadbare from here. All the Elian ships had taken extensive damage. Ships in such disrepair never would have been cleared to launch if the fate of the whole system hadn't been hanging in the balance.

LeMaine had to tear his eyes away and focus on the Axichis. They kept their distance from the Elian-Imoliv standoff.

The Axichis kept running sorties through the system testing what little remained of the Elian defenses. The Axichis didn't maintain a defensive posture against anyone. They didn't have to anymore. They had this whole conflict in the bag.

LeMaine's anger hardened when he saw how casually they treated this war. They didn't have a care in the world as long as the Elians and the Imoliv fought amongst themselves. They would weaken each other and make each other ripe for the Axichis' picking.

That needed to change right now and no one was better positioned to smack them down than the Hellhounds. He checked all their readings on his controls. They were ready. They just needed the word to go.

The tension mounted to the breaking point. LeMaine found it difficult to breathe. When would the assault begin? He fought to control himself....just a little longer.....

A blip flashed on his controls. "Deploy!" he called. "Launch the assault—all fighter craft!"

He hit the throttle, but as usual, Buca beat them all. He gunned it to the front of the pack as the Hellhounds and the Imoliv fighter craft rocketed out of formation.

The Elian Military spun around fast targeting their line, but the Imoliv fighters soared straight past them making for the Axichis. The Axichis had become so complacent that they didn't see the attack until the Imoliv fighter contingent got right on top of them.

LeMaine raced in line with the other fighters as phase cannons opened up throughout the Imoliv ranks. The Imoliv pilots streaked down the system pelting Axichis fighters and warships in a steady pounding rain of shots.

The Hellhounds burst out the other side as the Axichis closed into a defensive barricade. They got caught with their pants down halfway to their own territory. They were nowhere near Elia and weren't likely to get there with the Imoliv in the way.

Imoliv destroyers that had been confronting the Elian Military caught up a second later. The Imoliv blockaded the Axichis near the planet Morea and turned all their guns to drive the Axichis back into their own system.

LeMaine ran one more pass targeting Axichis warships and fighter craft. "Deploy the frequencies!" he called. "Phase cannons aren't doing any damage."

"The frequencies *are* deployed!" Sindra called back from somewhere behind LeMaine's fighter. "They aren't working!"

LeMaine raced through the Axichis position one more time trying to understand what was happening. He bombarded another warship, but he had to retreat when the same ship returned fire. Its lasers peppered his hull and he turned tail.

He spiraled out of the battle and paused behind the Imoliv assault to check his controls. He scrambled to find the frequencies that should have been loaded into his communications system.

Sindra was right. They were transmitting just fine. They should have been disabling the Axichis and making them more vulnerable to phase cannon fire, but they didn't. The Axichis were as invulnerable as ever.

"*Excursion* and *Lucidity* incoming!" Peterman called from somewhere. "The Imoliv defensive line is moving in!"

"No!" LeMaine yelled and pounced on his controls trying to contact.....anybody. He fumbled back and forth between trying to open a communications channel to Sehiri's destroyer, the *Excursion,* the *Lucidity*—anyone he could contact.

"Retreat back to Imoliv space!" he called. "The frequencies are ineffective! Don't put the fleet in danger...."

No one answered him and his worst nightmare came true when the Elian Military sprinted out of position to fall in line with the Imoliv fleet. Colonel Nicholson must have communicated to the Military to join this surprise attack.

LeMaine watched the disaster unfold from his cockpit. He couldn't do anything to stop it. He couldn't even appreciate that the Imoliv fleet and the Elian Military were working together at last.

The combined Elian-Imoliv force rushed across the system heading for the battle. The Imoliv fighter craft flew rings around the Axichis doing everything possible to damage them, but nothing worked.

LeMaine wavered between joining in a battle he knew he couldn't win and trying another desperate attempt to contact the fleet before this whole campaign went down the crap shoot in the biggest possible way.

He made up his mind and attacked the communications controls again when a shattering blow struck his fighter from behind. He glanced back to see Axichis craft charging him from Ar'el. Six Axichis craft rained lasers all over his fighter.

He pulled away running in the only direction where he could get away from them. He punched the throttle to the center of the battle trying to shake them off.

Other Imoliv fighters distracted the Axichis, but that only made LeMaine a target for more Axichis. They had a field day with all these defenseless Imoliv.

He wheeled hard to the port and dumped phase cannon fire all over another bunch of Axichis ganging up on Heckler. "You bastards!" he bellowed and returned fire, but he couldn't stop them from surrounding him.

They pushed him closer to the edge of the battle. The Axichis changed their strategy, now that they knew their enemies' weapons didn't do any good.

The Axichis completely ignored the Imoliv shooting back at them. The Axichis pretended the Imoliv weren't firing at all. They might as well not have been.

LeMaine pushed his throttle to the wall heading for Heckler, but LeMaine realized a second before he got there that shooting at the Axichis wouldn't do any good—for him or for Heckler. LeMaine needed to try something else.

He swerved away and then came hurtling back. He took a chance and plowed between Heckler and the Axichis. LeMaine's fighter collided with the noses of four attackers and he smashed them away from Heckler.

"Holy shit, people!" Heckler yelled. "Did you see that? Captain LeMaine, the badass!"

"Don't give me too much credit," LeMaine replied and winced as the Axichis turned their guns on him.

He'd been planning to go back in for another pass, but that one collision did the trick. All the Axichis veered out of line and raced to catch up with him.

"Pull it out, Hellhounds!" Heckler called. "Captain LeMaine is under the gun!"

"On our way," Lemon replied. "This battle is getting us nowhere."

The Imoliv fighter craft drew away from the Axichis as the Elian and Imoliv fleets moved in. Another hellish assault broke out, this time with Elians and Imoliv fighting the Axichis instead of each other.

Fighter craft whirled all over the place and Elian attack cruisers joined in, but the attackers didn't make any headway to drive the Axichis out of the solar system. If anything, the battle went the other way.

LeMaine lost sight of the battle behind a curtain of lasers. More Axichis fighters cut him off from returning to the battle.

The Hellhounds revolved around the Axichis hitting them all over with phase cannons, but the Axichis just ignored them, or worse, fired back and swatted the Hellhounds out of line.

"There has to be a way to destroy these cocksuckers," Monk growled.

"Who cares?" Kellogg called back. "Lead them away from the battle. Maybe we can set up another front somewhere and draw these fighters away from the fleet."

"Good idea," LeMaine replied. "There's Ar'el ahead. I'll lead them there."

He plunged for the planet and skimmed its orbit with the Axichis hounding him all the way. They raced up on his tail and laser shots batted him back and forth. The Hellhounds dogged the Axichis, but no one could unseat these fools.

The whole group screamed around the planet and LeMaine spotted the main battle ahead. He couldn't lead the Axichis back there. Distracting these fighters might not do any good, but it was all he had at this point.

He yanked his throttle away from Ar'el and spotted the planet Halira ahead. Its four moons created a labyrinth of obstacles leading to the solar system's outer reaches.

He raced for it, squeaked between the planet and the first moon, and slalomed between them trying to shake the Axichis pursuit.

They dropped back into the Hellhounds range. At least the Axichis were too far away now to rejoin the battle.

He cut a tight turn through the fourth moon's orbit and nearly collided with an Axichis warship stationed there. Another five warships sat parked in a tight grouping behind the moon where no one could see them.

LeMaine's stomach dropped. He tried to avoid colliding with the warship and barely grazed its sides before all six warships opened fire. The Hellhounds were flying way too fast to get out of the way in time.

The whole squad funneled right into the Axichis' line of fire. Yells and a few screams shattered LeMaine's mind and then a laser stabbed through his fighter. It barely missed the cockpit and smashed through the fuselage, the controls, and straight through the floor.

"I'm hit!" he yelled. "I'm steering for Aora! I gotta get into the atmosphere before this thing...."

An explosion went off somewhere and the controls died completely. He hauled the helm from port to starboard and back again trying anything and everything to control the ship, but nothing worked.

It wheeled through space, tilted at a dangerous angle, and he stared down at the planet Aora's blue and green surface. He was already in the atmosphere, thank Heaven.

His instincts kicked in and he wrestled the controls in all directions. His senses didn't want to register that his fighter was miles up in the atmosphere and totally out of control. He was going down with no way to save himself.

End of Book 2.

Keep Reading

H ellhounds Series: Book 3: Return of the Hero

With the Axichis invasion turning against the Elian m=Military and the Hellhounds caught in the middle, Captain Owen LeMaine and his squad of Special Forces badasses will have to take it home to the place where the adventure first started. The Axichis are bringing in more ships than the Elian-Imoliv alliance can possibly defeat. The Hellhounds try to launch a knockout strike against the Axichis staging area on the planet Ziea. So how can such a tiny squad defeat the whole invasion force?

LeMaine needs a bigger army to tip the advantage in his favor. Fortunately, there are thousands of native Maczhi already on the planet. They're they're loyal Elian citizens and also under threat from the invasion. They have every reason to fight back . Too bad they're weak, pacifistic, and incapable of even holding a weapon, much less fighting back. They'll all get killed if they go into battle against an enemy as dangerous as the Axichis. Can the Hellhounds find a way to swing these people to their side and win the war after all?

You can find it at your favorite book retailer.

Sign Up Once--Get all Theo Mann's free books including brand new releases

Sign Up Once--Get all Theo Mann's free books including brand new releases

Humanity on the brink of annihilation.

A mysterious package, a corrupt officer, and a conspiracy that goes all the way to the top? What could possibly go wrong?

When a routine mission goes horribly wrong, Warrant Officer Ewing Archer and a handful of faithful friends get trapped in a battle to save the last survivors of Earth.

The human race has abandoned the ecological disaster of Earth. Now all that remains is a network of interconnected ships, stations, and satellites surrounding the planet.

But when war breaks out, Archer becomes a firebrand that could destroy it all....or save it.

Sign up at www.theomann.com to read it for free

About Theo Mann

I write 70 books per year—and yes, before you ask, all these books are my original creative work. Nothing written under my name is AI-generated or ghostwritten because I write better than AI and any ghostwriter out there.

People don't read fiction for entertainment or to escape from reality. People read fiction to see their humanity reflected in another person's character and story.

This is my promise to you. When you read my books, you'll see your own humanity reflected in the characters and stories. I take this commitment to my readers very seriously. My books are an intimate form of communication between us. I would never disrespect my readers by turning that over to a machine or another writer. This is my bond between me and you as my reader.

I write 20,000 words per day as my daily work output. If anyone with a public platform would like to challenge me to prove this in a controlled environment, feel free to contact me on this website's contact page.

I worked as a professional ghostwriter for fifteen years. Now I'm on a mission to set a Guinness World Record by writing 700 books over the next ten years and 1400 books over the next twenty years, all originally written by me. See my website for the full book list.

I'm also the author of *Proof for the Existence of God* and the *Crimes Against Fiction* blog. You can find all my nonfiction work at www.crimes-against-fiction.com.

If you have a story idea, or if you would like me to explore a series in more depth, or if you'd like me to explore a character by writing a spinoff series about that character or world, leave me a message on my website's contact page. I answer all reader emails, so ask me anything, tell me what you liked and didn't like, and let me know where you'd like your favorite series to go. I would love to hear your ideas and find out what you'd like to read next.

Find out more at www.theomann.com.

Also by Theo Mann (so far)

Standalone Novels
Kingdom of Heaven
The Verge

Series
Onyx Series (Books 1-6)
Prideland Series (Books 1-4)
Ultra Meridian Series (Books 1-7)
Hellhounds Series (Books 1-7)
Battlefleet Series (Books 1-4)
Highland Heroes Series (Books 1-6)
Battalion 1 Series (Books 1-5)
The Network Series (Books 1-6)
Corrupted Coil (Books 1-5)
Rise of the Giants Series (Books 1-10)
The Edge of Chaos Series (Books 1-5)
The White Series (Books 1-7)

www.ingramcontent.com/pod-product-compliance
Lightning Source LLC
Chambersburg PA
CBHW061438030726
47503CB00005B/1463